A NOVEL

LAST LIGHT

A. LAWRENCE

Last Light

Copyright © 2024 –A. Lawrence

This book is a work of Fiction. Any references to historic events, real people, or real places are used fictitiously. Other names, characters, places, and events are the products of the author's imagination. Any resemblance to actual events, places or persons (living or dead), is entirely coincidental.

All Rights Reserved –No part of this book may be reproduced or transmitted in any form without written permission of the author

Published by: Cloaked Press, LLC
PO Box 341
Suring, WI 54174
Cloakedpress.com

Cover Design by:
Carmilla M. Ravensworth
carmillacreates.carrd.co

ISBN: 978-1-952796-40-1

For the librarian that gave me my first fantasy book.

Chapter 1: The Library

Andi waited in a vampire's library.

It was relatively small, not even a tenth of the size of the library that she worked in back at the coven hall. Dark wooden shelves lined cream walls, interspersed with heavily curtained windows.

There was something charming about it. Cozy.

And it had a crystal.

Every library she'd ever been in, which was sparingly few, had a crystal orb roughly the size of her fist floating somewhere within its halls. It glowed a soft white, surrounded by golden bands. They were always in a different formation, like an astronomer's ring. She'd never quite figured out what it meant.

In the coven hall, it was under glass.

Here, it hovered above a table, completely open to the air. She tilted her head, trying to get a better view, but she'd never seen any of the symbols etched on the bands anywhere else, and without a cipher she had no way to break the code. She glanced at the door, but it was still firmly closed, and activated her archive.

Her magic looked like golden sand. It shimmered around the rings, but never got close, forming loose rings of its own around the slowly rotating bands. Strange planets around a small sun.

She frowned and pushed harder, leaning across the table, but some invisible force stopped her magic from even brushing against the symbols.

The door opened.

Andi squeaked and only grabbing the edge of the table stopped her from toppling to the floor. Her magic scattered across the table-top and dissipated.

Chrys stared at her, one eyebrow raised. "Am I interrupting something?"

She sighed and flopped down into the chair behind her. "Oh. It's just you. Where's our host?"

"She'll be along shortly." They sat next to her. "What were you doing?"

"Just curious about something." Andi shrugged.

Chrysanthos was the head of the Rose Briar Coven. Andi had been studying under them since she was very young, but they looked nearly the same. Their brown skin was smooth and ageless. The only difference was their thick, dark braids were streaked with more silver than they used to be.

They had been one of the most powerful healers in recent memory.

Before magic began to fade.

In that moment, they looked tired and older than ever. "I need you on your best behavior."

"I am absolutely on my best behavior." Andi sat up straight, tucking a stray strand of her unruly, carrot-colored hair back under her hat. She hated wearing it, it always pulled on her bun and kept trying to slide over her eyes, but Chrys insisted it made her look professional. "I could not be better behaved if I tried."

"Please try," Chrys said. "We need her help."

"You think a vampire can help break the curse?" Andi asked. "Aren't they a symptom of it? Are we studying her? That's been done before, you know, twenty years ago they did a very thorough investigation on an entire colony of the afflicted, I think I have the information, if I just—"

Chrys put a hand on her shoulder before she could activate her archive again and pull up the relevant information. "I know, Andi. I was there."

"Oh. Right." She primly folded her hands in her lap. "Of course. Then…what exactly are we doing here? And why me?"

Andi was an archive witch. Any book she read or scanned was stored in a magical archive she could access on a whim. She was one of the few witches who wasn't affected by the fading of magic, though she hadn't been particularly strong to begin with.

"All in good time," Chrys said. The door opened again and Chrys turned to face it. "And here is our lovely host. Blythe, thank you for agreeing to our meeting."

"I didn't have much of a choice."

The first thing Andi noticed was the cane—black, the silver handle shaped like a raven's skull. Blythe held it in her left hand, its foot tapping softly against the carpet with each step she took.

Blythe herself was dressed in reds and blacks, contrasting her pale skin and short, white hair. Her eyes were an unsettling shade of gray, so light that if it weren't for the red ring around her irises they would have been indistinguishable from the whites.

"You always have a choice." Chrys stood to greet her. Andi hurried to follow their example. "I want to introduce you to someone. Blythe Camden, this is Andrea Madsen."

"Charmed." Blythe held out a hand. She was wearing a heavy looking silver ring with a dark stone.

"Likewise." Andi accepted the offered hand in a short, firm shake. Blythe's skin was cool to the touch.

"Andi is the archivist for our coven," Chrys explained.

"I've already told you everything of note, but if you insist I repeat it to your assistant I suppose I can oblige." Blythe sat down, indicating they could do the same. The crystal's light painted her like she was carved from marble. "It's not like I have anything better to do, being your…domesticated vampire."

"As fascinating as I'm sure Andi would find that, it's not why we're here," Chrys said. Andi did her best to keep her expression neutral, fighting the pout that threatened to purse her lips. "I bring news."

"And you came all the way out here to deliver it? Must be juicy." Blythe inspected the handle of her cane. "Did you leave your dog in the car in some ill-fated attempt to let the blow land softly?"

Andi bristled, but Chrys shot her a warning look before she could say anything.

"Yes, I know you and Lexa aren't on particularly good terms," Chrys said, smoothly.

"What a kind way to put it." Blythe looked amused.

Lexa was Chrys's personal guard, Andi's best friend, and a werewolf. Before most of the packs had been wiped out, werewolves had been the best weapon against vampires, other than the sun lamps that surrounded the few remaining strongholds.

They became the only thing keeping humanity safe when darkness began to cover the sky two decades prior.

Vampires had existed before then, but with the daylight faltering, their numbers swelled until only a decade after the darkness began. It was nearly impossible to leave the cities safely.

The elder vampires were hardly a concern, locked away in their towers and haunts. Regular vampires like Blythe were dangerous, but they could be reasoned with.

The afflicted were the true threat. The vampire curse spread through bite, and if it wasn't done properly, there was a high chance the person bitten would become one of the afflicted—so consumed by blood madness their reason was burned away.

Judging by her white hair, Blythe must have been one of the afflicted at some point in her life.

"Well, consider me mollified by your supposed show of goodwill." Blythe leaned back, regarding Chrys down her strong, aquiline nose. It gave her otherwise soft face character. "What's the news?"

"We've uncovered the library."

Blythe glanced around her bookshelves. "Have you, now? Well. Make sure to get me a card if you ever let me leave this house, but as you can see…"

She gestured to the shelves around them with her cane.

"Not that kind of library," Chrys said. "The library. The great tree."

Andi stared at them. She had no idea how or why they'd kept that information from her. She was supposed to be their archivist. She held every spell that every member of the coven had ever learned. All of the names. All of the research.

"But that disappeared…centuries ago," Andi said. "Three-hundred and ninety-seven years to be exact. What do you mean its back?"

"I mean that the great tree has once again unfurled her branches to shade us with her knowledge," Chrys quoted a very old book. One Andi had read so many times she didn't need her archive to recall it.

The library. A massive, hollow tree that held all of the knowledge of the world and connected to everything through its roots.

When she was younger, Andi tore through every piece of information she could find, but there had been sparingly little. When it disappeared, it took so much knowledge with it, that it had taken decades for witches to get back to where they had been. Andi was certain that there was information still out of their grasp.

"How do you lose a giant tree full of books?" Blythe asked.

"That's the mystery, isn't it?" Chrys smiled a bit. "But it's reappeared. And if I'm right, it holds everything we need. Including the origin of the vampire curse. That began around the time this library disappeared. I can't believe that it's a coincidence."

Andi was glad she was already sitting.

"So you think you can waltz into this big tree, find a book on vampires, and break the curse." Blythe didn't looked convinced, or impressed. "If that really is the case, which I highly doubt it is, the elder vampires will never allow it. They'll get wind of it and burn the place down."

"Which is why we need to beat them to it," Chrys said. "And I don't think we'll find the origin in any book, but at the library's core."

"Not much of a library without books." Blythe waved a hand dismissively.

"Oh, there are books, just—"

Blythe cut them off. "No. Thank you. I might not be enchanted with my life, but I'm in no hurry to end it. Anyone who goes to this tree is going to die."

"I have to believe you're wrong," Chrys said. "Things are more dire than I care to admit. Our magic is fading, Blythe. The sun lamps grow weaker every day. Without the werewolves, it's no longer just a possibility that the elder vampires will take the continent. It's a certainty. This is our last shot."

Andi knew things were bad outside of the coven hall, of course she did. She wasn't blind to the dark clouds that covered the once blue sky, or that the sun lamps were pulled back a little more every year, tightening the defenses of the city.

She hadn't known it was quite so bleak.

"Then make more werewolves." Blythe shrugged

Chrys sighed. "You know it's not that easy. The art was lost a long time ago, only naturally born—"

"I don't care," Blythe said. "What exactly do you want me to do about your library situation?"

"I have a theory."

"I am not staking my life on a theory," Blythe hissed, and the room seemed darker for just a moment. Her pupils flared. They were red, like rubies, or perfect drops of blood. Chills crawled up Andi's spine.

"It's the only choice we have." Chrys's voice was cold, ice breaking on a winter morning. "Either you can help us, or you can be at Carmine's mercy when she razes the city. It's your choice."

Blythe slumped back in her seat. "Fine. I suppose I can at least hear you out. What's this theory?"

"That's better," Chrys leaned back, their tone thawing. "I know that there is only one way to find the information we need. And that's why I brought Andi today. She's an archive witch, she can access the core, and with you along, I am completely confident that she can find the curse's origin."

Chapter 2: Agreement

ndi's elbow slid off the arm of the chair. She'd known, of course, that an archive witch would be the most useful person in a library, and particularly The Library , but Chrys hadn't even run the idea by her. "Excuse me. What?"

"Hm." Blythe didn't look impressed. "Seems to be news to your archivist. Let's say I go along with your plan, as terrible as it sounds, and for a wild minute we can even pretend that you actually do break the curse. What happens to me?"

"I'm not saying that we'll break the curse." Chrys leaned forward. "I'm saying we'll find the information to do so. You have my word that your safety will be paramount. And, of course, during the expedition we will take every precaution. I am preparing a team. I understand that I'm asking you to put yourself at great risk and I'm willing to compensate you."

"Fancy way of saying you don't know," Blythe said. "So, if you're just finding the information, why do you really need me?

Seems to me like you'd be better off not worrying about what happens to me."

"I'm not that cold," Chrys said.

"Agree to disagree," Blythe shifted her cane. "Don't be coy, Chrys. I'm not in the mood for your little games. Not today."

Chrys sighed. "There are concerns that there is a blood seal—"

"And there it is," Blythe cut them off. "Let me guess. Only a vampire can get in."

"Yes." Chrys sighed. "I had hoped to convince you to join out of the goodness of your heart."

Blythe put a hand to her chest and shrugged. "Still not beating. Can't appeal to my better side if I don't have one. I assume we're leaving immediately?"

"Then you'll help?" Chrys perked up.

"You—" Blythe tapped their knee with the beak of her cane "—need to stop playing things so close to the vest. Besides, Miss Archivist hasn't agreed."

"It's Andrea." Andi knew that Blythe couldn't have possibly forgotten her name already, but she felt like she should say it, anyway. "Of course I'll go."

"It will be dangerous, I won't lie to you," Chrys said. Blythe muttered something that suspiciously sounded like there was a first time for everything. Chrys ignored her. "The library disappeared a very long time ago, and we have very few records of what it was like on the inside."

"Really? How convenient," Blythe said.

"There was an invasion, the library was hidden to keep it safe." Andi accessed her archive. While she knew most of the information, she could easily check it, golden sand moving through the air around her. "And it worked. The Empire of the Dawn retreated soon afterwards. Of course, this was shortly followed by the first known vampires, and the very beginnings of the curse—"

"And now the whole sky is black, and you think this library can solve things," Blythe interrupted her. "Why hide a library?"

"It wasn't the library, not exactly," Andi explained. "I mean, don't get me wrong, it must be an incredible wealth of knowledge, particularly on magic. It's the roots. They're magical lines. They connect the entirety of Obrye."

Blythe nodded. "Take the library, take the island. Whatever that's worth, sea battered hunk of rock in the middle of an eternal night."

Andi frowned. "While it is an island, Obrye is several hundred miles long, and before the darkness there was more magic here than anywhere else. Not to mention important agriculturally. So not just a hunk of rock, thank you very much."

"Oh, I stand corrected." Blythe was definitely doing her best not to laugh at her. Andi's cheeks flushed with heat. "My apologies, Miss Archivist."

"Andrea."

"Miss Andrea Archivist." Blythe was smiling too widely. "I'm well aware. I've been alive for quite a bit longer than you have, and I doubt you've ever left Rosewood."

"I was born out in the country," Andi murmured.

"Well, we have a world traveler here, I'm feeling better about this expedition already," Blythe said. "Fine. It's not like I have anything to do around here. I'll break the seal and get you into your little library. But I get to make a few demands in turn."

"I was counting on that," Chrys admitted. "Thank you."

"Don't thank me yet," Blythe said. "You haven't heard my requests."

Chrys ignored her. "Andi, go back to the car. Warn Lexa we'll be down soon."

"I…" Andi actually wanted to be there for the negotiations. And she wanted to have a word with Chrys herself. She knew they didn't tell her everything. Coven head was a position that was rife with secrecy.

But this was the biggest thing they'd ever kept from her.

She glanced at Blythe, who gave her a warning smile, fangs showing. She knew nothing she said would keep her in the room. Or make any difference at all. "Okay."

She stood up, brushed non-existent dust from her skirt, and left the library. The house was large, but it was easy to navigate her way back to the grand entrance and through the front door.

She walked down the steps, her heels clicking on the stone.

The house loomed behind her, like it was a sentient thing that was aware it was a prison. The spires of the roof pierced towards the ever-dark sky. The only light on was the library, soft and golden. An island in a dark sea.

When they'd driven up, she'd thought it was a little ridiculous to house one person in a huge house, so far out of town. Even if it was a vampire. Leaving, it felt lonely and sad, opulent.

"Where's Chrys?"

Andi squeaked and jumped when Lexa threw an arm around her shoulders. As usual, she hadn't heard her approach. Lexa cackled at her pout, giving her shoulders a squeeze. "Man, you are too easy. How was the leech? Was it scary? Were you scared?"

"Oh please, I wasn't scared." Andi shoved Lexa's arm off of her shoulders. "I was just thinking that it must be terrible, being alone like this."

"Eh. Some people really like the privacy." Lexa shrugged.

"Maybe." Andi wasn't so sure.

Lexa shoved her hands in the pockets of her sturdy jacket. "What are they talking about?"

"Arrangements," Andi said. "They'll both be down here soon."

"Both?" Lexa's eyebrows rose. "You sure you heard that right? The vampire doesn't leave the house."

"She does now," Andi said. "This time. Did Chrys tell you? About the library?"

"What library?" Lexa asked. Andi hated to admit that she felt a little better.

They sat down on the steps. Lexa sprawled out like it was the most comfortable lounge in the world. Andi wrapped her arms around her knees.

Where Andi was short and all curves, Lexa looked like she should be taking on a dangerous expedition through long lost ruins. She was six feet tall, all of it lean muscle. Her silver and red hair was pulled back into a ponytail, showing off her knife sharp ears. As sharp as the teeth in her lazy grin.

And that was before she transformed.

She was one of the last werewolves. Most of them had been wiped out by a colony of vampires over a decade ago. Lexa had survived, two long scars on her jaw a testament. The population decimated, most of the remaining wolves fled, leaving Lexa as the lone protector of the Rose Branch Coven.

She had every reason to hate vampires. More reasons than Blythe had to despise werewolves.

Andi had reasons of her own, but she couldn't find it in her to hate Blythe. She seemed rude and sarcastic, but she was still just a person.

That drank blood. And couldn't stand the sunlight.

Andi finished recapping their conversation, trying to keep it as short as possible. "I just don't understand why they didn't tell me."

Lexa grinned. "Really, Ands?"

"What?" Andi glared at her. Lexa laughed. "What does that mean?"

"This has only been your special interest since you were, what, seven?" Lexa asked. "I bet they were just avoiding the babbling until the last possible moment."

"I am capable of not babbling." Andi's cheeks were growing warm again. She hadn't told Lexa about her attempt to correct Blythe, but it was repeating in her mind to the point that she wanted to sink into the steps.

"And the sun is capable of rising. Doesn't mean that it does."

Andi tried valiantly to hold it in, but the words burst out, almost of their own accord. "It still rises, just behind the darkness."

"Ha." Lexa snapped her fingers and pointed at her. "See?"

Andi pretended to find her knees incredibly fascinating. "That has nothing to do with the library."

"Yeah, but you can't help yourself. It's cute."

"I just…don't like people to be wrong," Andi said. "Because I wouldn't want to be wrong. I don't mean to…babble."

"That was a bad word for it," Lexa admitted. "But you know Chrys. They're kinda…eh. Eh meh. Weh."

"None of those were descriptive words." Andi realized a moment too late that she was doing it, again.

"They can be kind of an asshole," Lexa said.

Andi supposed that was true. Only a few years before, Chrys had been one of the most powerful witches in all of Obrye. They had been made coven head before she even came into the city from a tiny village up north when she was still a child.

That was before the darkness, before they lost the werewolves, and before her parents had been killed.

In two decades Chrys had lost nearly everything. Most of Obrye was coated in darkness, and if other towns had survived there was no way of contacting them. Vampires had gone from being an occasional danger to being a constant threat.

And the only witch with magic that worked consistently and well was an archive witch who just wanted to work in a library.

"I guess." She supposed she ought to answer. She rested her chin on her folded arms and looked up at the sky. Nothing pierced through. It was late afternoon, the world should have been gilded. Instead, it was a mass of shadow. "At least maybe we can do something about all of this. I'm kind of surprised she agreed to help us."

"Cause she's a leech?" Lexa asked.

"You are aware that's incredibly offensive, right?" Andi asked.

"That's the point." Lexa sighed when Andi glared at her. "Fine. Because she's a vampire? I mean, yeah, self-interest or whatever. But she owes Chrys huge. They saved her from being afflicted."

Andi stared at her. "…How?"

"Dunno, it was a few years back, when they still had their sauce."

"Don't ever call it that." Andi wrinkled her nose.

"You are so picky today. When they had their magic," Lexa said. "She must have been a normal vamp to begin with, and she fell. Happens, sometimes. I don't know the details."

"I wonder how," Andi said. Blythe seemed to be quite in control of herself. She hadn't even tried to attack them.

"Well, they're about out, you can ask her yourself, if you're feeling brave," Lexa stood up and stretched, offering Andi a hand.

She accepted it. "I don't think it's really a matter of feeling brave."

Chapter 3: Chase

Andi watched the sunlamps through the window.

They always overlapped, just slightly. Enough that the road was always bathed in light, only small wedges of shadow cutting into the road. Light like midday always filled the center of the city, but towards the edges the dark leaked in.

Chrys and Blythe had left the house with a bag each. Chrys hadn't said what was discussed, just told Lexa to drive them back to the coven hall.

The only sound since was the rumbling of the car's engine.

Andi snuck a look at her seat neighbor. The lights made Blythe's hair glow and shone on the metal handle of her cane. Her eyes glinted like a cat's in the moment between the lamps. Vampires could be in the sun, even the sun lamps, but they irritated them and caused them to weaken, losing a lot of their strength and agility.

Blythe looked over and Andi whipped her head around to stare out the window.

The car bounced over a particularly large pothole, jerking her against her seatbelt.

Road maintenance had been the least of anyone's worries for the last several years. Cars were a rarity, Andi had only ridden in one a few times. The first time had been on her way to the academy, a boxy thing that made the car Chrys was using now seem sleek and streamlined in comparison.

"The plan is to head back to the coven hall for the night, we'll head out first thing in the morning." Chrys's voice broke through her thoughts. "We'll be meeting Ingrid and Gilbert there. Do you remember them?"

"They're in charge of city defense." Andi had met them a few times. Ingrid's specialty was warding magic. She was kind, but fierce. Taller than most witches and able to swing a sword as easily as she used to be able to use magic. Gilbert was strong in light magic, which seemed odd for a man who looked like he had wrestled a bear and won. He'd become one of the most useful witches in the Rosewood in the last handful of years.

"Not leaving anything up to chance, are we," Blythe said. "Are you bringing her, too?"

"Of course I'm going." Lexa didn't take her eyes off the road. "And if you have a problem with that, you're free to jump out."

Blythe's fingers tightened around her cane. "I don't have a problem, merely getting a feel for what will be expected of me."

"Nothing much, just try not to bite anyone."

"I'll be on my best behavior if you are."

Andi tuned out their sniping, leaning back to stare out the window again. The only thing to see was the vague shape of bushes on the side of the road and the ever-present lamps, one after another.

And tiny lights, out in the darkness.

She frowned and sat up a bit, peering through the glass, trying to see past her own hollowed out reflection. It was far too late in the year for fireflies, but that was all she could think of what they looked like. Tiny flecks, moving and bouncing in pairs.

The cold realization that they were eyes reflecting the light hit her just as the sunlamps went dark.

"What the—" Lexa was cut off by something slamming onto the hood with a loud clang. Andi shrieked, leaning as hard as she could against her seat. A pale face with bright red eyes pressed against the glass. Lexa jerked the wheel and the vampire slid off.

"Why are the lights out?" Chrys yelled, rolling down the window. Cold air burst into the car, the wind overtaking the rattle of the engine.

"Why would I know that?" Lexa swerved to avoid another vampire leaping at the side of the car. They slammed right below Andi's door. She bit down another scream. "Get your head back in here!"

She grabbed the back of Chrys's sweater and hauled them back into the car, shifting with a quick jerk of the stick. Every dial on the dash whipped quickly to the right and back to the left in a way that Andi was fairly certain it wasn't supposed to.

She really should have learned something about any type of vehicle.

Chrys struggled to roll up the window. Another vampire threw themselves at their side of the car, latching onto the top of the glass. Chrys cursed and put all their weight on the handle. The vampire reached for them, but Blythe's cane lashed out, slamming into their arm and smashing it into their face. They howled and lurched back. Chrys hurried to roll the window up.

"Where to, boss?" Lexa shifted into the next gear, the entire car shuddering under the stress.

"Turn left next chance you get," Chrys said.

Lexa paused. "That's not towards city center."

"Those lights will be out, too," Chrys said. "This is an all-out attack. We need to get to the library. Right now."

"What about your friends?" Blythe asked.

"They'll know to head that way," Chrys insisted. "We're out of time. There's enough blood in these bags to hold you over and Andi has anti-venom in your bag. That's all that we need."

Andi put a hand on her bag. She did have four bottles of anti-venom, standard equipment for any witch leaving the coven hall, but she'd never thought she'd actually be in danger of using them.

"We had a deal—"

"The time for deals is over," Chrys snapped. "Turn left."

"Yeah, I don't think they're going to let me!"

Andi immediately saw the problem.

She wished she hadn't.

There was a barricade in the road, right where the fork was just visible. One of the bushes on the side of the road had been hauled to the middle, surrounded by vampires, all of them afflicted judging by their white hair. The afflicted weren't known for planning ahead, but Andi didn't see the normal vampire that must have been controlling them.

"She's not built for off road." Lexa hadn't taken her foot off the gas. "Gonna have to use the lights."

"Those are experimental, they—"

"Sorry, can't hear you!" Lexa slammed her other foot down on a pedal she hadn't used yet.

The round headlights flooded the entire road in front of them with blinding, searing light. The vampires shrieked and scurried out of the line of fire.

The bushes caught, flames roaring in the dry leaves and twigs. The barricade lit like it had been doused in gasoline.

"Okay, yeah, experimental." Lexa shifted again, spinning the steering wheel. A horrible screech of rubber and they didn't so much turn as slide to face left, drifting through the flames and coming out the other side. The car shuddered when Lexa threw it into another gear, stopped just long enough for Andi's stomach to catch back up to her, and lurched forward.

"You have quite a grip there," Blythe said.

Andi realized she'd grabbed her arm and immediately let go, holding onto the door handle with a grip that hurt her knuckles. "Sorry."

"Gonna need directions soon!" Lexa yelled. The engine let out a high pitched whine and rattled ominously.

"Right!" Chrys yelled, and they were all thrown to the side when Lexa turned again. If it weren't for the rope-like seat belt, Andi would have gone flying through the window.

They were in the city again, but not the one that Andi had become used to. As Chrys had predicted, all of the sunlamps were off. Only the interior lights kept the dark at bay.

With a crack and a pop, one of their headlights went out.

"Turn those off!" Chrys yelled.

"Don't know what to tell you, I've been hitting the pedal for the last five minutes," Lexa said.

"I told you they were experimental."

"Eh, we're alive." Lexa spun the wheel at Chrys's next barked out direction, nearly slamming into the curb. The streets were narrower, meant for pedestrians, not vehicles. The dark city streets were completely abandoned.

The wheels bounced and jerked on the cobblestone. Andi almost bit her tongue and kept her mouth closed after that.

Chrys instructed Lexa to pull over and she slid the car to a stop, the wheels bumping the curb so hard that the other tires left the ground before bouncing back down, yanking Andi against her seatbelt.

"Why do I let you drive, again?" Chrys muttered, head in their hands.

"Because you can't." Lexa gave them a winning smile, turning off the car. The remaining headlight went out, leaving them in darkness. "…Chrys, this is a school."

An all-girl's school for the gifted, according to the sign atop the wooden double doors.

"I know." Chrys opened the door and stepped out onto the street. "The doorway is inside. Come on, it's only a matter of time before we're overrun. I think we only just beat them."

"How did they know about it?" Blythe asked. "Who have you told?"

"No one," Chrys said. "Only present company, Gilbert, and Ingrid. Before you say anything, I trust them with my life."

"The librarian?" Andi suggested. "The teachers?"

"Have all been at coven hall since the opening was reported." Chrys pulled out a key and unlocked the door, leading them all inside.

The school's high ceiling was lost to gloom, despite the lights lining each doorway all the way down the hall. They glowed feebly, unable to penetrate the miasma that seemed to have fallen over the school. The smell of ozone was thick in the air, along with a tension that made Andi step closer to Lexa.

Only one door was ajar, at the very end of the hallway. Light leaked across the scuffed and well used floorboards.

Chrys walked straight to the open door. Andi followed, her hand on her bag. Lexa locked the doors behind them, though Andi doubted it would even slow a vampire down. Blythe's footsteps were silent, but her cane tapped softly with each step.

Chrys pushed the door open the rest of the way.

On the other side was a small library, the walls lined with books.

A doorway took up most of the back wall, surrounded by thick roots.

Chapter 4: Doorway

Andi touched one of the roots. Magic thrummed under her fingertips, ancient and deep. She peered into the doorway. The roots twisted into a tunnel beyond it, stretching out into darkness.

"It really is The Library."

She hadn't doubted Chrys, exactly, but there was a large difference from being told it was back and seeing it with her own eyes.

"How long until Ingrid and Gilbert get here?" Lexa asked, strapping on her sword belt and slinging her bag over her shoulder.

"I'm not sure, it depends on if they were held up or not," Chrys said. "We might not want to wait very long, it won't take the vampires a lot of time before—"

Lexa shushed them, holding up one hand. She turned her head to the side, listening, her ears twitching. Blythe was listening, too.

Andi didn't hear anything.

Lexa motioned for them all to stay put and moved towards the door, carefully, her boots not making a sound on the floorboards. She listened at the gap of the door, then pulled it closed. A screech rose from somewhere inside the school. Andi's heart beat faster and she wished she was safe at home. Or at the library.

Both of those places might have been overrun already.

"Dammit," Lexa muttered. "Vamps. Lots of 'em. I don't think Ingrid and Gil are getting through."

"I knew they'd find it eventually." Chrys was surprisingly calm. "I'll stay back, hold them off as long as I can. You three get to the core. Quickly."

"What?" Andi's voice cracked. "But we can't just leave you here, we—"

"There's no time, and we're out of options." Chrys put their hands on her shoulders and steered her over to the side. There was no doubt that Blythe and Lexa could hear every word regardless, but there was at least the illusion of privacy. "I wouldn't do this if there was any other choice. Andi, you are an amazing witch."

"I'm just an archive witch," she said.

They shook their head. "No, you're so much more than that. I believe in you. I know you'll find the curse's origin and fix all of this."

"I'm not a curse breaker!" Andi's voice went up an octave without any input from her. She wanted to cry, or maybe scream. She dug her nails into her palms and tried to even out her breathing.

"I know," Chrys said. "But you're the only hope we have now. Lexa will help you, and Blythe is…she can be very reliable, when she chooses to be. I'll buy you as much time as I can. Ingrid and

Gil are probably on their way. Everything will be okay, I promise you, but you have to go."

She knew they were right, she knew she needed to get moving. Her fingernails stung her palms. She bit her lip and nodded, jerkily. Chrys pulled her into a hug, squeezing her tight, then turned and released her, pushing her towards the doorway. "I'll be there as soon as I can."

She knew they were lying.

She didn't call them on it. They were already perfectly aware.

"Keep her safe." Chrys pulled the bag off of their shoulder and handed it Lexa.

"Of course." Lexa nodded. "C'mon, leech, let's get going."

"That's not a nice way to speak to someone who is here to help you," Blythe said. She looked at Chrys and something like concern crossed her face. "I still don't like you. Don't die."

"Trust me, I don't plan on it," Chrys said.

"Have to make sure you can help us?" Blythe asked.

Chrys snorted. "Don't flatter yourself. I have a husband waiting at home who will turn to necromancy and kill me again. Go. Hurry."

Blythe nodded and followed Andi and Lexa into the doorway.

Andi only didn't trip into the darkness beyond thanks to Lexa grabbing her arm, keeping her from falling flat on her face. Lexa carefully moved around her. "I should probably lead the way. Blythe, you take the back."

"Oh, we're using names now?" Blythe asked.

"Just shut up and guard the rear before I stick my foot up yours."

"Noted."

"I can't see anything." As if it had heard her, it brightened. They were in a tunnel made of the twisted roots of the tree. The lights were mushrooms, jutting from the walls, coming up from the floors, and hanging from the ceiling. They glowed in a myriad of colors, too soft to be much use on their own, but together the light was strong enough for her to move forward without bumping into anything.

"Interesting." Blythe touched one of the mushrooms. The cap wobbled slightly, shedding glowing spores.

Lexa reached around Andi to grab her wrist. "Are you going to touch everything you see? Because if you are, we're going to have a problem."

"And if you don't get your hand off of me, we will definitely have a problem." Blythe bared her fangs.

Lexa's lips pulled back from her own sharp teeth and her voice took on another layer, a deeper tone that was more of a growl. "Is that so?"

"Guys!" Andi stepped between them, separating them, holding her hands out between them. It was not her best decision ever, getting between an angry werewolf and a vampire. Either one of them could kill her with essentially no effort, even if the emotional toll would be pretty severe on one side. Blythe barely knew her. "Stop it! Chrys is…Chrys could die for us, do you know that? They could die and—"

And the tears were stinging her eyes. She blinked hard, valiantly, hoping that they wouldn't notice.

"—and we should get moving and stop arguing."

"…Sorry, Ands." Lexa patted her shoulder. "You're right. No more fighting, just moving."

"Agreed," Blythe nodded.

Andi nodded, not trusting her voice, it had already sounded wrung out. They kept walking and hot tears flowed over her cheeks. She tried to wipe them away, but they kept coming, stinging her cheeks raw. Everything she had ever known was behind her, and she had no idea if any of it would be there when she came back.

If she came back.

"Hey, they're gonna be okay," Lexa reassured her. "Chrys is scrappy. Even without magic. Don't worry about them, all right?"

She nodded.

A cold hand settled on her shoulder. She glanced back, but Blythe retracted her comfort before Andi could acknowledge it. All she could do was nod. Blythe nodded back.

At least she stopped crying. It still felt like something was stuck in her chest.

She stepped down somewhere else. The shift was so quick that she only felt it like a breath too close to her ear, sending a shiver down her spine.

It was a large, wide-open room. The walls were lined with bookshelves made of dark wood. In front of them a set of stairs led to a lower level. A fire crackled in an ornate stone fireplace. A silver chandelier hung over the tables set in front of the hearth. A crystal like the one in Blythe's library was suspended above the mantle.

She looked back. The tunnel full of mushrooms twisted away between two bookshelves, back the way they came.

"…Is this the library proper?" Blythe asked.

"Weird that it just appeared." Lexa pulled a book off of the shelf. It had no title. She flipped it open, but the pages were blank. "Well. That's useful."

Andi walked down the stairs, towards the fireplace. The mantle had an intricate carving of a tree, spreading its roots down and around the sides, the branches stretching up across the ceiling, incorporating the rafters so it looked like the chandelier was hung from a limb.

"Another blank book." Lexa tossed it on the floor.

"Put that back," Andi scolded her.

"You're always telling me to not put the books back," Lexa argued.

"Yes, well, that's in my library." Andi looked at the fire. No warmth came from it, and even though it crackled and popped, it didn't seem to actually be consuming the wood. She stepped closer and put her hand in the flames. It felt like a gentle breeze flowing between her fingers. A ghost trying to hold her hand.

"Andi!" Lexa vaulted over the railing and grabbed her wrist, yanking her hand back. "What are you..."

"It's not hot," Andi explained. Her hand was perfectly fine, her sleeve unmarred. "I don't think this is real."

"Really? What gave you that idea?" Blythe reached over and pulled a cord on one of the lamps on the tables. It came to life with a flicker and Blythe yanked her hand back like had burned. "...Strange, it's a candle."

"Next time, how about the person who's closer keeps this little idiot from sticking her hand in the fire," Lexa suggested.

Blythe blinked at her. "Far be it from me to hinder the scientific process."

"There is nothing scientific about sticking your hand in a burning fire—"

"As opposed to other kinds of fire?"

"I thought we agreed to not fight," Andi reminded them. They both stopped talking for a moment, at least. "And I wouldn't have done it if I thought I would get burned. We must have taken a wrong turn somewhere, or...or maybe..."

"There were no turns," Lexa said.

"I mean maybe we missed one." Andi knew it wasn't likely, but she didn't see a way forward. There were no doors, just the single enclosed room without any windows. She walked up the steps and stopped short when she realized what was missing.

The doorway was gone, leaving behind a solid wall of shelves.

"But it was right here," she said, dumbfounded. She placed a hand on the shelf, but all she felt was the stiff leather of the books and the wood of the shelf. "It was, wasn't it?"

Lexa gently moved her out of the way before slamming her shoulder into the shelf. The thud was terrific, but all it accomplished was knocking books off of the shelf. "Well. Now what?"

"I assume there's another way out," Blythe said, calmly. She hadn't followed them up the stairs, leaning against the railing. "But unfortunately, magic is not really my strong suit, so it's probably up to the witch."

"Andrea," Andi said, knowing it wouldn't make any difference.

"You're right, it's up to Andrea," Blythe said. The way that she said Andi's seldom used full name made her feel strange, like she'd stepped off of the stairs and expected another stair to be there. A jolt. She shook her head and decided to ignore it.

She closed her eyes, trying to feel the magic of the room, but it just seemed like any other room she'd ever been in. One without an entrance or an exit, but otherwise a normal room.

"Maybe one of the books can help us," Lexa said. "If they aren't all blank."

"Right." Andi nodded. She sat down on the stairs and accessed her archive, letting the magic flow through the library, checking the books. She knew what it looked like — golden sand in a stream, sliding in the gaps between the books, dusting the pages, before pulling back to check the next shelf.

All of the books were blank.

She frowned, searching harder for even the barest impression of a pen, the tiniest splotch of ink, anything to indicate that the books were anything but for show, but nothing returned her call.

"That's beautiful," Blythe said, quietly. Andi barely heard her, like she was speaking in another room.

"I love it when she does this," Lexa agreed.

At least they were agreeing, but Andi couldn't let it distract her.

A few more minutes and she found something, a book with some sort of writing in it. A motion with her hand had it flying off the shelf and flipping open.

The page turned black.

Chapter 5: Archive Magic

The book fluttered gently into Andi's hands. She closed it and ran her fingers over the soft green leather of the cover. There was no title, only a golden tree with delicate leaves embossed on the front. She flipped it open again, trying to find a page that wasn't black. Faint, spidery handwriting scrawled across the creamy paper.

She squinted at it, but she only read the words "the library" before the letters ran together and ink bloomed across the page.

"What's happening to it?" Blythe asked.

Andi jumped. She hadn't realized Blythe was so close, nearly leaning over her shoulder.

"I don't know," she admitted, hoping that Blythe hadn't noticed the rise in her heartbeat, but judging by the small smile on her face she most certainly had. "I've never seen anything like this, it's like—"

The book collapsed into glittery black sand. It streamed between her fingers. It scattered across the floorboards with a soft hiss.

She blinked at her suddenly empty hands. All that remained were dark smudges on her palms.

"Well. That's never happened before." Lexa crouched down, scooping up a handful of sand. It trickled out of her fist like an hourglass counting the seconds.

"I was about to ask if this was normal, I'm glad we've cleared that up," Blythe said. She looked up and grabbed Andi's arm, dragging her to her feet. Her fingers were like cold iron through the thin sleeve of Andi's blouse.

Andi was about to protest, but when she looked up and the words shriveled on her tongue.

A shadow spread across the surface of the chandelier, tarnish eating away at the silver. The candle flames burst impossibly high for just a moment, the light throwing the staircase and its occupants into sharp relief. Andi squeaked and moved closer to Blythe, who stood as still as a pillar. Lexa drew her sword, standing between Andi and the rest of the room.

The flames flashed to purple and extinguished, leaving behind nubs of charred wax in crumbling holders.

"What just happened?" Andi asked.

"Don't think it's over." Lexa didn't turn to look at her.

The chain the chandelier was suspended from groaned horribly.

"We should move." Blythe's voice was calm, but she practically dragged Andi up the stairs, leaning hard on her cane for the last few steps.

The entire chandelier toppled to the floor.

It crashed on the floor and exploded into more black sand. The table lamp exploded with a pop. The tables tilted drunkenly towards the center of the room, their legs eroding away. The fire roared and blinked out. The mantle above it cracked, tiny pieces of stone hailing down to the floor.

The stairs sagged and cracked. The railing melted like wax on a hot day. Andi glanced down, sand was moving over her boots, trying to pull her off of the balcony and down into the pit below.

"I think now would be a really great time to get out of here!" Lexa yelled over the roar of the sand steadily filling the bottom part of the room.

"How, exactly?" Blythe slapped her cane against the shelves. "The entrance is gone and if you saw an exit you certainly didn't share it."

Lexa snarled and took a swing at Blythe, who barely got her cane up in time for the blow to glance off of it.

"Stop it!" Andi had to yell just to hear her own voice. "Stop it, both of you!"

She stepped forward, though what she intended to do next exactly she wasn't sure.

There wasn't time to think of it. Her boot hit a soft spot in the floor and she stumbled into what was left of the railing.

It didn't hold her.

For a moment she was weightless.

Before she could process that she was falling she hit the sand, hard enough that it knocked the air out of her, pain crackling through her side. The particles pulled greedily at her, dragging her towards the center of the room. She fought weakly against it, yanking one hand free and grabbing onto the edge of a shelf that hadn't disintegrated.

The sound was incredible, as if she was teetering at the edge of a waterfall. If Lexa was yelling for her, she couldn't hear it. The only thing that reached her ears was the sand, rushing towards the middle of the room into a massive vortex, trying to pull her with it.

Her fingers were slipping from the bookcase. She clung to it with all of her might. Her mind raced, but it was like a fluttering bird, not landing on a single thought.

She slapped a hand on the surface of the sand, trying to heave herself up more.

The space around her hand glowed.

The noise stopped. The sand halted its progress so abruptly she yanked herself forward and only the shelf failing in the moment kept her from braining herself against it.

The stillness was so sudden her ears rang.

The sand drifted slowly towards the center of the room with a quiet sigh.

It wasn't sand.

It was magic.

Archive witch magic, quite a bit like her own. She pressed her hand deeper into the grains. She couldn't control it, but she could nudge it to take the shape it wanted to.

It formed into a massive tree, the branches spreading out in a thin lace of empty twigs.

"Andi!" Lexa landed next to her with a soft thud of her boots. "Are you okay?"

"I think so." Andi's voice was steadier than she expected. She accepted Lexa's hand up. She'd lost her hat and her hands felt scraped and raw, but she was breathing.

"Amazing." Blythe walked carefully down what remained of the stairs, her eyes on the tree. "Did you do this?"

"It's…it's archive witch magic," Andi said. "Kind of. I think it made this room."

"Since when can you do that?" Lexa asked.

Andi flushed. "No. I'm not even controlling it. I just nudged it a bit."

"Well, nudge it a bit more," Lexa said, like it was obvious. "Get us out of here."

"Or you could figure out where exactly we're supposed to be going," Blythe suggested.

"Which won't matter if we don't get out of here." Lexa glared at her.

Andi put a hand on Lexa's arm. "Look, I get it, you hate each other, but can you please stop."

"I'm indifferent, honestly," Blythe said. "But I suppose you do have a point, since she almost got you killed trying to take a swing at me."

"And next time I promise I won't miss." Lexa bared her teeth. Andi gave her a look. Lexa sighed, shoulders dropping. "I'm sorry. I should have been protecting you. I'm really glad you're okay."

"I'm fine." Andi patted her shoulder. "Just a little shaken up. You both have great points, we need to get out of here and find out where we're going, so let's see if I can do anything."

She stood up, a bit unsteady, the heels of her boots sinking in the sand. Lexa held her elbow until she got her footing. Andi flashed her a grateful smile and Lexa beamed back.

Andi walked carefully towards the tree, putting a hand on its trunk. It was incredibly detailed, the bark was rough underneath her fingertips. It must have been the tree, the one that the library was in. She'd never seen it.

It was beautiful.

She'd hoped for some detailed map, or maybe an arrow pointing at where they were, but instead a purple light glowed at the top of the tree. The sand moved towards it, forming a giant sphere, surrounded by rings.

She recognized it.

"It looks like one of the library crystals. Are you trying to tell me that's the core?" She reached out to touch it, and it collapsed, the magic blowing away, covering her with a fine glitter. She squeezed her eyes closed against it, but it felt soft against her face, like fingers brushing against her cheek.

When she opened her eyes again, they were standing in the same corridor as before with no sign of the room. Not a single bit of the magic remained.

Chapter 6:
Focus

"What just happened?"

Andi had no idea how to answer Blythe. She brushed the last remaining black sand from her skirt. The grains disappeared before they could touch the floor.

"Air smells different." Lexa sheathed her sword. "This isn't the same spot we entered at."

Andi had to take her word for it. Everything looked the same to her, the walls of twisted wood and the mushrooms providing just enough light that she wasn't stumbling into the walls. It trailed off into darkness on either side of them. Shadows swallowed up the details.

"Well, then, if this is a new area, which way do we go?" Blythe asked.

"Why would I know? I'm not a vampire," Lexa said. "Lead the way."

"I thought you were our fearless leader?" Blythe leaned on her cane, giving Lexa a little smile that was designed to be antagonizing. "I believe you should be taking point."

"Oh no, I insist, you do it." Lexa smiled back.

"I wouldn't dream of getting in the way of your decisiveness."

"Yeah?" Lexa's eye twitched. "How's your face?"

"I'll be the leader." Andi couldn't take the conflict anymore. It had nearly gotten her killed. They both looked at her like they'd forgotten she was here. "Yeah, hi, I've only been reading about this place my entire life. I'm pretty sure I should be in charge."

"Great." Blythe's smile didn't change, but Andi wasn't going to rise to the bait. "And we're going this way."

She picked a direction, the way she was facing, and started walking.

If Blythe and Lexa had complaints neither of them voiced them, following her. For a while all Andi could hear were her own footsteps. Lexa and Blythe both stepped silently.

If she had more magic she could have moved silently, too, but doing that would burn through her reserves quickly. She wasn't sure what she needed to save her magic for, but she'd rather have it.

"So, tell me," Blythe's voice broke through the silence like a window cracking. "How does archive magic work? Chrys was never particularly forthcoming."

"Well, it's a little complicated," Andi admitted. She'd never had to explain it to anyone before. Lexa had never shown much interest, and she was the only person Andi talked to at length. "But essentially, I can take in information and store it using magic."

"So you just know things?" Blythe asked.

Andi had to laugh, a little bit. "I wish! That would make my life so much easier. No, the information ends up in a magical archive that I can access at will. I still have to learn it."

"That sucks," Lexa said. She looked at Blythe. "Kind of like you."

"Adorable."

"I am, thanks."

"Anyway, I was trying to find information in that…that room back there." Andi wasn't quite sure what to call it. It hadn't been real. "I thought I had, but…"

Her magic had quickly scanned through the faint handwriting, but it wasn't enough for her to really understand what it was trying to say.

"Unfortunately, nothing to find." Blythe nodded. "What other sorts of things do you have in that magical storeroom of yours?"

"Nuh uh." Lexa stepped between Andi and Blythe. "Nope. None of that. Those are Coven secrets, and you don't get to know those."

"Oh please, what am I going to do with Coven secrets?" Blythe rolled her eyes. "I don't even talk to other vampires, I—"

Whatever she was about to say was cut off by another abrupt change of scenery.

Bookshelves rose up on either side of them, all the way to an arched ceiling so high above her she almost couldn't make it out. The floor was made of dark tile and marble busts sat at the end of each shelf.

Andi leaned in to read the nearest one, but the plaque was too faint and worn. The stern looking scholar didn't look familiar.

"Is this just a thing we have to deal with?" Lexa asked. "Random libraries just appearing? Is this one fake, too?"

"I think so," Andi said. The light coming from between the shelves didn't look like sunlight, even filtered through clouds. It was too flat to even be a sun lamp. "I don't think we're in the library proper yet."

"Really? So we just stepped into a vine tunnel for fun, then?" Blythe asked.

Andi shook her head. "No, before it disappeared the library connected the entire continent, through other libraries. I think we're seeing the memories of those places, like an echo."

It was the only thing that made sense to her.

"So we're stuck in the echoes?" Lexa asked. "How do we get out of here and into the actual library?"

"I…I'll figure it out," Andi said, but she had no idea. She had never expected to set foot in any part of the library. The information on it had always been sparse, probably by design. A quick glance through her archive didn't reveal anything new. "Maybe it's related to the seal Chrys mentioned. The one we have Blythe here for."

Blythe shrugged. "I don't know what you expect me to do about it. I'm not an elder vampire, I don't know any magic or spells."

"Maybe it's linked to something else, not spells." Andi could only hope that was the case. She doubted she could nicely ask one of the three elder vampires for a door into the library proper. "Does this place look familiar to you?"

Blythe considered the tall, dark arched ceiling and the long passageway between the shelves that they were currently standing in. "Possibly. I'm not sure."

"How can you not be sure?" Lexa motioned to one of the statues. "You're telling me you've never seen this guy and his fabulous mustache?"

"A lot of my memories from before are…vague," Blythe said.

"Before you became a thrall?" Lexa asked.

It was like a window had closed in Blythe's expression. She pulled herself up straight, her cane held tightly in her hands. "The correct term is afflicted. And yes, my time before that is not as clear as it once was. I've already been poked and prodded for it enough, nothing you do will get that part of my past to be any clearer."

"I'm sorry." Andi knew she must have been afflicted, judging by her hair and eye color. Normal vampires kept their hair color and their eyes were red. Elder vampires had white hair, but their skin was gray like stone.

Only the afflicted lost the pigment in their irises.

Blythe stepped closer to the bust Lexa had gestured towards. It was a heavily jowled man with a thick, curling mustache and a bald head. A silver monocle had been screwed in front of one eye, the lens catching the strange light. Blythe patted the dome of his head. "You're right. It would be awfully hard to forget this face."

"He looks like a walrus," Andi said.

"He certainly does." Blythe smiled at her, and for the first time it looked almost genuine. "So, what I'm gathering from all of this is that you still think I'm the key to getting us into the library proper, correct?"

"More like a library card," Lexa said. No one laughed. "Ooh, tough crowd."

"I mean, yes, to both analogies," Andi said. "If the library disappearing is linked to the vampire curse, then yes. Only a vampire would be able to access the library."

"So what do I need to do?" Blythe asked.

"Focus on where you want to go." Andi hoped she sounded like she knew what she was talking about. "On the core. It will look a lot like the crystal in your library. But bigger."

"The floating one?" Blythe asked. "Is that what the sand was showing us earlier?"

"I believe so," Andi said. "I think it's at the top. The crown. Where the branches spread from the trunk."

"I know what the crown of a tree is," Blythe said.

Andi's cheeks were warm. "Right. If we're anywhere in the physical tree, or the metaphysical of the tree, I think we'd be in the roots. So…up? Up is good."

"You sound so certain. Up it is." Blythe closed her eyes. Her eyelashes were barely visible against her pale cheeks, like snowflakes. She opened them after a moment. "Hm. That didn't work."

"How about you think and we walk, genius?" Lexa suggested.

Blythe didn't answer Lexa, stepping between Andi and the library behind them, holding up her cane like it was a sword. Andi hoped her heartbeat wasn't too loud. It was a fast staccato in her own ears.

"What is it?" Lexa peered into the shadowy shelves behind them. The passageway seemed to stretch on forever, the shelves layered on each other.

"I'm not sure," Blythe relaxed, her cane resting on the floor again. "I thought I saw something."

"One of these guys?" Lexa gestured to walrus man.

"Maybe." Blythe didn't seem convinced. "I think we should take your suggestion and keep moving forward."

They started walking, Blythe in front and Lexa behind Andi, an arrangement they came to without even speaking, which Andi was grateful for. She wasn't sure she could take much more arguing.

Andi would have rather had the bickering than the silence. She'd always liked the quiet of a library - it was calming, a presence all of its own. This was nothing like that. There was an ominous cast to it. The light was harsher, the shadows deeper, their edges sharp as knives. Andi glanced back, once, and thought she saw something move at the end of a shelf, but when she looked again nothing was there.

Only the busts changing showed they had been moving at all. Instead of a man who looked like a walrus, it was an older woman who looked like she'd eaten a lemon before she was immortalized in marble.

Just as she was certain she'd seen the woman before, they were back in the corridor. She hadn't realized how tightly her shoulders were wound until she relaxed them. She sighed and leaned against the wall, the grain of the wood rough against her palms, but comforting and solid.

Blythe leaned next to her. "Don't look, and don't be alarmed, but there's something behind us."

Chapter 7: Castle

It took every ounce of willpower for Andi to not look back. "How, exactly, am I supposed to not be alarmed by that?"

"It's a vampire," Lexa's voice was quiet, for once. "Must be regular."

Andi nodded. An elder vampire would have already confronted them. A confrontation they wouldn't have survived. A thrall wouldn't hesitate to attack. Still, she moved a little closer to Lexa. "It must have slipped past Chrys."

She had to believe that they were still alive. Most likely they had been forced to retreat and await reinforcements, only able to buy them time.

"If we keep moving forward, we should enter another room, correct?" Blythe's voice was low in her ear, her fingers cold at Andi's elbow, even through the fabric of her sleeve. "We may be able to lose them that way. Particularly if I keep focusing?"

"Right." Andi nodded. "If my theory is correct."

"Oh, this is a theory now?" Blythe asked.

Andi avoided eye contact. "Magic is largely theory and very little practice."

"Somehow, I don't believe that," Blythe said.

"How about we use our quiet voices, pretend we didn't see anything, and keep moving." Lexa didn't wait for them to comply, just started walking again, her hand on the hilt of her sword.

Andi tried her best not to crowd her. Something scraped in the tunnel behind her. A shudder worked its way up her spine.

"Don't worry." Blythe's voice was so close it made her jump. "I'll keep you safe."

"Y-yeah." Andi wasn't sure if that was entirely true. She trusted Chrys, and they had recommended bringing Blythe along, but that was with an entire team. Not just her and Lexa.

And Chrys was much stronger, even without magic.

"I'm just saying, you don't need to be scared." Blythe hadn't moved farther back, staying as close to Andi as she could and still walk without tripping over her. "You look delicious, but I promise I won't bite."

"Is now really the time to be teasing me?" Andi looked at her. Out of the corner of her eye she caught movement, not far enough behind them for her to feel safe. She wasn't sure if such a distance existed.

"When else will I have the opportunity, miss archivist?" Blythe laughed, softly.

"You're supposed to be focusing."

Blythe shrugged. "Luckily for you, I'm a woman of many talents. Besides, it's working, isn't it? Distracting you?"

"Unfortunately, I'm also a woman of many talents," Andi said. "I can easily be terrified and annoyed at the same time."

"Incredible." Blythe pressed a hand to her chest. "I can't believe I'm in the presence of such greatness."

Andi smiled, despite herself. "You are. Don't forget it."

"I could never."

"Are you two done flirting?" Lexa asked. "I'm trying to listen to our little friend, but I can't really do that over whatever this awfulness is."

Blythe laughed.

Andi's face was on fire. She was going to die of mortification. "I'm not—"

She never got the chance to finish her denial. The scenery around them changed abruptly.

They were in another room full of shelves, the books layered thickly, some of them stacked on the wooden floor. An arched window looked out on a rain slicked city street, the sky above gray and low, nearly touching the spires of a castle at the end of a cobbled street.

"I know where we are." Blythe leaned heavily on her cane and nearly upset a pile of books when she walked towards the window, putting a hand up to the water speckled glass. "That's Carmine's castle."

"The elder vampire?" Andi asked.

There were only a handful of elder vampires, the first to be turned. Carmine was infamously cruel and bloodthirsty. She'd ruled from what was once the capital city of Obrye, sitting on a throne soaked in the blood of the royal family.

There had been no monarchy in Obrye since.

"She was the one who turned me." Blythe was still staring out the window, her hand against the glass. "Years and years ago. Back when the world still looked like this."

"Carmine was your…the Butcher of Obrye changed you?" Andi didn't know how to feel. She didn't know Blythe, or what kind of life she must have led, but it was completely at odds from the person Andi thought was in front of her.

"Does that surprise you?" Blythe finally turned to look at her. She looked tired, delicate purple blooming underneath her eyes.

"I suppose that would be a shock. That was a very different time, before…well. That's behind me now, and here I am, helping witches to save the world from the dark. But, I have been in this library. I remember it fondly."

"Then we must be getting somewhere," Lexa said. "So, you lived up in that big castle, huh?"

"For a time," Blythe said. "I wouldn't go back for the world, if it means anything."

Andi wasn't sure that it did. Blythe was a puzzle that she could only find the corner pieces for, the frame not matching up to the picture.

"You're staring," Blythe told her.

"Sorry." Andi looked away, her face heating up again. She knew she must be bright red, she showed her emotions too easily. "Yes, we must be getting somewhere. Just keep concentrating, and—"

Lexa held up one hand, signaling them both to be quiet. Blythe nodded.

Andi hadn't heard a thing. She strained her ears.

A faint, almost inaudible scrape.

In a fake library specifically created from Blythe's memories.

The hair on the back of her neck rose. Had they been followed? Had whatever was in the hallway gotten into the room with them? It hadn't seemed close enough, but vampires were fast.

If she was incredibly optimistic, she could have hoped that it was Chrys. Possibly Ingrid or Gil.

But even she wasn't that hopeful.

Another scrape, closer, louder, but she couldn't tell where it was coming from. There were too many shelves. Whatever it was, it could be anywhere, the sounds echoing off of anything. She tried to peer through one of the shelves, but all she saw were shadows and more books.

A skittering sound, the scramble of claws on wood. It sounded too close.

Lexa nodded at Blythe before she stalked forward, silently. Blythe moved in front of Andi, crowding her against the cold window. Andi grabbed the back of her jacket. Blythe glanced back. Her pupils were huge, rubies lined with silver.

She wasn't safe, either.

Somehow, Andi wasn't afraid of her. Or maybe Blythe was just the evil she knew.

Blythe motioned for her to be quiet. She realized her breathing had gotten ragged, her heart pounding against her ribs. She struggled to stay quiet, to calm her drumbeat of a pulse, trying to remember every single calming exercise that Chrys had ever given her. Saying it might save her life one day.

They had been right, but every single lesson slipped from her like water.

If Blythe noticed her heartbeat, she gave no sign.

That, more than anything, helped. Andi breathed in, counted the books on the shelf closest to her, and breathed out.

It was too quiet.

Lexa didn't make a noise when she moved among the books. Blythe didn't even breathe. Andi pressed her forehead against Blythe's shoulder, willing her heart to slow even more, for her mind to stop racing. The cold grounded her, but she couldn't help the unease prickling across her scalp and down her neck.

"I lost it." Lexa admitted, stepping back into their little alcove. "Can't get a scent on it, either."

"Wonderful," Blythe said. "What could it have possibly been, then?"

"Magic feeder, maybe," Lexa said. "Sometimes they get into places like this, gorge themselves, fall asleep for a few centuries, get woken up when the magic comes back to life. Wouldn't be the first time."

Andi nodded. "She's right, it could have been. Magic feeders would have been more common when the library was around, and they can hibernate for an indefinite amount of time, as far as we're aware."

Magic feeders were pests. They looked like moths, in their most basic stage, but with enough magic they could become big enough to be a hazard. Andi used to beat them out of the curtains in the library with a stick.

She hadn't seen one for a long time.

"That's your best guess?" Blythe asked. "I don't think they get that large."

They both looked at Andi, who shrugged. "Theoretically it's possible."

"There you go with your theories again," Blythe said. "Can you give me something a little more concrete?"

"Look, if you wanna go find it, then you can be my guest." Lexa motioned to the space between the shelves. "If it wasn't a magic feeder, it was probably one of your little friends."

"I don't have any friends," Blythe said, coolly.

"Now that's a shock. I'm shocked." Lexa pressed a hand to her chest. "It might just kill me."

"I hope it does, the world would be a much better place—"

"Please stop fighting." Andi's voice was very small. She felt small. Blythe was still standing straight to attention, like she was expecting a fight.

Lexa sighed, running a hand over her hair, shoving a few loose strands back. "Yeah. Sorry."

"I apologize as well." Blythe didn't relax at all. "Whatever it was, maybe they were just terrified of what they'd be facing."

"What, you?" Lexa snorted. "Or me?"

"Oh, please, I've been punched by you," Blythe said.

"To be fair. I wasn't actually trying to hurt you."

"I hope not, you would make a poor bodyguard otherwise," Blythe said. "Regardless, I meant our lovely little archivist here."

"That's not funny," Andi told her. "Are you just trying to distract me again? Because it won't work."

"No, she's right, you're very scary, you got between a werewolf and a leech," Lexa said. "No offense."

"How could that be anything but offensive?"

Despite how calmly they were talking, Andi knew that the danger hadn't passed. Blythe and Lexa were standing too stiffly, and she was still so close to the window the cold radiating off of it was like frost creeping up her back.

Something dripped on the floor.

A leak? It was still raining.

Andi slowly lifted her eyes to the ceiling.

A horrible, pale thing leered down at her.

Chapter 8: Monster

Andi didn't even have a chance to scream before she was shoved back toward the window.

The thing fell to the floor with a thud, hard enough the glass shuddered under Andi's fingertips.

It was humanoid, standing on two short, bowed legs, but hunched over onto its thick forearms. That was where the similarities with a person ended. It was huge, nearly twice her height even with its head bowed. Its skin was so pale it was see-through, a dark tracery of veins forming patterns across it. The only color on its face was the wide, red mouth, full of sharp, yellowed teeth. Above the mouth it had only slits for a nose. It had no eyes. Large, bat-like ears rose on either side of a scalp covered by thick, silvery hair that sprouted over its shoulders. A thin membrane flapped between its arms and sides.

It sniffed the air, a loud sound, and moved forward. Long claws scraped against the floorboards.

Blythe lifted her cane.

It lunged forward with no warning at all.

Blythe slashed at it with her cane, knocking it into a bookshelf. Pages exploded from their bindings, fluttering through the air. It let out a high-pitched screech that had Andi clamping her hands over her ears.

It swung itself around to the top of the shelf, stalking along the top like an angry cat, complete with a hiss.

"Stay behind me," Blythe said, quietly.

Its ears swiveled around, not towards them, but behind it where Lexa had landed on the shelf. It shrieked again and threw itself at her. She slashed at it, catching one of its arms with a glancing blow, but it knocked her off of the shelf. She landed and slid back from the force of it, still holding her sword. The blade was black with blood.

The creature launched itself from the top of the bookshelf, slapped Lexa's sword to the side and grabbed her head. It slammed her into the opposite bookshelf and tossed her to the side. It whirled at Blythe and slashed at her with its claws. She sidestepped easily and hit it with her cane. It didn't even seem to feel it, grabbing her arm and yanking her to the side with a wrench that would have broken a normal person's bones.

Leaving nothing between it and Andi.

She was too afraid to move, even as it charged at her, mouth wide and horrible.

Blythe slammed into it, not bothering with her cane. A click and the handle pulled away, revealing a dagger the length of Andi's hand.

Blythe slashed at the monster, clipping the thin skin between its arm and side. It shrieked and lurched back into the shelf. Blythe's dagger shimmered with black blood.

The air was thick with the stench of iron and rot. Andi covered her nose and mouth, trying desperately not to gag. Blood ran freely from the creature's torn wing.

It shrieked and lunged at Blythe again, swinging at her with its long, dark claws. Blythe blocked it with the shaft of her cane, driving the dagger deep into the monster's abdomen. It shrieked again and lurched back.

Right into Lexa, who was ready with her sword, stabbing it in the base of the neck.

It reached for the blade with one clawed hand, but it went slack and fell to one side. Lexa yanked her sword from it. Dark, foul-smelling blood splattered on the floor and coated the length of Lexa's blade.

"Oh, that's disgusting." Blythe made a face. She pulled out a red handkerchief from the depths of her coat and wiped down her own blade before handing the silken square to Lexa. "Clean that off."

"Thanks, fangs. I thought I'd leave it. Let it rust right through." Lexa cleaned her sword and sheathed it. If Blythe was offended by the nickname, it didn't show on her face. "What is that thing?"

Andi took a cautious step forward, but the thing didn't even twitch. Now that it wasn't moving, it was fairly obvious what it was supposed to be.

"It looks like a human bat hybrid," she said. "If humans were routinely nine feet tall. But bats aren't blind."

"That's what you're hung up on, the blind thing?" Lexa nudged it with her foot. "We're lucky that this one is. If it could see us, we'd be dead already. Some new kind of leech? You ever heard of something like this?"

"No," Blythe admitted. "Well, I have heard of vampires that can shift, but as far as I'm aware that talent lies solely with the elders. Carmine has a bat-like form."

"…That's not her, right?" Lexa crouched down next to the creature. Andi couldn't understand how she could stand to be so close to the smell. She was several feet away, and human, and she thought she might throw up.

"Fortunately, no." Blythe put her cane back together with another solid click. Andi couldn't even tell where it had come apart. She leaned hard against it.

"Right, she was your—"

Blythe cut Lexa off. "We wouldn't survive against her."

"Right." Lexa straightened. "Some sort of proto-vampire?"

"We are not bats," Blythe said, long suffering tinging her voice even if her expression didn't change.

"Worth a guess," Lexa said. "Well. Great. Just how I wanted to spend this trip. Fighting fun and exciting bat monsters."

Andi couldn't tell if she was joking or not. "But how did it get in here? Where did it come from? Could it have been whatever was following us? Maybe some sort of parasite or…"

Andi knew that wasn't right. She wasn't even sure what it was. Finding out was probably important, but she didn't want to get any closer. Even dead, it was horrifying, and the smell was even worse. Like something that had been rotting for a very long time.

"I don't think so." Blythe frowned. "Are you all right?"

"I'm fine." Andi held the strap of her bag tightly, so her shaking fingers didn't betray her. "Thank you. For keeping me safe. Both of you."

"Just doing my job," Lexa said. "That cane packs quite the wallop. I'm impressed."

"It's made of ironwood." Blythe smiled a bit. She was using both hands to grip her cane, tightly enough that her knuckle bones showed through her pale skin. "…Did you hear that?"

"Must have more friends." Lexa's hand felt to her sword hilt. "We need to get out of here."

Blythe nodded and strode to the window. She hit it with her cane. The glass cracked into a spiderweb. Light speared in from the other side. She hit it again and the entire illusion fell apart, leaving them back in the hallway. Nothing had followed them there. The corridor was completely empty, aside from the mushroom lamps.

"Why were those things there?" Lexa asked. "But not out here?"

"It could be part of the seal, if it's attached to a vampire." Andi had read up on vampires, but had never heard of anything like that. It was worse than the afflicted. At least they were largely human looking, and there was some veneer of what they had once been covering what they had become.

That thing had been a monster.

"I guess," Lexa said. "Makes about as much sense as anything else here."

Which was a very kind way of her saying that it didn't make sense at all.

"Could it possibly mean that we're getting closer?" Blythe asked. "You told me to focus, but I'm not actually sure what I'm supposed to be focusing on. I assume it's a point of magic, somewhere up above us, but I can't sense these things like you and the mongrel."

"Hey," Lexa's protest sounded half hearted at best.

"Right." Andi wasn't sure how to describe it, and checking her archive didn't help. Magic had always been a part of her, ever since she could remember. When she was little it had been easier than forming her own words. "It's...a little how this tunnel feels. But it's much stronger."

She could feel the residual magic in the tunnel walls, even standing where she was. If she'd pressed, she was sure that it was much more potent than it seemed.

"That doesn't mean anything to me. It's just wood," Blythe admitted.

"Right. Let me…" Andi hesitated, but after a moment reached out and took Blythe's hand. It was cool, not nearly as cold as Andi had expected. Her skin was soft. Andi's hands were rough from pouring through dusty old books that sucked the moisture from her fingertips. She regretted never remembering to use the cream one of the potion masters had gifted to her.

She let her magic spark around her fingertips, trying her best to emulate what the core would feel like. Golden sand danced around their joined hands, sparkling with its own light.

"Oh." Blythe blinked down at her hand. "Do you mind if we stay like this for a moment?"

"I don't mind," Andi said it too quickly. Lexa huffed, but didn't voice her probably disparaging opinion.

Blythe closed her eyes. She held Andi's hand like it was a delicate thing. To her, it probably was. She was so still Andi could have been holding hands with a statue. With some ethereal being that had decided to take notice of her, if only for a moment.

The fingers in Andi's hold twitched, breaking the spell.

"I think I have it," Blythe said.

"Good." Andi bobbed her head, feeling a little stupid. "Great. I'm glad that worked. Shall we go?"

Blythe looked down at where Andi was still holding her hand. "If you plan to keep holding my hand I think you should probably move to the side—"

Andi let go of her hand like it had burned her. Blythe laughed, but she found she didn't really mind, even as the heat bloomed across her cheeks again.

"Great, you two held hands and found the meaning of the universe in each other's eyes or whatever," Lexa said. Andi made a noise of protest. "Can we go? We haven't even gotten into the library proper and Chrys needs us."

"You're right." Blythe stepped forward. "I'll do my best to make sure little miss librarian's efforts weren't in vain."

"See that you don't," Lexa said, before Andi could say something incredibly stupid. She kept her mouth shut and followed close behind.

A few steps forward and their surroundings changed again.

It wasn't a library.

Chapter 9: The Forest

It was a forest.

Bare black branches shattered the dully overcast sky, stretching skeletal fingers to the clouds. Thick tendrils of mist hugged the ground, ebbing around the trunks and over roots. White mushrooms spotted the leaf litter and the trunks of the trees. An owl hooted, somewhere far away.

It wasn't a forest from the last few years. It must have been another memory.

"Are we still in the library?" Lexa asked.

"We must be." Andi trailed her fingers over one of the trunks. It felt real enough — the roughness of the bark, the damp of the air. "Does this mean anything to you?"

She directed the question to Blythe, looking at her for the first time since they stepped into the forest.

Blythe was normally pale, but her skin was almost ashen, the darkness under her eyes standing out in stark contrast.

It could have been the light.

Andi didn't think that it was.

"Blythe?" Andi put a hand on her shoulder.

Blythe started, badly, staring at her with eyes so wide her pale irises were completely surrounded by white.

"Are you all right?" Andi asked.

Blythe shook herself and seemed to come back to the present. "Yes. I'm fine. Merely distracted. What were you asking?"

"I just…asked if this place was familiar." Andi frowned. "Are you sure—"

"I said I'm fine," Blythe cut her off, a little more harshly than Andi expected. "Yes. I've been here before. Why is this showing up? I thought only libraries did."

"I don't know," Andi admitted.

"Well, what do you know? I focused, and it brought us here," Blythe said. "Clearly, your plan isn't working. Or do you have any other bright ideas? Theories? Plans that might lead nowhere?"

Andi shrunk back at the harshness of her tone. "I'm sorry. I don't have all of the answers. I'm doing my best."

"Well, your best hasn't been exactly show stopping, now, has it?" Blythe snapped.

Andi took a step back. Leaves crunched under her foot.

Lexa moved forward, the tip of her sword under Blythe's chin before either of them could blink. "You do not get to talk to her like that."

"Why not? You're thinking it, too." Blythe had a horrible smile on her face.

Andi had forgotten, for a moment, that being a vampire wasn't just being cold and still. Or maybe it hadn't fully hit her that Blythe was no different than any other vampire. Vicious, blood thirsty, angry at the world.

"I'm not thinking anything like you," Lexa said.

"You just can't admit it because you're her little guard dog." Blythe rolled her eyes. "We're stuck in this nightmare with all of these grand theories and ideas that won't get us anywhere. You're just too submissive to say anything."

"Anything about what?" The hilt of Lexa's sword creaked under her grip.

"The witches, they're all broken." Blythe laughed. "Sure, she can put on a light show, but she doesn't know what we're doing! She can't fix it, either. The world is going to end and we'll be stuck wandering around this place until we eventually rip each other apart."

"That is not going to happen," Lexa said. "Andi is one of the best witches I know and she's definitely the smartest. You can't even remember her name, can you? What do you know about anything?"

Andi knew, on some level, that Blythe was scared. That the forest had shaken her, allowing her fear to rush up to the surface. It was a feeling Andi understood all too well. She couldn't imagine the words that would come out of her if she was faced with a dark memory without any warning.

But the hurt and betrayal welled up, anyway, even as she told herself that it had nothing to do with her. She stepped back again. The stark reminder that Blythe was barely different than any other vampire more sobering than a slap to the face. She didn't want to be there anymore, listening to Blythe and Lexa argue like she wasn't even there.

They were still saying things. Yelling. But a roar filled her ears, drowning everything else out.

She needed to get away.

Andi turned and started running through the trees before she even processed the thought.

There was no thinking after that. Just the pounding of her feet against the ground and the burn of the cold air in her lungs.

She didn't stop until her foot caught on a root and she hit the ground. The leaf litter cushioned her fall, but it still winded her, and all she could do was lay there for a moment. She blew a leaf away from her mouth and turned over, lying on her back in the middle of the forest, the mist flowing around her in little waves. Her heartbeat slowly calmed from thundering in her ears to steady and slow.

It took a lot more than ten breaths for her to feel like she could sit up.

Everything looked the same. The close, heavy sky. The trees. The mist. The world smelled like rain, but she didn't think any would ever fall.

She had no idea where she was or how far she was from Lexa and Blythe. Logically, she should have burst back into the tunnel. This new room seemed to go on forever. Yellowed leaves coated the ground. Dark trees rose towards the sky. Pillars holding up a delicate lace roof.

It didn't make sense. The other rooms had only been a fraction of what they appeared.

Nothing made any sense.

She wanted to scream, or cry, or do anything but just sit there in a pile of dead leaves. Hot tears burned at the corners of her eyes and she swiped angrily at them with her sleeve, trying to soak them up before they fell. They sealed up her throat and bowed her head, driving her forehead to her knees. She got in a breath around the hitch in her chest.

Everything felt like it was crashing down around her.

Chrys, her own inadequacies, the enormity of her situation. It slammed over her in a wave that left her dizzy.

Blythe was right. Theories and ideas weren't going to save them.

It was all she had.

She needed to pull it together. Any moment now Lexa, or worse, Blythe, would walk through the trees and see her sitting there. The thought didn't help, adding itself to the pile of anxieties threatening to bury her alive.

Something moved in the trees to her left.

Andi's head snapped up and she wiped at her damp cheeks, shoving a loose piece of hair behind her ear. Any attempt to look presentable failed. She knew she was covered in leaves. "Lexa?"

Silence greeted her. She pulled herself to her feet, brushing leaves off of her skirt and blouse. "Lexa, I'm fine. Breakdown all over. It doesn't matter what she thinks."

It did matter, but if she kept saying the opposite, maybe it would come true.

No answer. Andi frowned and turned around. She couldn't see anything. The trunks stretched back as far as she could see until they were lost in shadow. The mist was thicker, hugging the ground and swirling around her.

"Lexa?" She tried again. Something scuttled between the trunks, too quick for her to see what it was. "…Blythe?"

No matter how Blythe felt about her in the moment, she would have said something.

It wasn't either of them.

Movement on her other side. She whirled towards it.

Gone.

A new fear overwrote everything she'd been overwhelmed with, creeping up her back like icy spiders.

Something was in the woods with her.

She needed to go back, but she couldn't remember which way was back. No matter where she turned, everything looked the same. The dark trees, the mist. It was growing darker, whatever passed for a sun must have been setting. Or the clouds were growing thicker.

She could barely see. If it got darker, she'd be completely at the mercy of whatever was near her.

A few stumbling steps backward and she was pressed against a tree. Damp bark scraped at her shoulders, but she didn't care. Something ripped past her, so close she felt it, but all she saw was the mist billowing in its wake.

She heard a growl and looked up. A creature very much like the bat in the library before was crouched in the branches above her. It glared down at her with glowing red eyes.

A scream tore its way out of her throat. She pushed herself off of the tree as it took a leap at her. It landed awkwardly, slipping in the leaf litter. She turned to run but a second one was behind the tree. It lunged at her.

A knife sprouted from its temple.

It staggered and fell, blood spreading in a sticky pool beneath it.

Andi scrambled back, staring at it.

"Watch out!"

Blythe was next to her an instant later, her cane coming up and smacking the first creature away from her. She hadn't even heard it come close.

"Are you okay?" Blythe yanked the knife out of the monster's skull, tossed it to catch it by the blade and threw it at the second, pinning it to a tree by the membrane of its wing. It let out a shriek that left Andi's ears ringing.

"Andrea." Blythe had a hand on her shoulder. "Are you all right? Did they hurt you?"

"I…" Her mouth didn't want to work. She wanted to say she was fine, but she couldn't form the words. "You said my name."

She was so focused on Blythe she didn't notice the sand pulling at her feet until she was falling.

It was like missing a stair, but the feeling of her stomach flying into her throat continued, even as she jerked to a stop, Blythe holding onto her hand.

The ground beneath Blythe crumbled, and they both tumbled down. Blythe slammed her cane into the side of the hole.

It was the last thing she was aware of before she was swallowed by the dark.

Chapter 10: Magic

The echo of something dripping was the first thing to permeate Andi's consciousness.

She wrinkled her brow, fighting to keep her eyes closed, to drift back off before her alarm began to blare.

She'd been having a dream, something about a library. Something dangerous.

And falling.

Her eyes snapped open and she sat up, too fast. The world spun around her and she bowed her head, willing the dizziness to retreat.

"Take it easy." Blythe's hand landed on her shoulder. It was so dark Andi could just barely see her. The other rooms had been full of light, even if it was muted. This one was pitch black beyond the feeble circle of light cast by the small lantern next to her. Blythe must have taken it from her bag. They were sitting on a smooth, concrete floor. At least, Andi was fairly certain it was too uniform to be a cave floor.

It smelled of damp and old dust. And something strange she couldn't identify.

"What happened?" Andi asked. "There were those things, and we were falling—"

Blythe nodded. "Good, you remember. Let's start small. Are you okay?"

Andi blinked. She felt sore, like the time she'd slipped on the ice in front of the library, but not like anything was broken or seriously injured. Her head hurt with the dull, pounding sort of headache she always got after a cry. She touched her cheek, but it was dry. "I think so. Wait, are you all right?"

"We fell, I did my best to stop our fall," Blythe said. "You just disappeared, back in the forest. Not even your werewolf could find you. We split up and…well. I chose the correct direction. I don't know where we are now, I just woke up myself."

"Oh. Do you…she has to be okay, right?" Andi knew Lexa could take care of herself. She'd seen it time and time again.

"I'm sure she's fine. I hate to admit it, but she is perfectly capable," Blythe said. "I suppose it falls on me to keep you safe."

Andi didn't know what to say to that. Everything Blythe had said before came rushing back. And now they were trapped together in some dark place. She didn't know what to say. Best to start with apologies and hope that it wasn't too horribly awkward. "I'm sorry."

"For what?" Blythe asked. "If it's about what I said before, I'm the one who should be sorry. I didn't mean it. Your magic is beautiful, and I'm sure you're perfectly capable without. I know you can't possibly know everything, and I'm aware that I'm not particularly easy to deal with. That place brought back bad memories, but I shouldn't have taken it out on anyone. Least of all you."

"It's okay," Andi said, and surprisingly, it was. The tension between them deflated. "I should have been more upfront that I was working on theories, and you saved my life. I think that makes us even."

Blythe smiled, tentatively. "That's awfully generous of you."

"I'm in a generous mood," Andi said. "You stabbed two monsters for me. And kept me from breaking my neck."

"I suppose I did." Blythe's smile faltered. "Unfortunately, I'm going to have to ask you to risk your unbroken neck. I'm not sure where my bag fell, so I don't have any blood, and I don't believe I can walk without assistance."

"What do you mean?" Andi asked with a sinking feeling. "You said you were fine."

"Ah. Well." Blythe bit her lip. "Physically, yes, I am just as capable as I was before our fall."

Andi didn't like the sound of that. "…Where's your cane?"

"As I said, I tried to break our fall." Blythe picked up her cane from where she'd had it beside her and held it out.

It had snapped in two, the ends splintered.

"Oh no." Andi looked up at her. "I'm so sorry."

"I suppose even ironwood has its limits," Blythe said. She was trying to sound light, but her voice caught. She cleared her throat. "Which is apparently trying to break the fall of two adult women. If you could find something to…to bind it together, or perhaps something that I can use in its place…I haven't seen anything moving. It should be safe."

Her hands shook slightly, and her grip tightened around the two pieces.

Andi put a hand over Blythe's. "Before we do that, can I try something?"

"What are you planning?" Blythe asked. "Do you have a glue spell in that big brain of yours?"

"It's my archive, and no," Andi said. She thought for a moment. "Well, yes, I do, but that's not what I plan on using."

Blythe handed her both pieces. "I supposed you can't cause any more harm."

Andi ignored her, closing her eyes and accessing her archive. It was second nature, like recalling a memory, but when she'd first started using magic she'd had to imagine a large room full of books that she had to carefully sort through. She did that now, if only to calm her frazzled nerves, but it took her mere moments to find the spell she was looking for.

It was old, something she'd taken from her predecessor's archive. He had been an ancient man who had been bent nearly in two with gnarled hands by the time Andi met him. He'd received the spell from a witch who'd died well over a century before Andi was even born. She was certain it was even older than that.

And as long as she lived long enough to pass down the archive to whoever took over from her, it would be preserved for centuries more. Witches weren't vampires, but they lived much longer than the average human.

She needed to concentrate on the spell.

Golden sand swirled around her. It turned green when it reached the cane, mimicking flowering vines that curled all the way down the length of both halves. The magic felt out the wood of the cane, reminding it that it was once a living thing. That it had been whole.

Both halves lifted from her hands. The magic moved faster, pulling the two pieces together.

The wood fused back into a single piece, like it had never been broken.

The cane settled back in her palms. Green leaves unfurled down its length, turned yellow, and scattered around them before she could cut off the magic.

"Oops." Andi smoothed her hand over the wood. She couldn't tell where it had been broken. "Here."

"How…that was incredible." Blythe accepted the cane. She ran her fingers over it, but if she was worried about the new knots and whorls, she didn't say anything. "Thank you. I can't believe…I thought you were a glorified librarian."

"…I mean, to be fair, I am a glorified librarian," Andi said. She felt hollow and tired. It wasn't often that she used any of the spells in her archive, and it left her fingers twitching for the feel of more magic. She glanced down. Tiny shoots of green defied the concrete floor, curling around her fingers. She gently tugged her hand away.

"I didn't mean…I'm sorry." Blythe used the cane to pull herself to her feet. "I have been incredibly rude, and you have been nothing but kind. I don't believe I can ever repay you for this."

Andi flushed. She'd done it without really thinking. All that had mattered was she knew she could help. "I just happened to have the right spell in my archive."

"My cane is everything to me," Blythe said. Her voice caught again and she looked away. "So again, thank you."

Andi nodded, awkwardly, relieved when Blythe stopped talking and offered her a hand up. She accepted it, but the moment she moved her ankle throbbed and her head spun. She sagged against Blythe. An arm around her waist held her in place.

"What's wrong?" Blythe asked. "You are hurt."

"Just got a little lightheaded," Andi reassured her. "I think I might have hurt my ankle—"

"Right." Blythe helped her to move a few feet over. A chair loomed out of the dark, tall backed with a cushion so coated in dust and softened by cobwebs she couldn't tell what color it was. Blythe helped her sit down. "Wait here. I need to find my bag."

"Right." Andi didn't really want to sit in the chair. She didn't even want to think about what horrors the cushion held. It was marginally better than the floor, and logically the floor had far more spiders, but her skin still prickled at the thought.

"Take this." Blythe handed her the tiny lantern. It was collapsible, and Lexa had put it in her bag more as a joke, but Andi wasn't going to complain. "I can see well enough without it."

It was a few minutes of sitting alone, hearing a soft scuffling in the dark and hoping that it was Blythe and not something much worse. Finally, Blythe came back, her bag slung over her shoulder.

"May I?" she asked.

"Yes?" Andi wasn't sure what she meant until Blythe was sitting on the floor in front of her, unlacing her boot and taking off her stocking. Her face felt hot again.

"That heartbeat of yours is going to get you in trouble if you meet any vampires half as charming as I am," Blythe commented, almost airily if it weren't for the undercurrent of something hungry in her voice. "Luckily for you, I have excellent manners."

"Yeah." Andi wished she didn't show her emotions so readily. Or that she could crawl into a hole and never emerge. "Lucky me."

"It doesn't seem to be sprained, you must have landed on it wrong." Blythe probed her ankle carefully. Her cold fingers felt like heaven. She moved it back and forth. "Does this hurt?"

"A little bit." Andi had braced herself for it to hurt quite a bit more, but it was more of a twinge. "I think it surprised me, more than anything."

"Well, we can't be too careful." Blythe pulled a silky sash out of her bag. She bound up Andi's ankle before she replaced her stocking and shoe, ignoring Andi's stammered insistence that she could do it herself. When she stood up again her ankle felt much more stable, even if her head was still cottony. "Better?"

"Much." Andi nodded. "We need to figure out where we are and find Lexa. What do you see around here?"

"Honestly, there isn't much to see," Blythe said. "Bookshelves, but that's not exactly a surprise. Quite a few tables, all covered in white sheets. Equipment, but I don't recognize any of it. It's so covered in cobwebs I couldn't begin to guess what it was for. I'm more concerned about the smell."

"What smell?" Andi had noticed something on the air, something musty, but she didn't have supernatural senses.

"Old blood," Blythe said. "Fear so potent it soaked into the walls. Whatever that equipment was for, I doubt it was anything good. Experiments of some kind would be my guess. Experiments on humans."

"We don't experiment magic on humans." Andi frowned.

"Really? And what do you think that thing that attacked you was?" Blythe asked. "Because underneath everything, it certainly was human. Once."

Cold and nausea spread through Andi, filling her completely. She quickly sifted through her archive, but she couldn't even find an instance. Either it had never happened, or someone had scrubbed it from existence. "I'm going to need to see that equipment."

Chapter 11: Jars and Vials

Andi hesitated when Blythe offered her arm, but she linked elbows with her and was escorted across the room. Her ankle held up surprisingly well, only a twinge.

The room was much larger than Andi had expected. It was populated with a plethora of long, low tables and squat, round platforms that might have held the equipment that Blythe had mentioned, at one point, but it was all broken metal and wires sticking out of the middle of each one. Great, spidery contraptions had been shoved against the wall, so shrouded in cobwebs that Andi couldn't even begin to decipher what they were supposed to be. The tables were covered in white sheets that almost glowed in the tiny ring of light whenever it caught the edge of one, fluttering in their passing like a ghost.

Together they wove around the outer edge of the room, navigating through a small labyrinth of tables and chairs. They reached the bookshelves, but Andi's hopes were dashed immediately. Most of the contents had been strewn across the floor into mildewed piles of slowly rotting paper and leather covers.

"I suppose we won't be finding any answers there." Blythe poked at a book with her cane. The cover sloughed off and she made a face.

"It's fine, I didn't expect much," Andi said. Unless someone had left a detailed log of exactly what happened, she doubted any book would give her the full story. If she was lucky, she could divine something from the equipment.

Andi pulled Blythe to a stop next to one of the platforms.

"Something catch your eye?" Blythe asked.

"I'm not sure. What could this be for?" She frowned at it. It didn't look like any of the equipment had been there. It was wide enough that she could have laid down and and spread her arms and legs and not touched the edges. A metal ring stood in the center, large enough for her to stand in. The whole thing was covered in a thick layer of dust, softening the details.

She let go of Blythe's arm to walk around it. Putting her full weight on her ankle made her wince, and it turned into more of a limp. She ignored the pain as best as she could, trying to focus on the puzzle the platform presented to her.

"What do you think it was?" Blythe asked.

"I have no idea."

The next platform had shards of broken glass sticking up like jagged teeth from the center. She didn't get near it.

"Have you ever seen a place like this?" Blythe asked.

"No," Andi said. "It doesn't feel like the rooms from before."

Once she said it, it seemed obvious. There was a charge in the air, despite its heavy stillness. An energy that was an undercurrent to the cold and the damp.

"So…we've made it?" Blythe asked. "This is your great library?"

"I think so." Andi wasn't sure if she should feel triumphant or not. She'd always imagined that if she ever made it to the library, it would be the most incredible moment of her life. That so many of her questions would be answered.

"Then your theories were correct after all." Blythe looked at the empty bookshelves. "This isn't quite what I imagined."

"Me either," Andi admitted. "I don't even know where this is, but…so much of the library has always been shrouded in mystery. By design, I'm sure, but…"

"But you hoped you'd know more. Well. It is a big tree," Blythe said, like that explained everything. "Maybe we're in the roots. It feels like we're underground, at least. What do you know about the inside?"

"Honestly I only know of a few rooms, because they were mentioned in passing in a book that wasn't even about the library." Andi hated how little she knew. She had scoured the coven's library and her own archive for any mention. Whoever had decided to hide the library had done too good of a job.

Blythe winced. "I'm guessing this wasn't one of them?"

"Definitely not. But it means we're closer to the center. We just need to find…a door? Stairs? I'm not sure. I…I'm sorry. I wish I knew more."

"It's not your fault." Blythe was clearly struggling to keep her tone even. "How long has it been since anyone was here? Four hundred years?"

"Three hundred and ninety-seven."

Blythe seemed to find the exact number amusing. She smiled, at least. "See? You're doing amazing. So. A door. Or some stairs."

"It might be hidden, or inside something else," Andi said. "If the person who hid the library was so secretive, we can't expect everything to be obvious."

Blythe nodded. "Well. I can see a fireplace."

"That's a start." Andi had read about the fireplaces in the library in a very old and dense tome, once upon a time. "There should be a way to light it on the edge. Lead me over there?"

"Of course." Blythe held out her arm again, and together they made their way to the fireplace, accompanied by the soft tapping of Blythe's cane. It wasn't as far as she'd expected, just a short distance around the edge of the room.

Andi ran her fingers over the dust and cobwebs, trying hard to not think about hundreds of little legs scuttling over her skin.

She found a raised bit that felt like a circle on one of the stones. She pressed down on it. A click, but nothing happened. She frowned and fed it the tiniest amount of magic, a few grains of golden sand.

Flames took residence in the hearth like a fire had been lit there for hours. One by one, the lights around the room blazed to life. They were shaped like gas lamps, even though their source was clearly magical. Somewhere, a venting system whirred to life, choking and coughing.

"How did you know that would be there?" Blythe asked.

"Because I'm a librarian," Andi said. "And it was standard practice. Several centuries ago. I've never actually seen one, though, so that was actually really exciting. I wonder how they did it, it took so little magic, but it produces such incredible results. Look at all of this!"

The room was huge, much larger than she'd ever anticipated. It was a circle. Blythe had led her around a sunken middle.

"I'm looking." Blythe was looking at her, not the room around them, so Andi was sure she wasn't getting the full effect.

Or she was staring, because Andi was rambling. "I'm um. I just knew."

"Oh, well, I bow to your several centuries of random knowledge." Blythe inclined her head, slightly. If she was annoyed by the beginnings of a full-blown information dump, it didn't show on her face.

"Well. Let's take a look."

The sunken area was lined with wide, shallow steps on one side. A railing circled the other. It had crumbled in several places, whether from rot or some long past violence, Andi couldn't say. There was a chair in the middle, covered with a darkly stained sheet, hiding whatever was sitting there. The higher part of the room was ringed with the platforms, some of them had nothing on them, others had wires dangling from the ceiling. One had a piece of machinery that poised over it, a horrible spider of metal parts and gears, long straps dangling from its arms.

Most of the machines had straps, some of them were ripped short, but they must have been used as some sort of restraints.

Only one platform had an intact glass tube, too close to them for comfort. Something dark and rotten had slowly evaporated to the bottom. She didn't want to go anywhere near it.

"I found the stairs." Blythe pointed behind the fireplace.

The staircase spiraled tightly up into a shadowy ceiling.

Andi wanted to hurry to the stairs and leave the room behind, but she stayed right where she was. "Okay. Well. Now that the lights are on we can…find out what was going on in this room. Right?"

"Do we particularly want to know?" Blythe asked.

"I…" Andi turned to look at the table nearest to them. It was covered with a white sheet. Or it had been white, once. It had horrible looking stains, spots that spread like flowers with petals made of rust.

Every table was like that.

Andi walked towards the first one, her steps faltering in a way that had nothing to do with her injured ankle, though it burned with every step. She wanted to sit down, but she didn't dare stop moving.

Her hand trembled when she reached for the edge of the sheet.

Blythe grabbed her wrist. "Don't."

"I have to see," she said. "I don't recognize the equipment, and the books are all over the floor, this is all we have left. I have to know."

"You don't," Blythe said. "I don't think this is something you should see. That anyone should see."

"I'm an archive witch. I…I have hundreds of years of magical history stored in my archive," Andi said. "I'm not delicate. If it's because it smells like blood—"

"Old and rotten." Blythe made a face. "Everything in this room is. I don't think it's of historical note."

Andi wanted to go. She didn't want to spend another moment in that horrible room.

"Just…just this table," she said. "And then we can go."

Blythe bit her lip. "At least let me move the sheet?"

Andi swallowed and nodded, bracing herself.

Blythe pulled the sheet to the side. It was stiff with whatever had stained it and a thick layer of dust that billowed up into the air around them, sour and stale.

The stench without the sheet was so rank that it stung. Andi covered her mouth and nose with her sleeve, but it didn't help very much at all.

The table was covered in bottles and jars. Some of them had broken, the source of the stains. Whatever had been in them had long since rotted away, black sludge left in the bottom of shattered glass. The intact bottles had not escaped the ravages of time.

Only a few were clear.

Organs and bones floated in a liquid that cast them in an emerald sheen.

Andi wanted to back away, but she forced herself to look closer.

She was well versed in anatomy. Her archive had a large amount of healing spells locked away in it, and most of those required knowledge of human physiology.

So, she knew, without accessing her archive, that every single preserved specimen was wrong in some way.

There was a lung with bronchioles fanning out from it like a delicate fern. A heart with too many chambers, lumpy and misshapen. A curve of a rib, serrated with spines.

Andi stepped back to the fireplace and sagged against the side of it, heedless of cobwebs and dust. Not caring about any spiders that still called it their home. The warmth of the fire should have been a welcome balm, but it exasperated the queasy rolling in her stomach.

"I didn't want to look." Blythe pulled the sheet back over the table.

"I know," she replied, her voice small. She wished she had listened to Blythe. "How did…were…is it all human?"

"As far as I can tell." Blythe nodded. She was paler than ever, her face rivaling her white hair. "What do you think they were doing? Why do any of this at all?"

"I don't know," Andi admitted. She straightened, clearing her throat, but it didn't do anything to dislodge the smell, or the acrid taste of bile that was trying to rise in the back of her mouth. "But I think I know where we can find answers."

"You said one table," Blythe reminded her.

She had, but she couldn't just stop. Not if so many horrors took place there. Not if there was something to prove, even if it was just to herself. "It's at the center. I think…I think we need to see what's there."

Chapter 12: Corpse

"We really don't."

Andi expected the protest. "Fine. I do. I need to see it."

"Why?" Blythe asked.

"Because I can't just ignore whatever this all is," Andi said. "What if it has ties to the curse? What if it's why the library disappeared? I can't just leave."

"You can, actually," Blythe said. "The stairs are right there. We can just go. Whatever you learn here isn't worth it."

"It could help," Andi argued. "It could even help keep you safe."

Blythe sighed. "Do you really believe that, or do you just think I'll agree if you beseech my survival instincts?"

"I don't know, but I have to at least try." Andi was done arguing about it. She started down the steps. Blythe took her hand before she got far.

"Fine." Blythe's tone was deeply unhappy, but she looked resigned. "Let's go."

Going down the steps together was easier than trying to go alone. Blythe's hand in hers was more reassuring than she wanted to admit.

A single metal pole anchored a reclined chair to the floor, covered in a stained sheet. A stalactite of broken metal stabbed down from the ceiling. Whatever had been there was long gone. The dust was thick and free of any footprints.

They reached the chair and Andi stared at the marred cloth. Her hand trembled when she lifted it.

"Are you really sure about this?" Blythe asked.

Andi didn't have words. All she could do was nod and reach over to pull the sheet off herself. It crumpled on the ground.

A mummified corpse had been propped up underneath. Its chest was cracked open, ribs spread like petals of a flower. The chest cavity was empty, scooped out and hollow. The curve of bone was tight against dark, desiccated flesh. The face was lined and gaunt, eyes shut. Long white hair spilled down to the floor.

Andi looked away.

"I suppose we know who donated to those jars." Blythe's voice shook. "I mean. Probably. I'm actually not sure. I don't want to know. Can we go now? I don't think we're going to find anything."

Andi shook her head. "There could be something in those books, or on the other tables, or..."

"Andi." Blythe tugged her close, letting Andi hide her face against her shoulder. She smelled like cloves and very faintly of smoke. Andi closed her eyes and let Blythe hold her there, trying to even her breathing, but it kept hitching in her throat, like there was something stuck. Blythe's hand made comforting circles between her shoulder blades. "It's okay. We'll find answers at the center, or crystal, or whatever it is."

"The core." Andi knew she was getting it wrong on purpose, trying to distract her. She turned her head so she wasn't completely muffled by Blythe's jacket. It was surprisingly soft under her cheek. "What if I'm wrong about that?"

"Then we can always come back," Blythe said. "But for now, I think we should leave."

Andi nodded. "We should have left right away."

"I'm glad you're finally seeing reason." Blythe stepped back, but kept herself carefully between Andi and the corpse, so all she could see was the long white hair and the ornamental brass at the top. "Besides, I have complete faith that nothing we find here will be useful to anyone. Ever. I propose we never speak of it again."

"Proposal accepted."

Andi knew it wasn't that easy, but she was willing to let it go, for the moment. To get up the stairs and away from the awful smell and dust.

"Well, Andi, I think it's about time we get out of here," Blythe offered her hand again. Andi didn't hesitate to take it. It helped, reminding her that there was someone with her, someone solid and real.

A knot of tension loosened in Andi's chest once they reached the bottom of the stairs. "You go first. In case. You know."

"In case I fall?" Blythe's eyebrows rose. "I'm not quite as delicate as you seem to think I am."

"Well, that. But mostly in case there's spiders." Andi shuddered. "I have dealt with enough today. I'm not dealing with spiders, too."

"…Fair enough." Blythe started climbing the stairs. It was clearly a struggle for her, and Andi was glad she'd volunteered to follow. It was several turns of the stairs before Blythe spoke again. "You're dying to know why I need a cane, aren't you."

"I wasn't going to ask," Andi said. "My social skills aren't exactly amazing, but I know that much."

"I'm afraid it's not terribly exciting," Blythe admitted. "I fell off of a horse when I was young and my leg healed crooked. It turns out becoming a vampire doesn't fix that, which honestly, makes the exchange incredibly less fair."

"Really? I thought it might have happened…after."

"Being a full vampire was considerably less painful, yes," Blythe said. "Falling to afflicted status did not help me in any way. It was either the change in status or wandering around the woods for twelve years as a mindless thing. You can decide which."

"Twelve years?" Andi asked, quietly.

"Give or take, I'm not really sure, but that was Chrys's estimate after they found me," Blythe said. "I don't know why they decided to save me. I don't know how they even knew that they could. That was almost ten years ago now. I've been their little experiment ever since. A rehabilitated afflicted. Of course, it only worked because I was a vampire first. And that's essentially my whole life story, give or take a few details."

"Probably more than a few details," Andi said, but learning more about Blythe was a warmth that staved off the cold and the nausea.

"Oh, nothing important," Blythe said. "Cross dressing. Gallivanting about. Breaking hearts and causing my family all sorts of grief."

"That sounds like a very long and important story I would like to hear," Andi corrected her.

"Another time, maybe." Blythe flashed a grin over her shoulder. "Now for the other question you're dying to ask—"

"Honestly I'm still back with the gallivanting," Andi admitted.

"I can move quickly if needed, but it takes quite a bit out of me," Blythe ignored her. "I am still a vampire."

"That makes sense." Andi wanted desperately to press for more details. Blythe had led an incredible life before becoming a vampire.

Blythe stopped, so suddenly that Andi nearly ran into her. "Did you hear that?"

Andi wasn't sure why Blythe bothered to ask her. She went quiet and strained her ears, anyway.

They were probably halfway up the stairs, on the side facing the room. Andi gripped the railing and looked around, trying to find a source for any noise. As far as she was aware, they were the only living things down there.

It took her far too long to realize the chair was empty.

Any warmth left her immediately.

"Blythe, the chair—"

"Get in front of me." Blythe stepped back to give Andi room. "No arguments. Go. Now. Don't worry about me, just run."

"But—"

"No arguments!"

Andi could protest all day. It would just give the corpse more time to get to the stairs. She moved past Blythe and ran up. The steps clanged under her feet. Her ankle throbbed but she couldn't worry about it, not now. The ceiling was visible above her, dark and soot stained, but she could see a trap door. If she could get through it…then what? What would she do?

She didn't get to find out.

Blythe shouted, too far below her for comfort.

Andi looked down.

The corpse scaled the side of the stairway like it was a ladder. Its ribs, splayed spider legs, clicked against the bars with every movement. It was moving too quickly for something that looked like it shouldn't have been able to even twitch.

It launched itself up, landing almost delicately on the railing in front of her. The head rolled back, but the ribs quivered, reaching for her. She screamed and backed away, her shoulders hitting the post holding up the stairs.

It lurched forward and she barely got out of the way. She slid down a few stairs, catching herself on the railing. The ribs stabbed into the post, puncturing the metal like it was paper. The head tilted to the side, facing her.

Behind a curtain of long, dirty white hair, its eyes glowed crimson from deep within dark sockets.

She took another step back and nearly tumbled, but Blythe was next to her, grabbing her shoulders and keeping her from falling the rest of the way down the stairs.

With a horrible crunch the neck snapped up into place. The corpse wrenched itself and sheared the post to free its ribs. The entire staircase shuddered.

The corpse shambled down the steps for them, reaching with one hand and its ribs. Its mouth fell open, revealing a rows of needle-like teeth.

Blyth swung her cane at the corpse. It grabbed it and jerked her forward. One of the ribs stabbed her in the shoulder and she kicked it just below where its chest was open, sending it sprawling back. She staggered down a few steps, her hand over the wound.

Andi still had the lantern, hooked to her bag. She yanked it off and threw it at the corpse. A dry hissing, a bug slithering over dead leaves, filled the air. It was distracted long enough for Blythe to yank her cane free. She slammed the corpse into the post. It grabbed her bag. The strap snapped.

She shoved the whole thing into its chest cavity.

It made a horrible, high pitched keening noise.

"C'mon!" Blythe grabbed her wrist and hauled her up the stairs. Her leg nearly buckled underneath her.

Andi wrapped an arm around her waist, hauling her the rest of the way up the stairs. Her breath burned in her lungs. Her ankle shook underneath her. She didn't stop. She didn't look back.

She reached a door set in the ceiling at the very top.

She let go of Blythe to shove against it with all of her might.

It didn't budge.

"No!" She pounded a fist against it, uselessly.

"Move." Blythe got her shoulder under the door and heaved. A hand snuck between the stairs and Blythe paused long enough to smash it with her cane. She shoved against the door again and this time it cracked open. Something heavy in the room above them slid away. Blythe threw the door the rest of the way open, clambered into the room, and hauled Andi up with her. She slammed the door and hauled the bookshelf that had been on top of the door over it again.

The door rattled once, twice, and went still.

"That…that thing it…" Andi wanted to cry. "You shoulder! We need to bandage it, I know you heal fast but—"

Blythe turned to look at her. She had a strange expression, one that Andi had never seen. Like she hadn't understood her at all.

"Blythe?" Her voice came out as a cracked whisper. Her heart hadn't had a chance to calm down.

Blythe's pupils were blown wide, her eyes glowing a brilliant red.

She bared her teeth.

Chapter 13: Blood Mad

"Blythe?" Andi's voice was a squeaky whisper.

Blythe dropped her cane.

A low, inhuman growl rippled from her throat.

Andi turned and ran.

The room was a maze of bookshelves. Stacks of books became shadowy lumps in the soft light from the lanterns hanging overhead.

She darted into a small space between two shelves, twisting around the corner. Her boots thundered on the wood floor. Her heart pounded too hard.

There was no way she could lose a vampire.

A vampire in full blood madness, at that. She'd read about it, of course she had, but she had no idea what to do. Blythe's bag had been ripped off in the other room, and Lexa had been careful to make sure Andi wasn't carrying any blood bottles.

For her safety. She could have laughed.

She ended up in a narrow space between two shelves, her back pressed against the books, trying to breathe without making any noise. Each lungful of cold, stale air burned horribly. Her ankle throbbed so badly the sensation was in her head. She couldn't keep running.

If she could just think. Maybe check her archive. Or at least slow her racing thoughts, but she couldn't focus, the terror driving out any useful thought.

A noise in the next aisle.

Andi froze.

A footstep.

So soft that if she hadn't been completely still and on the alert she never would have heard it. She didn't dare to move. The seconds ticked past, stretched out to excruciating lengths.

Blythe slammed into the shelf, fingers scrabbling madly through the gap at the top of the books. Andi screamed and shoved the shelf the other way.

It rocked, dangerously, and she rammed it with her shoulder. It toppled and fell, pinning Blythe between the shelves. The next one teetered and dropped, too.

Andi didn't wait to see if the domino effect continued.

She ran back to the trap door. If she could get the shelf off the trap door, maybe she could get Blythe's bag from the corpse. With any luck the corpse had gone back to its chair. Or at last stopped moving. Long enough that she could get the bag.

If she was fast and lucky, maybe they could get out of the room alive.

She almost cried with relief when she saw the trap door.

Until she noticed it was rattling.

If she was going to survive, it would have to be against Blythe.

She wasn't sure she cared for those odds. She snatched Blythe's cane off of the floor and looked for another path out of the area.

The shelf she'd shoved over Blythe tipped back over, crashing into the next one and spilling books across the floor.

Andi didn't wait to see Blythe. She turned and ran in the opposite direction.

She couldn't get the bag and she had nothing on her to help besides a few bottles of antidote that weren't going to do anything if she was dead.

She needed a better plan.

She turned a corner and tripped.

She was stunned for a moment. She'd landed hard on her hands and knees on the wood floor, the dust doing nothing to cushion her fall. She turned and had to swallow a scream. It went down like ice.

A corpse had been leaning against the shelf, blanketed in cobwebs. She'd knocked it over in her mad dash through the stacks. It was old and mummified, the skin a dark gray. Or maybe the dust marred its features.

For a moment she was frozen, just waiting for it to move.

But it didn't even twitch, sprawled like a broken doll, its desiccated hand on a journal with a spotted green cover. She snagged the journal just as Blythe came around the corner and threw it right in her face.

It hit her in the forehead, ancient pages exploding out of it. Andi didn't stop to see where it landed. She dashed forward, gripping the cane so hard her fingers hurt.

She couldn't keep going like this. She was already flagging, her breath coming in ragged gasps. A knife twisting in her side would have been less painful.

It came to her like a thunderclap.

She couldn't keep going, and neither could Blythe.

Even as a vampire, she had a bad knee. A very bad knee. And she'd been flagging for a while. If Andi could keep ahead of her, eventually it would drop her, blood madness or not.

And if she could get higher, maybe it would help.

She took the next right, heading deeper into the stacks. She picked one at random and kicked the books out of the way, shoving them farther back in the shelf so she could get her foot on it. The shelves were tall and made of wood, but it rocked underneath her, threatening to tumble into the next one.

She kept climbing regardless, the cane hindering her progress, but she didn't dare let go. Her bag hit her hip hard enough to bruise, swinging wildly from her shoulder.

A strong hand closed around her ankle.

She kicked back, but Blythe dodged it. She sliced down with the cane and that freed her ankle long enough to pull up to the next shelf. Blythe yanked on the shelf.

Andi fell.

Along with everything else.

Andi hit the floor and covered her head. She only knew she was screaming because her throat felt torn raw. The cacophonous crash of bookshelves echoed all around her. Books pummeled every part of her.

Silence.

It took a moment for Andi to feel safe uncovering her head. The dust was still settling, and she was surrounded by books, but she'd ended up in a small space where the bookshelf she'd been climbing was leaning against the shelf next to it.

She slowly crawled out. Dust tried to choke her. A few more books fell and she started at the noise. The wood floor pressed painfully against her already bruised knees. The moment she was out she used the shelf to pull herself to her feet.

A wild snarl made her leap back with a startled squeak.

Blythe was trapped under one of the shelves. She only had one arm free. She reached for Andi, but she couldn't budge.

"All right." Andi still had the cane. She found the catch and the head popped off, but the dagger was gone. "Right. You left it up there."

She had her own dagger. It was small with a silver edge. Lexa insisted that she carry it, even though werewolves were largely extinct. Even if they weren't, there was no moon to turn them.

Thanking Lexa's need to be prepared, she unsheathed it from where it was hidden in the side of her bag. She rolled up her sleeve and sliced her arm open, just below the elbow, trying to keep it shallow, but it was still a line of fire across her skin. Red welled up and pooled in the crease of her elbow.

Blythe made a horrible noise, straining even harder.

Andi ignored the noise. Blythe was distracted enough she could kneel next to her head and hold her arm above her face. The blood dribbled from her arm into Blythe's mouth.

Blythe strained for more. Her fangs seemed longer, sharper.

"I really need you to get back to normal, because I don't think I'm getting out of here by myself," Andi told her. She doubted Blythe understood. "Please."

It took two more cuts before Blythe's stopped straining against the shelf. The red of her pupils shrunk down to pinpricks. She coughed and turned her head to the side. Andi pulled her arm back. "Blythe?"

"What…what happened?" Blythe looked down at the shelf pinning her to the floor. "…Did we destroy the library?"

"Part of it." The relief Andi felt made her want to lie down on the floor. She hadn't realized, until that moment, she was terrified that the blood wouldn't be enough. That Blythe had tumbled back to being afflicted. It hadn't even occurred to her until the moment was gone. "Glad I'm not on shelving duty. Are you okay now?"

"Am I…?" Blythe blinked, heavily, like she was waking up from a very deep sleep. She had more color than before, her cheeks almost rosy. "Did I bite you?"

"I mean, you tried." Andi admitted. "Can you get—"

Before she could finish asking, Blythe was already shoving the bookshelf off of her, and with a little help from Andi she pulled herself clear of it.

"Did you cut yourself?" Blythe accepted Andi's hand up.

"Well, it was either that or let you bite me, so this seemed like the better option." Andi shrugged. The movement hurt. She needed a long, hot bath full of pain potion. She didn't think that was anywhere near in her future. "Was that enough? We lost your bag…"

"I'm okay now." Blythe stared at her. "You…you probably should have left me on the floor. Let me see it."

"See what?" Andi asked, even as Blythe was taking her wrist with gentle fingers. "Oh. Right."

"This is going to seem odd, but I promise it will help." Blythe lifted Andi's arm and licked the cuts.

What blood Andi hadn't dribbled into Blythe's mouth went straight to her cheeks and ears. "I uh. Um."

"Vampire saliva has antiseptic qualities," Blythe reminded her. "It can also act as a coagulant. But I'm sure you already knew that."

"Uh huh." Andi did know that, but her brain had stuttered to a stop.

"You should sit down." Blythe still had blood around her mouth. Andi had the strangest urge to wipe it away. "Wrap your arm with something. Do you have food?"

"I have some granola bars—" Andi sat on the ground. There was nothing to sit on, at least not that she had seen. Now that it was over, the adrenaline was draining from her, leaving her cold and exhausted, and her ankle hurt. She stretched it out in front of her.

"That will do," Blythe said. "You need to eat something. Did I…do all of this? I am so sorry. I should have had blood back in the laboratory, but I was so focused on getting out, and that thing took my bag…"

"Hey." Andi grabbed her hand. "It's okay. We're okay."

She knew she should have been running screaming, but even if she had been inclined to do so, she was far too tired.

"How can we be okay?" Blythe's voice had a horrible edge to it, but Andi knew it was directed inward. "I just tried to kill you."

"Luckily, I'm really smart."

"If you were smart, you would have left me under that shelf."

"No, because I'm smart," Andi said. "All we have is each other right now. I don't know how to get out of here, and…and all we can do is keep going, right? So we're going to keep going."

Blythe was looking at her like she'd started screaming, regardless. "I…suppose that's right."

"If you feel really bad—"

"I do," Blythe said, quickly.

"I threw a book at your head, back there Next to um…another corpse." Andi handed back her cane. "He was holding onto it. I think it might be important. Could you go get it for me?"

Blythe nodded. "Yes. Of course. Eat something, please. Rest. And bandage up that arm. I'll be right back."

Chapter 14: The Journal

The cuts were on her left arm, but Andi had to admit her bandaging skills were clumsy at best. The salve stung when she applied it, but cooled a moment later, leaving her with a dull ache under the thick padding of gauze.

She ripped open a granola bar with her teeth and chewed mechanically. She knew Blythe was right, she needed food and water, but she wasn't hungry. During her mad flight through the library her nausea had burned away, at least. Hopefully food would keep it at bay.

The room provided little distraction. It was huge, the ceiling far above, but it still felt claustrophobic. The blond wood shelves were too close together. Old-fashioned lanterns hung from the ceiling, putting out just enough light for her to read the titles of the books that had fallen off of the shelf Blythe had upended. Most of them were very old, very outdated medical texts. She picked up "The Maladies of the Four Humours", but the text was so dense and faded she closed it and put it to the side, like an apology to every book that had scattered across the floor. Each one left a shiny swath in gray dust thick enough it could have been a carpet.

Andi realized, very suddenly, that she was very grimy. Every part of her was covered in dust. She brushed futilely at her skirts, sending up little clouds with already dirty fingers.

She was starting to miss her tiny bathroom above the Coven library, even if she couldn't lay down in the tub completely.

Blythe returned a few minutes later with a handful of yellowed pages.

"Well, there was one casualty of our little tussle." She waved the paper, gently. "The spine didn't make it. I'm fairly confident I found all of the pages. Now I know why my forehead hurts."

Andi winced. "Sorry."

"Please, don't apologize, I tried to murder you." Blythe sat down next to her. "The cover looked familiar. Quite a bit like the book you found in the library made of sand."

"Did it?" Andi tried to remember what it had looked like, but she had only glanced at it. She supposed it must have been green at one point, and maybe what she'd assumed was age spots was actually tarnished gold leaf. "I just figured if they died holding it…"

"Then it must be important." Blythe nodded.

"Or at least…at least it should be preserved."

She was lucky, the pages were numbered in a familiar looking, spidery handwriting. Some of them were still held together by ancient glue. The paper had a strange feeling, a charge that felt familiar and foreign all at once.

Maybe it was just a feeling. She didn't sense any magic beyond preservation spells on them, repelling the oil and grim of her fingers.

She could have used magic, but putting them back in order manually was a quick job. She tapped them into a thick bundle once she was done

"Are we safe here?" she asked.

"As far as I can tell, the only danger appears to be me," Blythe said.

"So that's a yes, then." Andi took a deep breath and activated her magic.

Using archive magic was much easier than trying to copy someone else's spell, but the exhaustion still weighed heavily on her.

Golden sand, its glow much warmer and comforting than the lanterns above them, wove through the fluttering pages, pouring over each word.

And the magic that was on them. She realized too late that it wasn't a preservation spell, but some sort of leftover archival magic that had been infused in the pages. Her own magic absorbed it easily enough.

It hit her archive like a brick.

She doubled over. Pain seared behind her eyes, so intense for a moment that it blinded her. Terror washed over her, but it was gone an instant later, leaving her weak and shaking.

She realized Blythe had a hand on her shoulder and had been saying her name.

"'M okay." It came out in a drunken sounding slur. She cleared her throat and tried again. "There was a protection spell on the words, should have figured that, should have just read it like a normal person."

"You scared me!" Blythe looked terrified. "You're bleeding…"

"Am I?" She felt something wet under her nose. She wiped at it. Her fingers came away slick and red. "Oh. So I am. Do you want some?"

"What? No." Blythe made a face. "I'm not going to…here."

She pulled a handkerchief from one of her pockets and handed it to her.

"How many of those do you have?" Andi asked.

"Just take it, please." Blythe put it in her hand and sat next to her, heavily. "That was almost enough to get my heart going again. Here. Give me those."

She took the pages and tucked them into Andi's bag. She pulled out a water bottle Andi had kept in there just in case. "There's not a lot here. Will you be okay?"

"I think it's too late to worry about that," Andi admitted. She had the handkerchief pressed under her nose, staining the white linen red. "I'm ruining your handkerchief. You know, there's this great invention, it's called tissues—"

"Shush, you." Blythe sounded like she was smiling. "Handkerchiefs are timeless."

Andi couldn't help but smile herself. "I'm sure."

"I'm immortal, I think I know more about what's timeless than you do. You're what, twenty?"

"Twenty-eight," Andi corrected her.

"Oh, eight years, what a difference," Blythe said.

"Well, considering the developments that the brain goes through alone, there actually is quite a difference," Andi said.

"If you want to believe that, you can be my guest." Blythe patted her shoulder. "So. Are these more of the roots? Is it an actual tree or more of a metaphor?"

"A treetaphor," Andi said.

"Did you hit your head?" Blythe asked.

"No," Andi said. She thought for a moment. She had fallen from the shelf. It was possible she suffered a blow. It was hard to sift out what was pain from her magic and physical ailment. "I mean, maybe. Why? You didn't think treetaphor was funny?"

"Not in the slightest." Blythe was smiling.

"You're a liar," Andi said. "And a terrible one. No poker face at all."

"Maybe I just don't have a poker face when it comes to terrible jokes and potential head trauma," Blythe said. "Do you know what Chrys would do to me if you got hurt?"

"Murder, probably," Andi said. "I'm really okay, I just…need to sit here for a while. And it is a real tree."

"An actual tree," Blythe said. "I thought you were making a treetaphor."

"If it's not funny then why are you saying it?" Andi asked.

"Because I actually did hit my head."

Andi bit back the apology that rose automatically. "How is your head? And your leg."

"Well, luckily, even in life I had a thick skull," Blythe said. "As for my leg, as loathe as I am to admit it, drinking blood helps. It's a shame I lost my bag."

"We could try to get it?"

Blythe gave her a flat look. "That is a spectacularly bad idea. I'm convinced you have a concussion."

She prodded Andi's head gently. To her absolute mortification, Andi giggled. "Really, I just need rest."

"Are you sure?" Blythe turned her head back and forth. "You seem fine."

"I told you I was," she said. "I just…I knocked over so many bookshelves."

Blythe stared at her.

And burst out laughing.

"It's not funny!" Andi buried her face in her hands. "I was so focused on getting away I didn't even think! I have done so much damage to an irreplaceable ancient library."

"I think the only book that didn't make it was that journal." Blythe's reassurances were a little less effective when she couldn't keep herself from giggling. Andi had to admit, she had a nice laugh. "We'll come fix it later. I promise."

Andi narrowed her eyes. "You're just saying that to get me to rest."

"Is it working?" Blythe gave her an innocent smile.

"I guess I can't lift entire bookshelves by myself," Andi sighed.

"I'm just glad you're not nearly as badly hurt as you could have been," Blythe said. "The only irreplaceable thing in this library is you."

"That was so cheesy," Andi said. If she'd had any energy at all left, she probably would have blushed, but Blythe was clearly teasing her. "Besides, you're here, too."

"Vampires are a dime a dozen, but archive witches are very rare."

"Oh, it's not because I'm the only me, it's my magic." Andi huffed, pretending to be offended. "I see how it is."

She leaned her head against Blythe's shoulder, too tired to keep sitting up anymore, and she was the closest thing to a pillow that Andi had. She knew she should ask, she knew she was probably overstepping boundaries, but she couldn't even keep her eyes open.

Blythe went stiff. "Are you…comfortable?"

"Comfortable enough." Andi checked her nose. At least it had stopped bleeding, and the pain was gone. She was just so tired.

Slowly, carefully, Blythe put an arm around her shoulders so she could settle in more fully. "You should be terrified of me."

Maybe she was right. Andi should have been scared. Blythe had tried to kill her, not even very long ago. But her brain couldn't equate the person who had lunged at her with the intent to bite with the woman who teased her and saved her life multiple times.

It was possible she was simply tired, but Andi knew what she'd said before was right. All they had was each other.

"I don't want to be terrified of you," she said. "So I won't be."

"Just like that, hm?"

"Just like that. I have a will of iron and incredible focus."

"I'm sure."

Andi sighed, softly. Blythe still smelled like cloves. It was pleasant. "Are you okay to keep watch?"

"Of course," Blythe reached over and tucked a loose strand of hair behind her ear. Her fingers grazed Andi's cheek, leaving a cold trail on her skin. "Get some rest."

Chapter 15: Quietly

Andi woke up curled up on the floor, her cloak bundled up into a pillow, the material scratchy under her cheek. She moved her hand and her fingers bumped into the leather of her bag. She grabbed the hilt of her knife, just to make sure it was there.

She sat up, blinking heavily, not sure what had disturbed her. Blythe was missing.

Andi jolted to awareness, a charge crackling under her skin, urging her to pull herself up using the bookshelf next to her. It rocked slightly under her touch, completely unsteady.

She had no idea how long she had been asleep. Long enough her magic had replenished, her mind no longer hollow. She tested her ankle and was surprised to find it only ached dully.

The light had changed, golden like the sunsets that used to paint honey-toned bars across the floor of the library, glowing at the window of her tiny apartment, or simmering red on the horizon.

It had been so long since she'd seen a sunset.

She shook herself. It wasn't the time to miss the sun. It was time to find Blythe, or at least be ready for her return. She wouldn't have left without a good reason. Andi pulled her cloak over her shoulders and grabbed her bag.

It was horribly loud in the silence that coated the room as thickly as the dust. Every rustle of cloth sounded like a whisper from someone in the next aisle over. By the time she was done it felt like the old paper from the journal had been inserted under her skin, crinkling and crackling with each movement.

She held her breath, and it was so quiet that she felt the pressure of it in her ears.

Maybe she'd just woken up naturally. The library was getting to her, and who could blame her? She breathed out.

A bump. A scrape.

Andi's heart sped up and she hurried between two of the still standing shelves, pressing her back against the books. The shadows were a cold, dark blue. The lights overhead glimmered faintly. A sunset echoed a thousand times like dying stars.

She tried to concentrate on the titles in front of her, trying to stay calm even as anxiety prickled in her throat, but she couldn't make out the letters in the dark.

Blythe slid into the aisle next to her. Andi started badly at the sudden appearance. Blythe held a finger to her lips, her eyes wide.

She was scared.

All Andi could do was nod and keep her mouth shut. She didn't want to find out what scared a vampire.

Blythe motioned with her head farther down the aisle, then gestured to Andi's feet.

She blinked at her.

Blythe tapped one of her boots with her cane.

Andi mouthed a quick "oh" and crouched down, unlacing her boots. They fit well enough in her bag. The floor was freezing cold through her stockings, but when she stepped back there was no tell-tale clack of the sole.

They walked through the maze of shelves, quiet and careful. The dust further muffled Andi's footsteps. Blythe was as silent as she usually was. The only sound was the soft rustle of Andi's clothes.

They twisted and turned through the stacks until Andi had no idea where they were. They'd found a few dead ends, places where books had been stacked so high at the end of shelves that they'd slumped into cascading mountains of paper and leather. Passing over them would have been much louder than backtracking.

They had been walking for quite some time before Blythe finally spoke, her voice low and quiet, so close to Andi's ear she felt the coolness of her breath. "The bookshelf was almost off of the trap door. I moved more things on top of it, but I doubt it will hold. We need to find the exit."

"Do you think it's that…that thing?" Andi didn't even want to say it. The memory of the way the corpse looked at her was burned into her mind. She shuddered, hugging her bag to her chest.

"I have to assume so," Blythe said. She put a hand on Andi's shoulder. "I'm not going to let it hurt you. I promise."

"You don't even have your knife," Andi reminded her.

Blythe pulled back the collar of her coat. The inside lining had a set of sheathes, each one with a blade. One was already missing, presumably already attached to her cane head. "Don't I?"

"What don't you have in that coat?" Andi asked. "Don't answer that. Let me check the journal, maybe it has…something. Anything."

She closed her eyes, accessing her archive. The journal had been handwritten, and the writing was hard to read, but that wasn't the problem. It was as if she was being blocked, the words sliding around before they made sense. She frowned and tried harder, knowing she couldn't push it too far.

A shock made her lose the thread of her magic and it unraveled before she could grasp it again.

"Nothing." It wasn't a lie. It was better than the truth. She'd never had anything like it happen before. The protection spells on the journal must have been far more advanced than the magic she was used to. Archive witches used to have all sorts of spells to keep the wrong people from reading something, but those spells had been lost before she was born. She was certain she could work around it, but she would need time and quiet. Two things that would probably be in short supply.

"If you had to guess?" Blythe asked.

Andi closed her eyes, trying to concentrate, to think logically. Nothing came to her, but she found herself pointing, anyway.

"That way?" Blythe looked to where she was pointing, straight at a shelf.

"I'm not sure," she admitted. She hadn't made the conscious decision on a direction. "It just…feels right."

She cringed. It wasn't a convincing line of thought, and they'd already argued over that before. "I've never done any sort of dowsing before, but it could be similar. It could be that the journal is leading us, just not in a way that I'm used to, I believe it was written by an archive witch, and—"

"Andi." Blythe put a hand over hers. "That's good enough for me."

Andi blinked, surprised. "Are you sure?"

"I trust you," Blythe said, and something in her voice forced warmth into the cold spots that the anxiety had frozen inside of Andi. "I'll go find the stairs. You stay here. Be quiet. Don't draw attention to yourself. I'll be back as soon as I find them, okay?"

"But—"

"I can move a lot faster without you, no offense," Blythe said. "Especially with my recent…indulgence. I promised I wouldn't let anything hurt you, right? I'm keeping that promise."

"Okay." Andi nodded. "You be careful, too."

"Keep that knife out, just in case." Blythe drew the knife from Andi's bag and handed it to her, hilt first.

Andi accepted it. "I'll…I'll see you soon."

The words fell a little flat. They weren't enough to encompass everything that was laying between them. Something Andi didn't quite understand yet, but she wanted to.

Blythe just smiled like she already knew and was gone between the stacks, leaving Andi alone. All she could do was stand there, holding the strap of her bag and her knife that felt far too small, the hilt pressing into her hand.

A muffled crash echoed through the floor. The lights above swayed, shadows spinning across the floor.

Andi stood absolutely still, straining her ears for any sound at all.

All she could imagine was the corpse, moving silently from aisle to aisle, trying to find her. Her hands shook so badly she almost cut herself on the knife. Blythe had told her to keep it out, but she sheathed it, anyway. Fresh blood would attract it much faster, and she doubted she could do anything against it no matter what she was holding.

Minute after agonizing minute trickled past. She was too afraid to access her archive again, worried that the magic would attract it. There was nothing she could do but read the titles of the books in front of her. Books on human anatomy, on preserving corpses, and autopsies. She looked back down at the ground.

"Are those not to your liking?"

Andi squeaked and turned so fast she knocked the bookshelf with her elbow. A few books hit the floor with loud thuds.

A man was standing in the aisle with her.

He was tall, quite a bit taller than her, dressed in an old-fashioned billowing shirt and loose pants. His skin was gray. His hair was pure white, falling freely over his shoulders. In the low light his eyes glowed bright red against dark sclera.

An elder vampire.

She'd never met one before, but she'd read about them. There were only supposed to be three left — Carmine, Dahlia, and Tana. She'd seen artist renditions of them.

This man wasn't any of them.

"Are you going to pick those up?" he asked.

She nodded. There was nothing else she could do. Even if she had the knife out, he wouldn't even notice when he snuffed her life out. She crouched down, scooping the books into her arms, trying not to stare at his bare feet. His nails were black and too long.

Andi tried her best to put them back in the right spot. Freezing cold fingers brushed back the curl of hair that kept falling over her cheek, tucking it behind her ear. The man was too close, leaning towards her, and she knew her pulse was jumping in her throat.

"It's been a very long time since anyone has been here, and you seem to be very lost," he said. "This area is not for the general public."

She could have laughed. How many times had she said almost the exact same thing?

Andi wished Blythe was with her.

Just as she prayed that she stayed far, far away. Blythe was strong and fast, but she wouldn't stand a chance against an elder vampire. No one would. If she was going to die, she'd rather it be alone.

"Can you speak?" the man asked.

"Y-yes." Her voice came out breathless and shaky.

"Wonderful," he said. "And what's your name?"

"Andrea."

"Andrea, that's a very beautiful name." He hadn't moved away, but she turned to face him. A disconcerting stain darkened the front of his shirt. She didn't want to look at it, but she couldn't force herself to meet his gaze, didn't dare to look up any farther than the collar. "You can call me Silva. I'm the head librarian."

Chapter 16: Silva

"You're Silva Graham," Andi whispered.

"You know me?" He seemed legitimately surprised.

It wasn't any wonder that Andi knew who he was. Any archive witch would. "You were the head librarian when the tree disappeared."

"Ah." Silva ran a finger over one of the shelves, the dust pale against the dark gray of his skin. "I was sleeping. For much longer than I expected. How did you get into my library?"

"A door opened." Andi's mouth was so dry her words came out as a harsh whisper. She wanted to move away. He smelled of dust and rot. Of worse things. She didn't dare move an inch.

"And how many years did it take?" he asked, still standing far too close. He could kill her so easily. A thought and a twitch and she'd be dead.

"Three-hundred and ninety-seven."

"Ah. Longer than I expected." He sounded sad and tired, though his expression remained unreadable. "I was expecting…I suppose it doesn't matter now. There are more important things. Do you know what happened to the Empire of the Dawn? Are we under their control?"

"They retreated a long time ago, no one has heard from the continent since." Andi knew it was all connected, that the library had disappeared to stop the Empire from using it.

She'd never expected to get such direct confirmation.

"And Obrye? Is it safe?" Silva asked.

Andi didn't see any point in lying to him. "It's not."

Silva's hand clenched into a fist so tight his joints creaked. "I see. What new threat do we face?"

"A darkness has spread over the continent," she realized, as she said it, that an elder vampire wouldn't care. Would probably even welcome the dark.

"Then the Empire won't return and Obrye is saved." His grip relaxed. "I asked you how, but I've neglected to ask why. Why are you in my library? You stink of magic. You're obviously a witch."

"I…I've been interested in this library since I was a little girl." It wasn't a lie. She couldn't tell him she was there to try to break the curse. "I'm a librarian myself, I wanted to see it—"

He slammed a fist into the shelf. The books trembled and the wood cracked. "Why are you here? I will not ask again."

Terror had her by the throat. "The curse. I'm trying to find the origin of it."

"What curse?" He looked genuinely puzzled.

"The…the vampiric…" Andi wanted to close her eyes. She didn't want to see what was coming next. But she could barely even blink. "The vampire curse."

"They're calling this a curse?" He smiled, as if she was a small child who had said something deeply stupid. "Why?"

"M-mostly for the afflicted, they aren't…they aren't like you," she stammered out, lamely. "There are so many, and…and if we can help them…"

"Isn't the sacrifice of a few worth the safety of the entire continent?" Silva asked, quietly.

"It's not just a few—"

"They're alive, and safe from the Empire. That is enough." Silva shrugged. "I must apologize, I have been quite rude. You have found your way into my library, and that is quite the feat. What kind of witch are you?"

His hand was on her cheek. His fingers weren't the same cold as Blythe's. They burned like ice against her skin.

"Archive." It came out as a hoarse whisper.

He smiled. "Of course, I should have guessed. You are a librarian, after all."

She nodded, barely, wishing she could step away. That she could run for it and not die in an instant.

"Show it to me."

"What?" She knew what he was asking, but the word left her anyway, a moment of stalling, to gather up what little courage she had left.

"Your archive." His fingers wrapped around her skull, long and ragged nails digging painfully into her scalp. She swallowed a whimper. "All of it. Now."

She wanted to refuse, but she knew he would just kill her. At least this would buy her a few more seconds, though towards what end, she wasn't sure.

Andi spread her hands and activated her magic.

She let it pour out until she was empty.

Golden sand filled the space between the shelves, forming words and picture, unfurling and sliding wherever it fit, burning bright against the cold blue of the shadows.

Silva let go and she dropped to her knees. Then to her side, just trying to breathe. She'd never sent out this much information at once.

It hurt, like she had been scraped clean inside. Every breath felt raw.

"Incredible." Silva breathed, fingers moving through the sand. "So much information. So much advancement. It really has been a long time."

"Yes." It was all she could say. The only word she could get out. It was hard to think, her thoughts bleeding together.

"I believe I'll take it."

"What?" Horror filled up every spot Andi's archive had taken up.

"Your archive." Silva looked down at her. "I'm taking it."

"You can't." She struggled to sit up. Everything her Coven had ever learned, every spell, every story, were all with her. She was the very last archive witch, the only one who could pass them on to someone else.

She couldn't let him take it.

She pulled her archive back to her, like candles being blown out by a sudden rush of wind. The magic filled her to the brim, too quickly. She was left too dizzy to move.

He snarled and grabbed her collar, hauling her up to her feet.

"If you kill me, you won't get anything," she choked out. If the archive was lost either way, she'd rather be dead than have it in Silva's hands. Whatever had happened, whatever he had done, she had to keep it from him.

Chrys would understand.

"Oh, miss Andrea, you misunderstand," he said, calmly. "I wasn't asking for your permission. Nor do I require it. Unfortunately, you have chosen a path that is much, much more unpleasant."

His tone remained completely even. He undid his tie with careful, unhurried motions, leaving it to hang loose around his neck. He started undoing the buttons of his vest.

"What are you doing?" Andi scooted back across the aisle. She didn't know what he had planned. She didn't want to.

"I thought I made it quite clear." Silva undid his shirt buttons. Andi grabbed a rather thick book. She couldn't just let him do whatever he wanted. She couldn't count on anyone to save her. "And here I thought you seemed like a bright young witch. I will explain it to you, slowly. I want your archive, and as much as it pains me, I will have to consume you to get it if you won't give it over willingly."

His shirt fell open, exposing an ugly, gaping wound that went from his collar bones to his navel. His chest split open with a sound like tearing wet paper. His ribs fanned out, exposing the impossible emptiness of his chest cavity.. The smell of rotting meat and ancient dust was unbearable.

"I do have to thank you, for the blood. It revived me where nothing else could have," he said. "My rest was much longer than I ever expected. My assistant was supposed to return to me…but we're here now. Once I drain you, I'll be feeling much more like my old self."

"You're the thing from the chair." She wanted to scream, but all that came out was a whisper.

"And you're the first living person I've seen in centuries." Silva actually smiled at that. "How fortuitous that you were the one who came here."

She threw the book as hard as she could. He caught it with one hand and placed it back on the shelf. "It's a shame our conversation had to be cut short. I had a lovely time."

Blythe leaped down from the shelf above.

She slammed her cane into Silva's head with sickening, bone crunching force. She stepped back and smacked him back into the shelf. With the same motion she popped the top of her cane off and slashed him across the throat. The blade slid out of the cane head. She caught the handle, throwing it brutally hard.

It pinned Silva to the shelf by his throat.

He choked and tried to wrench the blade out, fingers scrabbling on what little of the handle was sticking out. It scraped when it caught on his collar bone. There was no blood.

"C'mon!" Blythe grabbed her wrist and yanked her down the aisle.

They ran.

It didn't take long before Blythe started to flag and needed to use her cane, leaving Andi to lead them.

They dashed around twists and turns that left Andi dizzy. A spiral metal staircase loomed out of the ever-deepening shadows, thick with dust and cobwebs.

A roar echoed behind them. The shelves rattled. The lamps vibrated and hummed.

"Up we go," Blythe said. "Witches first."

Andi didn't even pause to put on her shoes. She didn't even feel the cold of the metal steps as she dashed up to the next floor.

Chapter 17: Specimen

Andi climbed the final steps and stumbled away from the trap door. Blythe slammed it shut and drag a heavy looking oak desk over it. It wouldn't hold forever.

She leaned against it, anyway. Her lungs burned. The air she was gulping down barely touched them.

"Are you okay?" Blythe stepped closer, holding her shoulders to look her up and down. Andi wondered what she looked like. Pale. Dusty. Terrified. "That was the thing from the laboratory, wasn't it? Did he hurt you?"

"No." She shook her head. She didn't remember lifting her arm, but she had a hold of Blythe's wrist. "You stabbed him before he had a chance. I'm okay."

"You're shaking." Blythe's eyebrows drew up.

"I'm fine, we need to get moving, that won't stop him for long." Andi didn't move. She knew she needed to heed her own words. The stairs could be right next to them, or clear across the floor. She suspected the latter, even though the only illumination was a diamond shaped lantern on the desk, casting a pool of light around them. "The core is at the top, and…and that could be floors and floors above us, we have to go…"

Her cheek was wet.

She was crying.

"Sorry." She tried to wipe her tears away, but they kept falling. "Stupid chemical reaction. That's all. I'm fine. I'm really fine. I—"

Her next word was swallowed by a sob.

She wasn't fine.

Blythe pulled her into a hug and any semblance of calm shattered. Andi sobbed openly on her shoulder, clinging to the back of her jacket like it was a lifeline. She knew they weren't safe, but she couldn't stop the deep, horrible rending in her chest.

It took a while for her to be able to step back, wiping the last few tears from her face. "Do you have more handkerchiefs in your magic coat?"

"All out, sorry." Blythe pulled up the sleeve of her shirt over her fingers to wipe Andi's cheek. "There we go."

"I'm a little grimy," she admitted. "Sorry."

"You have nothing to apologize for," Blythe said. "I'm sorry I wasn't there fast enough."

"Honestly, you were right on time," Andi said. "Earlier and he would have just killed you. Both of us. We…we should get moving."

The door wasn't rattling, but she knew it was only a matter of time before Silva made his way up the stairs.

"You're right, of course, but I want to make sure you're okay," Blythe said. "This has been…a lot."

"I'm…well, I'm not okay," she admitted. Saying it out loud made her feel a little lighter. "And I'm worried about Lexa."

"She's your bodyguard. I think she can take care of herself," Blythe said.

"She's my best friend." Andi looked down at the floor. "I know she can take care of herself, but I'm…I'm just scared."

"Ah." Blythe didn't seem to know what to say.

Andi knew Lexa was probably fine. She'd probably made it out, all the way back to the entrance. Maybe her and Chrys were planning a rescue mission, even as they spoke.

She hoped not. She wasn't sure even Lexa could stand up to an elder vampire, let alone one like Silva.

She shook her head a bit. It was better to focus on what was ahead. "It has been a lot. But I can keep moving, I promise. Though, I can't see anything."

"That might be for the best," Blythe said.

Andi frowned at her. "What does that mean?"

"There aren't many books here," Blythe said. "Better to be prepared."

"This is a library," Andi huffed. "Why wouldn't there be any books?"

"Well, there seem to be a few, but it's largely wet specimens," Blythe said.

"Really?" Andi grabbed the lantern by the ring at the top, yanking it out of the corroded sconce with a little difficulty.

"Of course you're excited about that, I have no idea why I expected anything different," Blythe muttered. "Put your boots on, I know you're excited, but you already have a hole in your stockings."

Blythe held the lantern while Andi sat at the desk and pulled her boots back on. She hated that she could feel the hole in her stockings, but she hadn't prepared an extra pair of socks. Or nearly enough. She took a small sip of water, conscious of how little she had left. Once she was back on her feet, she took stock of the room.

They were in a small reading alcove full of dark wood shelves. There had been plants there, once, but they had long turned black and brittle, littering the space around their pots with long dead leaves. There were a few books, tucked into the shelves, but on one shelf was an array of amphibian specimens in dusty jars. Andi wiped away the surface of one of the smaller ones. A purple toad the size of her thumb was suspended in fluid, its colors still vibrant centuries later.

"Do you think the whole floor is like this?" Andi asked.

"I…hope so?" Blythe looked dangerously close to laughing. "Aren't we supposed to be finding an exit?"

"This floor is huge, and it's all different rooms, this was a study area, but there's a room dedicated to different specimens," Andi said. "We'll have to go nearly all the way through it to get to the main room, and that's where the stairs are. We are going to see so many amazing things."

Blythe's amusement crumpled into a frown. "How do you know that?"

"I…" Andi blinked. She hadn't known that, not until she was saying it. "I don't know."

"You know about this room. You pointed right to the stairs before." Blythe tilted her head slightly, regarding Andi with curiosity. "But you never told me how you knew that. I thought you said the journal didn't contain anything."

"I said it had nothing," Andi said. "Because I couldn't read it. Not in the way I normally do. I assumed it was because of the protection spell, but now I think it must have been made with archival magic, it interacted with my archive magic in a way I wasn't expecting."

"Has that ever happened before?" Blythe asked.

"No, but you have to understand, there are no other archive witches," Andi said. "There hasn't been a journal like this for centuries. I can check my archive for something similar."

"Please do," Blythe said.

"Does it really matter?" Andi did a quick check through, but nothing came up. "Nothing. But as I said, something like this simply doesn't exist anymore. We don't have the knowledge for it."

"I suppose it doesn't matter, I just…find it strange, that's all," Blythe said.

"Strange bad?" Andi said.

"Strangely useful." Blythe looked her in the eye. "You seem to be all right, but you also have another theory, don't you?"

Was Andi that easy to read? She supposed she must be. "The only other thing I can think of is this is a living library. It could be interacting with my magic."

"Is that how it works?" Blythe didn't seem convinced.

"I've never been here, so I'm as much in the dark as you are," Andi said. Blythe looked at the lantern she was holding. "…You know what I mean."

"Do I?" Blythe grinned.

Andi shoved past her, gently. Blythe laughed softly and followed her into the next room.

It was a lot like the room they'd just left, but with more desks and chairs, a few jars had been left on the desks, next to books that had been left open. Like someone was about to come in, brush off the dust, and resume their studies.

It made Andi's heart ache, a little bit.

The reading rooms formed a crescent around one side of the floor. The entrance to the next part of the room was huge, soaring above her head so she couldn't even make the details out around the edge of the frame.

They stepped into a hallway that was lined with resin full of fish as they would have been in life, swimming forward in colorful, kite shaped groups. A lobster sat on the sandy floor, another on top of a rock, surrounded by strands of kelp that threw long, watery shadows up on the ceiling when she moved closer.

The hallway opened into a room full of specimens.

Hundreds of jars glinted in the light. The first shelf was full of shellfish, some no bigger than her pinkie nail, but she could still see the way the shell interlocked into its fan-shaped tail.

"This is amazing," she said. "This area is ocean specimens. And all invertebrates! I bet some of these haven't even been seen for hundreds of years. Some could even be extinct, but they're still here! Perfectly preserved! Do you know how incredible that is?"

Blythe was looking at her, not at any of the shelves. "That is pretty incredible, yes."

"Oh! Look here!" Andi swung the lamp around, hurrying to the next shelf. "Sea slugs! Oh, this one looks like a little bunny, it's so cute."

It was tiny enough it would have fit on her fingertip.

"It's small," Blythe said.

"And incredibly toxic," Andi explained. "Because they eat sea sponges. And this one is a blue dragon. Look at its fins! Anemone! And look, a cuttlefish! I've never seen one in real life!"

"I'm glad you're having fun," Blythe said.

Andi sighed. "But we should get going, right?"

"I didn't say it," she said.

"But it's true." Andi straightened, brushing off her skirts, even though they were most likely a lost cause.

They moved through shelves of translucent fish, some of them so small she had to lean in close to see the fan of bones through its glass-like skin.

They reached the end of the aisle and she shrieked, stumbling back into Blythe and nearly sending them both careening into the shelf.

Chapter 18: A Moment

It was a huge glass tank, full of slightly murky liquid. Suspended in it was an enormous shark, easily twelve feet long, black eyes staring at Andi, jagged teeth on display in a slightly agape mouth.

"I think it's dead," Blythe said.

"It scared me!" Andi pressed a hand to her chest. Mostly it had surprised her. She walked closer to take a look. If it was alive and they were out in the ocean, it definitely could have eaten her.

Luckily, it was in a glass case in a library.

And it hadn't been alive for centuries.

Blythe sniggered.

The back of Andi's neck grew hot. "Shut up. I was just startled. It's not funny."

"It's very funny." Blythe grinned. "Watch out, the eel in that bottle might get you."

Andi glanced at the bottle despite her best judgment. An eel thicker than her arm was coiled up in the bottom, its head up, eyes clouded. Its teeth looked like jagged pieces of glass.

She glared back at Blythe. "I will turn this lantern into a sun lamp and then you'll see how funny I can be."

Blythe clearly wasn't intimidated. She leaned closer to Andi, expression interested. "Can you do that?"

"I was joking," Andi said. "I wouldn't ever do that to you."

"Oh, I know, but if I ever go blood mad again…" Blythe didn't finish that sentence. "But I am really asking, could you make that lantern into a sun lamp?"

Andi looked down at the lantern. It was a beautiful thing. A diamond of glass, surrounding an orb of magic simply meant to give off a warm, yellow glow. Copper flowed around the glass, oxidized to green everywhere but the handle and where the point had sat in the sconce for years. They looked like rivers on a map.

"Yes," she said. "It's a very simple spell, it would just be a matter of tweaking the components to change the value of the light. Why?"

"Elder vampires are much more susceptible to sunlight," Blythe said. "Silva will show up again. We both know that. When he does, don't even hesitate. Don't worry about me. Light him up."

"I'll try," she said. "He was the head librarian. Before this place disappeared. He must be where the curse started. He didn't care about the darkness. All he cared about was the Empire."

"The Empire of the Dawn wasn't even a problem when I was human," Blythe said.

"I guess if you've been asleep for four centuries…" Andi rubbed her forehead. "I mean, I suppose in a way he's right. The darkness drove off the empire. But…"

"But it's not any better," Blythe finished for her.

Andi nodded. She actually had no idea. The Empire of the Dawn had all but been scrubbed from their history, only mentions of the invasion and the subsequent retreat.

"If he's where the curse started, could he be the answer?" Blythe asked.

"I don't know," she admitted. "I don't think so. I think the core is where we need to be, but…there's more to this than we ever realized. I um. I…"

She realized she was shaking again when the lantern light became jittery.

Blythe put a hand over hers. "We don't have to talk about him."

"Yes we do." Andi tightened her grip on the lantern. "If he's part of this, if he shows up again, and he will, you know he will, then—"

"Hey." Blythe took her shoulders. Andi's entire body was shaking. She hadn't realized it was happening, hadn't noticed much of her the fear had frozen into shards that were trying to thaw in her chest. "I'm not going to let him hurt you, okay?"

All she could see was his open chest, ready to take all of her magic, everything that she was. Every part of her Coven's past and with any luck, their future. She could have lost it all in an instant.

"Andi."

The use of her name finally got her to look at Blythe and see her. She focused on her features - her thin lips, the softness of her cheeks, the red ringing her pale eyes, her crooked nose. Her thoughts slowed, stopped spiraling with each thing she noticed, until together it painted a picture of someone she was starting to really care about. The thought all on its own was scary.

"I…yes." Andi nodded. "Sorry."

"You have absolutely nothing to apologize for." Blythe smiled at her.

"You don't have to be nice to me," Andi said. "We hardly know each other, and we're only here for the mission, not by choice, I understand that."

She didn't want to be strangers working towards a common goal, but she knew that at the core of things, that was all their relationship was.

"You literally bled to keep me sane," Blythe said. "And you fixed my cane. I told you then I was in your debt, but I'd rather be friends. If you'll have me."

"Oh." Andi hadn't expected her to be so candid about it. "I mean, yes, I would like that. So, friends?"

"We already were." Blythe's smile was radiant. And contagious. Andi found herself smiling back before she realized it. "There we go, that's my girl. Now. Do you want me to hold your hand to keep you safe from the big bad sharks?"

"You—" Andi pushed her shoulder. "We were having a moment and you just ruined it."

Blythe laughed. "Aw, Andi don't be like that—"

"Nope, it's done. Won't ever come back." Andi started walking again, but she kept smiling.

There were several more cases containing sharks and fanged things that had never come up in books. Most of them were probably extinct or simply hadn't been observed in hundreds of years. It was hard to say with the ocean. Andi couldn't help but give commentary, on eating habits, on how one shark would leap from the water and twist itself around, on the way the mouth of another must have reconstructed after its death to resemble how it would in life. Blythe didn't tell her to shut up or look impatient, so she kept talking. About how most sharks weren't actually very dangerous at all and anything else that came to her mind. She wasn't particularly well versed in sharks, but she'd spent some time reading about them.

The next section was dedicated to the largest of the deep-sea creatures - an octopus that was bigger than her in an enormous round jar, its legs coiled into thick spirals along the bottom. The suckers were as big as her hand when she held it up to measure. An entire wall was dedicated to a squid. There were enormous crabs with long, thin legs and the long, silvery body of an oar fish.

"It's said they can predict earthquakes," Andi said, trailing her fingers along the glass of the column that mimicked the deep-water columns the oar fish hung in.

"Can they?" Blythe asked.

"You know, I don't think I ever found out if it was true," Andi admitted. She knew they weren't even seeing a small portion of what the library had to offer. The floor was enormous. She wanted to explore, but they didn't have the time. She hadn't heard anything, and Blythe hadn't said she did, either. But she knew Silva was still behind them. The thought made her shudder, and she pushed him out of her mind as best as she could.

The next hallway helped. It was lined with resin, just like the first one, but it was dedicated to insects. They started in the water, and moved up into the trees as they walked, until the space opened into the next room .

There were less jars, but no less specimens. Most of them were in display frames, all of them carefully labeled. Beetles and butterflies with their jewel wings spread. Fuzzy moths and caterpillars. Judging by how far the shelves went, Andi bet there were more species than she'd ever even heard of.

The darkness hadn't helped that. She wondered if the land would ever truly recover, even if she could break the curse. It had been deprived of light and magic for so long, it was impossible to say.

She supposed the only way to find out was to break the curse and do what she could with the spells she had.

"Spiders are next." Blythe's words cut through her thoughts. "Are you sure you don't want to hold my hand?"

"Spiders aren't even insects," Andi said.

"I'm aware," Blythe said. "I have read a book or two."

"Oh, that library wasn't just for show?" Andi asked.

"It was mostly for show, I'm afraid I'm not one for reading, but I've been known to flip through a picture book on occasion." Blythe shrugged. "Now as for the spiders—"

"I'm not that afraid of spiders." Andi looked up just as the light fell on the biggest spider she had ever seen. It was easily twice the size of her hand, even with her fingers spread out. Its mandibles were enormous. If it was venomous, she doubted she'd survive a bite. "Actually, it turns out, I'm very afraid of spiders."

Blythe grinned when she held out her hand. With a sigh, that was mostly for show, Andi took it.

She tried not to look at any of the spiders on display. Some of them were beautiful, like an enormous yellow and black orb weaver. She still didn't like the way it made her skin crawl. She kept wanting to brush at her arms even though she knew there was nothing on them.

"What, no facts about this cute little guy?" Blythe asked about a bulbous looking spider with fuzzy orange legs.

"Cat face spider, they spin webs, usually outside, usually high up, very important for the ecosystem," Andi rattled off. Someone had once told her that learning about something would help her with her fear. They'd been wrong, she'd never come to love spiders. "How much farther until the next room?"

"Looks like we're getting to the slugs and snails," Blythe said. "This place is huge. Are you sure we're going the right way?"

"We are," Andi said, with absolute confidence. She wasn't sure where the confidence was coming from, but she wasn't about to question it. "C'mon, I'd rather look at the snails."

"Wait." Blythe pulled her back. "There's someone over there."

Chapter 19: Rest

Andi froze.

"Stay here." Blythe stepped forward, carefully. She stopped just a few paces away. "Never mind. They're dead. It's safe."

Andi had no idea how to handle that information. "How is that safe?"

"…Would you rather the alternative?" Blythe glanced over her shoulder.

"If the alternative is no corpses, then yes!" Andi inched closer. She saw the shriveled figure, barely silhouetted by the light, and made sure to keep the lantern on the other side of her skirts. "That's just…that's unsanitary."

"Well, maybe not sanitary, but safe enough." Blythe gave the corpse a wide berth, wrinkling her nose. "Be glad you don't have a good sense of smell."

"Honestly, I'm grateful every day." Andi followed her. She glanced at the corpse, despite herself, but it was too lost in shadow for her to make out much besides the glint of hair and the tight, wrinkled skin stretched over one outstretched hand. She shuddered and hurried past.

"Looks like frogs are next," Blythe said, probably to distract her. "I hope he studied insects. It'd be sad if he was a frog scientist."

"A herpetologist," Andi said.

"I love that you just know that." Blythe grinned at her.

"And they're amphibians." Andi was well aware she was doing what Lexa had called "babbling" not very long ago. She had no idea how long they'd been in the library. It must have been two days, at least, with how long she must have slept. It felt like it had been years since then. "Not just frogs. And it's strange that the insects were between the fish and the amphibians, but then again taxonomy is not an exact science, and despite the wealth of knowledge here it was four hundred years ago, and it may have been common practice to order things in such a way. Going from gastropods to amphibians, now that I'm thinking about it there is a certain amount sense, I suppose, however…um. I like frogs?"

She wondered how long Blythe would have let her talk before she caught herself and was honestly not sure she wanted the answer.

"I noticed." Blythe didn't comment on anything else she said. Which was probably for the best. "I know we just passed…that, but I think we should take a break."

"We have to keep moving," Andi argued.

Exhaustion burned behind her eyelids, her feet hurt, and her ankle was beginning to throb again.

"We won't get there any faster if we push forward until you collapse." Blythe put a hand on her shoulder to stop her. "And don't you dare apologize."

"Right." Andi hadn't realized until Blythe said that they needed to take a break, but it was like hitting a wall. She was certain that she couldn't go forward another step.

Dizziness overwhelmed her, for a moment. The next thing she was aware of, Blythe had caught her around the shoulders to ease her down.

"I just got a little lightheaded. Did your vampire senses tell you that I need a break?" Andi was half joking.

Blythe got them both sitting on the floor, stretching her bad leg out in front of her, her cane across her lap. "Not so much. You just went pale. And you stopped talking about taxonomy so, I figured something had to be wrong."

"I didn't want to be annoying," Andi admitted, leaning against the shelf, glad that she had a support at her back.

They were surrounded by snails in jars. As fascinating as it was, the number of eyes back in the fish room had been getting to her. She doubted the amphibian room would be any better.

"You aren't annoying." Blythe leaned next to her. "I know I wasn't particularly kind when we first met, or in the hours that followed—"

"I already forgave you," Andi reminded her.

"Yes, but I…since then, well, I'm glad I'm here with you," Blythe said.

"Even if running and fighting isn't exactly my strong suit?"

"Miss Andrea, we are in a library, we shouldn't be running anywhere," Blythe pretended to admonish her.

Andi couldn't help but smile. "You're kind of a dork."

"I am a creature of the night, I am suave and sophisticated," Blythe corrected her.

"I take it back, you're definitely a dork. I'm…I'm glad you're here, too," Andi said, curling her knees up. "Well, not, here. Because here is really interesting but honestly kind of awful. But here as in, with me, but maybe not specifically here—"

Blythe nudged her gently with her shoulder. "I know what you're trying to say."

"Good, that makes one of us."

They both giggled. It felt nice, the tiny pool of light, sitting together and talking. She could almost pretend she was home, in her own library, trading secrets with a pretty girl late into the night.

If it weren't for the dust and the heavy silence that made their voices small and quiet.

Andi dozed, for a time, and when she woke up her head was on Blythe's shoulder. She sat up, carefully. Blythe's eyes were closed, the curve of her cheek shining gold, her eyelashes gilded.

"Good nap?" Blythe asked.

"Yes," Andi was stiff and sore, but she didn't feel like she was about to fall over. "Did you rest?"

"In the dark, I need a lot less rest than you," Blythe explained. "I was thinking."

"About what?" Andi was bold enough to ask.

"A lot of things. But one thing that I can just ask you. If we do find a cure, and it doesn't ah…if it works, will you visit me?"

"Of course," Andi didn't hesitate to answer. "Will you still be at the manor?"

"Well, I have been promised it as payment when all this is over," Blythe said. "Providing we survive that long."

"We will," Andi said.

"You're so optimistic." Blythe's smile turned wry.

"I'm really not," Andi shrugged. "I just don't have any other choice. Even if the curse is broken, if I die, my Coven would lose so much."

"Well, I won't allow that to happen," Blythe said. "But, surely there are other archive witches?"

Andi shook her head. "When I was very young there were a few. They were all much older than me. The last one passed when I was thirteen. Now it's just me."

"So you have…everything?" Blythe asked.

"Going back centuries," Andi said. "It would take lifetimes just to go through it all. My archive is only a little bit mine, most of it was given to me. And with magic fading, with no idea what happened to any other part of Obrye…well, some of the spells might only exist in me. That's why I have to live."

"That's a heavy burden." Blythe's brow furrowed. "How old were you?"

"I was twelve," Andi said. "My predecessor, Duncan, cut it a little close. He was ancient when I met him."

"What about those close to you?" Blythe asked. "Chrys? Your…your parents?"

It was still a sore spot, after so many years. Like a thorn that she forgot was still buried in a callous, until she stepped down wrong and it hurt all over again. "They were gone by then. Afflicted. My whole village was. I was hiding in a cupboard."

Her father had placed her there, in a secret cabinet. Chrys had found her, eventually, and taken her back to the Coven. No one else survived. She had no idea if her parents were still out there, stumbling along, driven by blood madness. The afflicted could live for a very long time, even with nothing to keep them going.

But many didn't survive.

When she was younger, she'd dreamed of finding a cure. Of her parents coming to find her. As she grew older, those dreams had faded. She doubted they were alive after so long.

"I'm sorry." Blythe put a hesitant hand on her shoulder.

"It was a long time ago." Because it was true. A lot of it was blank, softened by years and her own mind trying to protect her. She didn't remember what her parents looked like anymore. She'd cried for days when she realized she'd forgotten the sound of her mother's voice.

So many people had stories similar to hers.

She had to break the curse. For the sake of everyone, not just her parents, who were probably long dead. It still ached, a little, to think that. Having hope hurt even more.

"I can't imagine going through something like that and not giving up," Blythe said.

"Oh, I did, for a while," Andi admitted. "I didn't talk for an entire year after that. Lexa thinks I talk so much now to make up for it. Maybe she's right. It took a long time for me to come to terms with things. Longer still for me to start really living. But…I was twelve and given an archive. I didn't have a choice. So, I made the most of it."

"You are incredibly strong," Blythe said.

Andi blushed and ducked her head, though she doubted that would keep Blythe from noticing. "I don't know about that. You know, I was terrified to meet you."

"You were?" Blythe was clearly surprised.

"Oh, yes, but…Chrys helped," Andi admitted. "And then I met you, and you were just kind of a jerk, not monstrous."

"I'm wounded," Blythe said. "But mostly because that's a very accurate assessment of my character."

Andi was smiling again. She couldn't help it. "I'm not saying I'm over my fear entirely, but I'm not scared of you. Yes, even if I should be. I'm not. I don't think I can be."

"Brave, strong, and very smart," Blythe said. "It's funny, even after Chrys saved me, I was…resigned, I suppose. And yet, less than two days with you, and I feel like we can do anything."

"Do you really mean that?" Andi asked. Blythe's words ignited a strange fire in her chest.

"I really do," Blythe said. "It's a little cheesy, but…"

"But?" Andi prompted when she trailed off.

Blythe held a finger to her lips, turning her head and listening, hard. Andi didn't dare move. After a moment, Blythe relaxed. "I thought I heard something. If I leave you here, and go check, are you going to be okay?"

Andi wanted to say that of course she would be okay. That she would stay and wait, the only bit of light in an enormous room full of shelves and corpses. That she wouldn't spend every single second terrified out of her mind at what would loom out of the dark.

The words wouldn't come. They were locked inside of her.

It must have shown on her face.

"Okay," Blythe said. "That's a no."

"I—"

"I shouldn't have even asked." Blythe held up a hand. "Do you feel like you can keep going?"

Andi nodded, and together they got up to face the next room.

Chapter 20: A Particular Scent

Andi barely looked at the walls of the next hallway. The lantern light made the blue-green resin glow, piercing through thick vegetation. The next room was mostly jars again, like the fish room. Andi didn't take the time to look around.

Blythe held up a hand and they stopped at the end of an aisle, next to one of the biggest bullfrogs Andi had ever seen. She couldn't help but stare back at its eyes. Strangely beady, considering its massive size.

"Can you hook the lantern to your bag?" Blythe asked. "And dim it, please. Just enough that you can see."

She nodded and hooked the round handle to the clip for her strap. She pressed a hand against the glass, the light fading under her fingers until she could only see Blythe because of her white hair.

In the end, maybe it wouldn't help much.

"Do you want to hold my hand?" Blythe asked.

Andi shook her head. "You might need to fight. I'll just…I can follow you."

"If you're sure." Blythe sounded worried. Andi wished she could see her face, but at least Blythe could see her.

She tried very hard to school expression into something that could be brave and nodded.

Blythe's fingers brushed against hers. "Remember what I told you about the light."

"Light him up," Andi said. "I remember."

"Good."

Together, they stepped into the dark. Andi followed the flash of Blythe's cane, winking in the lamp light every time she stepped forward. Occasionally the eyes of something caught the light just right, pin holes in the dark. Every time it happened her heart attempted to seize up, expecting something to blink at her.

It was a long, dark nightmare.

"I think the stairs are that way," she whispered after the silence had stretched on.

"Okay." Blythe didn't question her, just turned to where she pointed. They walked past an empty snakeskin that still had luminescence, glowing a pale blue. She couldn't say when they'd entered the reptile room.

"I've seen a few more corpses," Blythe said, quietly. "But I haven't heard anything. I think we're okay."

Andi's shoulders relaxed. "Good. I think we're almost to the stairs."

"Great, let's keep on—"

Even Andi heard the noise, the clink of a jar hitting the floor, the ringing when it rolled towards them. It only stopped when it hit Blythe's boot, the tiny snake coiled inside jerking back and forth like it was still in its death throes.

Blythe backed up, as quickly as she could, crowding Andi back, but another jar hit the ground behind them.

A footstep.

Muffled and soft, but it couldn't be anything else. Then another.

"When I tell you to turn off your light, do it," Blythe whispered. "And please trust me."

Andi nodded.

Despite the horrible, gnawing dread deep within her, she did trust Blythe.

"Turn it as bright as you can and then off," Blythe said. "Now!"

Andi did as she was told, the lamp flaring to life. The light was scorching bright for an instant, and she saw exactly what was bearing down on them.

Corpses.

Dozens of them, coming down both sides of the aisle, their skin gray and leathery, their sunken eyes glowing a bright red. They didn't make a sound beyond a soft shuffling. The closest ones were only about an arm's length away, but they cringed back from the light, desiccated arms lifted to try and shield their cadaverous faces.

Andi turned off the light.

Blythe grabbed her around the waist and knocked the shelf next to them over with a thunderous crash. Jars shattered, displays broke, and they scrambled over all of it and into the next aisle. The unmistakable burn of formaldehyde hit the back of Andi's throat and dizziness clouded her mind a moment later. She covered her mouth and tried not to breathe. Blythe's hand slid to her free wrist and she yanked her along, running so fast her cane actually made a noise, thumping in time with Andi's heartbeat.

They had to stop a moment later, so she could breathe. The air was stale and dusty, but it helped clear her head, at least a little bit.

"Light!" Blythe called out to her, and she turned on the light again. There were more corpses there, a stepping between displays of feather, bone, and a huge taxidermy form of a flightless bird. Another blast of light sent the corpses cringing back, and then they were running again, the lantern barely showing Andi where her feet were hitting.

They hit the stairs going so quickly that Andi stumbled up the first few.

The lights above them flared to life. Lanterns like hers hung from the ceiling. Giant bones were thrown into sharp relief. They'd been suspended from the ceiling, by what she couldn't say, but it looked like the massive skeletons were swimming through a sea of lights. A whale took up the center of the dome room, so large its narrow skull nearly touched the staircase where it slowly twisted around the room above them. It was surrounded by smaller specimens — dolphins, a winding sea serpent that looked like delicate lace ribbon, and a narwhal with its spiral horn. The dome above was painted to look like the night sky, tiny stars glinting far above them.

Blythe turned and smacked a corpse that had been reaching for Andi's bag with her cane, sending it tumbling back down the stairs.

"Oh." Andi climbed up a few more steps. "Thank you."

"They're persistent, but they're slow, if we keep going, we should be fine." Blythe gave her a strained smile.

"Your knee hurts." Andi didn't have to ask, it was obvious. Blythe was leaning very heavily on her cane. "You need blood. It should be easy to re-open the cuts, or I have antidote, we could get up a bit farther and—"

Blythe lifted a hand to stop her. "No. Thank you, but no. If I need it, I will ask. I promise."

Andi had been ready to undo the buttons on her sleeve, but she let her hands fall to her sides. "Right. Make sure you do."

Blythe nodded. "Of course. It's painful, but it's manageable. Are you all right?"

"I think so." Andi's head still felt a little cottony, but it was already starting to pass. She wasn't sure if she felt sick because of the corpses, the formaldehyde, or because she'd eaten so little in the past however many hours.

"Good." Blythe started up the stairs. They were wide enough that they could walk side by side. So. Tell me about how you would arrange this place if you were in charge."

"I'm not sure," Andi admitted. "I'd probably leave it as is. It's part library, part history museum, and there's a charm to leaving it exactly as it was, I suppose. …Except for the shelf you knocked over."

"Yes, I'm so sorry for saving our lives," Blythe did not sound sorry at all.

"So, I would fix that, and…install elevators," Andi said.

"Great, when can you start?" Blythe asked.

"Really? You have the power to hire me, just like that?" Andi's eyebrows rose.

"Oh, yes, I fired the old head librarian." Blythe grinned. "He should consider that knife in his throat his termination letter."

"Well, I can't argue with that." Andi glanced back. None of the corpses were coming up the stairs after Blythe knocked the first one down. They all just stood around the room, staring up at them. "…That seems ominous."

"They act a lot like the afflicted, but they're much farther gone," Blythe said. "They might have decided this was their territory, and they refuse to leave it. They might not even…be vampires. They don't smell right."

"Smell right?" Andi asked.

"Vampires have…a particular scent," Blythe explained.

"Cloves?" Andi guessed. "Or is that just you."

Blythe blinked. Andi had a feeling she'd be blushing, if she could. "Oh. No. That's just me. It's a salve I use, which I should apply next time we're sitting down. Luckily, I kept that in my pocket."

She patted her right side, though it must have been masterfully tailored, because Andi didn't see anything.

Andi nodded. "Do you have anything else in that coat I should know about?"

"It just has a lot of pockets," Blythe huffed. She was decidedly not looking at Andi, who realized that maybe it was a personal question. Or possibly inappropriate. She was very bad at judging things like that. Blythe continued talking before she could mull it over further. "As I was saying, the vast majority of vampires smell…well, like iron. Like blood."

"Oh," Andi said. "That…makes sense."

"Yes." Blythe nodded. "But these ones barely smell of anything. Like dust, if I could pick one thing out. It's actually quite unsettling. If they had any to drink it might be different. After all, I found Silva rather quickly after he was ah…reborn. That's probably how he found you, actually. Because of your injuries. So. I apologize for that."

"It's not your fault, and I think he would have found me either way," Andi said. She didn't think a few shallow cuts on her arm made very much difference. Even if he hadn't been able to smell her, which after her dash through the library she very much doubted, vampires had incredible hearing.

"You're probably right," Blythe said. Her head snapped up and she stepped in front of Andi, holding up her cane. "Unfortunately, you are very right."

Chapter 21: Carmine

A shelf on the wall slid back.

Andi backed down a step, but that way didn't lead to safety, either.

Silva stepped through the opening.

He'd found new clothes — still old fashioned, the colors too muted. His tie was the only spot of color on him, a garish red and tucked neatly into his vest, cut in a way that hadn't been popular for centuries. Despite that, the clothes could have been new. He'd even combed his hair, tying it neatly back with a silk ribbon. He adjusted the cuff of his suit coat before he pretended to notice them. "Hello, Andrea. We meet again."

Andi barely heard him. Her ears pounded. Her chest felt like it might break from how fast her heart was beating — a bird wildly fluttering against its cage. She couldn't move. She wanted to run. Everything in her screamed to move.

There was nowhere to go.

Blythe glanced back at her. "I won't let him hurt you."

"I have no intention of hurting her. Blythe, was it?" Silva walked calmly down the steps.

"How do you know my name?" Blythe jabbed her cane at his face.

He caught the end of her cane and moved it delicately to the side. The smile crossing his face only made him more intimidating. "Did you really think that you were the only ones to make it into my library?"

Andi's first thought was of Lexa. Of her strapped to the chair, down in the laboratory. She wouldn't have given up any information unless it was pulled out of her.

She tried to squash down the panic.

"Say what you mean or I'll go for your eyes," Blythe snarled.

"I see you're still impatient."

The new voice came from the corridor behind the open bookcase.

Blythe flinched back, so hard Andi had to grab her shoulders to keep her from tumbling down the stairs. She was shaking.

Slow, measured footsteps echoed into the stairway.

Silva stepped to the side. "I suppose Carmine requires no introduction."

The elder vampire who stepped through the doorway had to duck slightly to avoid hitting her head on the high door frame.

She had the same gray skin as Silva did. Her white hair was neatly plaited into a thick braid that fell to the small of her back. She was easily a head taller than him, her shoulders much broader. Her well cut suit did little to hide her massive frame. She could have snatched Andi up in her clawed hands and snapped her in two with no effort at all.

Her size wasn't the most intimidating thing about her.

Power washed off of her in waves. It made Andi want to drop to her knees, in worship or in hope of a swift and merciful death, she couldn't say.

She tightened her grip on Blythe's shoulders instead.

"Hello, Blythe." Carmine's voice was calm and even.

"Carmine." Blythe sounded surprisingly steady. "It's been a while."

"You used to call me Cari." Carmine's smile was cruel, the light from Andi's lantern glinting off of shark-like teeth. "I know you fell, Bly, but I didn't think it was this far. Protecting a little witch?"

She spat out the last word like a poison.

"You abandoned me." Blythe's pain was so raw in her voice it made Andi's heartache. "You left me in those woods for twelve years. How could you?"

"You know the rules, pet," Carmine said.

"I thought you cared about me." Blythe's voice cracked and Andi's grip had to be hurting her, but she didn't even seem to notice it. "You told me you loved me, but you just left me. And then you left me with the witches. Why?"

"I did care about you." Carmine stepped down the stairs, moving slowly. "And that's why I'm offering you a second chance, right now. Leave the witch to Silva. She's not your concern anymore, anyway. Come with me. The dark is deeper than ever before, and Silva has promised us Obrye. What do you say? Put that cane down, and let's talk. We have a lot to discuss."

Carmine held out a hand.

Andi didn't know Blythe very well. That was more than apparent. If Blythe did turn her over, she couldn't even blame her. She'd wandered the woods for years, and then was trapped in a house by witches. Of course she would resent them. It made sense that she would want to rejoin Carmine, to start living her old life again.

Despite that, despite everything, Andi stayed exactly where she was.

It wasn't fear of what was below. It wasn't because she was frozen. Some part of her just knew that she couldn't leave. All she could do was let Blythe make her decision. She should have been pleading with her, but the words were stuck. The only thing left was to keep her hands on her shoulders.

The tip of Blythe's cane stopped wavering, and she stepped away from Andi, her stance shifting slightly.

"This isn't a hard decision," Carmine said. "Just come back to me. I miss you."

"Okay."

Blythe's voice held no emotion at all.

Andi was pretty sure she stopped feeling anything herself.

Blythe leaned on her cane to walk up the steps that separated them. She let herself be folded into Carmine's embrace, let her hair be stroked by thick, dark claws.

"We are reasonable creatures, when we need to be," Silva said.

"Are you going to kill me now?" It was the first thing Andi had been able to say, and her voice was hoarse. "If you are, get it over with, quick."

Silva sighed. "No. I've decided I have other uses for you and your marvelous archive. If you cooperate I'll let you live. See? Much more than reasonable. Now, how about we all go somewhere a little more comfortable?"

Andi's fingers ached from gripping the strap of her bag.

She needed to move. To run back down the stairs. The corpses weren't fast, she could avoid them. She could find help. Get out of the library, maybe.

She knew she wouldn't even make it a few steps before Silva was on her.

"There's just one more thing," Blythe said.

The meaty thunk of a blade sliding into flesh.

Carmine howled and ripped away from her. Blythe spun and slammed her cane into the side of Silva's head, knocking him into open space. He tumbled down into the dark.

"You little bitch!" Carmine roared. "I should have killed you when I had the chance! I'll rip you apart!"

She charged in low, but Blythe was ready for her, leaping at the last possible moment and swinging her cane down, bringing her entire weight behind it and slamming Carmine into the stairs.

"Run!" Blythe screamed. She started forward but Carmine grabbed her head and yanked, throwing her onto the enormous whale skeleton with a horrible clatter.

Andi dashed up the stairs. Blythe had to have a plan. She had to trust her.

Silva was in front of her before she could blink. She stopped so hard he had to grab her arm to keep her from falling over the edge.

"How unfortunate that it had to come to this," he said. Despite his light tone, his eyes were nearly all pupil, only a tiny ring of red left in the darkness.

"Andi! Now!"

She didn't see Blythe, couldn't turn her head to look, but she knew what to do.

She placed a hand on the lantern.

The spell it contained was simple. Just a little light spell. She took the threads of magic holding the spell together and twisted them, forming something new.

Sunlight blazed from the lantern, so bright it was daytime in the stairwell, if only for a moment. Wild shadows were tossed up against the wall. The skeletons were thrown into brilliant, sharp relief.

Silva screamed and threw himself back. Carmine reached for her and Andi jabbed the lantern in her direction. She shrieked and fell off the stairs. She grabbed one of the whale's ribs. The whole skeleton bounced, jerking her to a stop.

Andi held up the lamp, backing up so her shoulders pressed against the wall, the spines of books digging into her own.

Carmine clambered up onto the whale skeleton, her skin smoking. It creaked and groaned, but held her considerable weight. A bone snapped under her foot and fell to the floor, crashing into a display far below.

Blythe took a step back, barely balancing on two of the ribs, her cane wedged in the vertebrae.

Silva lunged for Andi, half his face hidden behind one hand. His other stretched towards her. She swung the lantern his way. He screamed, staggering back. "I don't want to hurt you! Just stop, we don't have much time before—"

Darkness, great clouds of it, full of red lightning. It came billowing up from the ground, surging through the room and up the staircase. Bottles shattered like gunshots. Skeletons toppled. Bones rattled across the floor.

The wires holding up the whale snapped.
Andi had just enough time to make eye contact with Blythe before it plummeted to the floor.

Chapter 22: Solitude

A scream wrenched out of Andi's throat.

She scrambled to the edge of the stairs on her hands and knees, leaning out farther than she should have, the lantern held high, as bright as she dared.

It didn't pierce the darkness.

Black clouds billowed up from the floor, slashed through with scarlet lightning. It boiled into the hollow space all the way up to the domed ceiling, just out of reach, but the light did nothing to it.

The stairs shuddered underneath her.

A hand wrapped around her upper arm like a band of iron, yanking her back and up onto her feet.

"You don't want to touch that," Silva said.

"Then make it go away!" She pulled her arm free. He let her back away until there were a few stairs between them. It wasn't enough.

She couldn't run away. Blythe was down there, somewhere. She might have been hurt. She could be dying.

Silva's face was pinched. With pain, with regret, Andi didn't care which. The skin around his left eye was darker, healing rapidly. "I can't."

"You called it here, didn't you?" Andi climbed up another step, holding her lantern up between them.

"If only that was the case," Silva said. "I will do my best to contain it. You need to go."

It was too much. Andi had too many thoughts, too many questions, all swirling up inside of her, threatening to split her open.

"Go!" Silva snarled at her.

She didn't understand. He'd been trying to kill her.

Blythe needed her.

The tree creaked and groaned, as if a high wind had picked up outside, strong enough to move the largest living being on the continent.

The realization that there was nothing she could do was heavy in her gut.

She turned and ran.

She hooked the lantern onto her bag. It banged against her back with every step, the light and shadows spinning around the walls. Scarlet light cleaved into the stairs behind her, splitting the dark wood. She stumbled and had to crawl up the next few stairs on all fours, her skirts dragging around her. She pulled herself up with a bookshelf set into the wall and kept running.

She reached a dead end.

The stairs tapered off against a bookshelf.

There was no door.

Andi checked the ceiling, but there was nothing above her, just carved wood and the dome. She hit the bookshelf with her hands. All she managed to do was make her palms sting.

The storm raged on beside her, the stairs were being swallowed up by the dark, one by one, and all she could do was cower in front of a bookshelf and wait for it to reach her, the wind howling in her ears and tugging at her hair.

She squeezed her eyes shut and leaned her forehead against the shelf.

It couldn't end like this.

She wouldn't let it.

Her entire Coven was counting on her.

There had to be something, anything. She took a deep breath. It came out shaky, but she was able to open her eyes and attempt to look at things calmly. She held up the lantern, it was still bright, the metal growing hot under her palm.

The bookshelf itself was rather plain, made of dark wood with a rich, swirling grain. She ran her fingers across the shelf but only got them coated in dust for her troubles.

The corners each had a rose carved into them. The top left corner looked a little different. She might not have noticed if she wasn't looking so hard, if she didn't have the light so close.

She pressed it.

Something clicked. With a terrible grinding the entire shelf swung into the room beyond. Andi slipped through as soon as the opening was wide enough. She had to yank hard to get the door to close behind her.

The moment it was closed everything fell silent.

Her legs shook, breath burning in her lungs, and she slowly slid down to the floor. She sat on the cold tile and just breathed. She dimmed the light until she was in a tiny bubble of it, the copper handle slowly cooling beneath her fingers.

She couldn't get Blythe's face out of her mind, her expression right before she fell, like she knew that she wouldn't make it back to the stairs.

Andi shook her head, using the door handle to pull herself slowly to her feet. She needed to look around, to see what form of awful the library had to offer.

She was standing in a large room. Far away light flickered dimly, but they were too far to provide any illumination. The only thing the pool of light from her lantern showed her was a black tile floor, mica and quartz in the stone glittering back at her. An upside-down night sky.

Her heels clicked on the floor, but she tried to walk quietly. She didn't have the energy to take her shoes off this time.

She found a table, with the same sconce as the one she'd found her lantern in. She dug the point into it, flexing her hand. She'd been holding on so hard it had cramped around the handle.

She'd expected the worst from the table, but the jars only held dried plants.

"An herbarium," she whispered, quietly enough that it wouldn't echo. She listened, hard, but she heard nothing at all. If there were any corpses in the room, they weren't close enough for her to hear their faint shuffling.

She sat down in the nearby chair, not even caring about the dust and cobwebs, put her head in her hands, and tried very hard not to cry.

Blythe had to be alive. She had to believe that. She was a vampire, a fall like that wouldn't kill her. Carmine had been hurt. And the dark…

She had to believe that wouldn't hurt her, either. Silva had stayed behind. He didn't seem the type to do that if it would kill him.

And there was the question of why Silva had ordered her to run, instead of killing her. Taking her archive. He'd said he'd changed his mind, but she had no idea what that meant. Had he been trying to warn her? But why? He said he had a use for her archive, but she couldn't imagine what it was.

There was so much she didn't understand.

Her hands were shaking and her breathing was turning ragged. She needed to do something to distract herself, to get her thoughts in order. She carefully cleared a space and upended her bag on the table.

Taking inventory would help.

Four antidotes for vampire venom, carefully wrapped up in soft cloth. A handful of granola bars. She opened one and chewed on it, barely tasting it. Her canteen, which she took a swig from. It did little for her parched throat.

It would have to do. She would have to ration what little was left.

Blythe's handkerchief.

The one she had bled on.

She dropped her half-eaten granola bar, staring at it. She hadn't even noticed Blythe slipping it into her bag. Some horrible, desperate feeling was crawling its way up her throat.

Blythe was okay.

She had to be okay.

Andi threw all caution to the wind, stood up, and marched back to the door, pushing on it with all her might.

Nothing happened.

She grabbed the lantern and searched every inch of the door. There was a carving of lavender sprigs in the middle of it. Pressing them elicited no reaction. There was no handle. She shoved her shoulder against it.

It didn't budge.

She swung her lantern back and forth. There weren't even bookshelves on the wall, it was all carved, pale wood. She tested a few of the carvings, but they were all solid.

She couldn't go back.

"It's okay," she whispered, even if it was only to herself. "She'll catch up to me. She'll find me. I know she will. She's really smart and…and she can smell me. Probably."

She had to believe that. If she didn't, if she let herself fall into believing she was gone…

Andi shook her head, hard. Thinking like that wouldn't do her any favors. All she could do was move forward and trust that Blythe would find her, and they would continue the journey together from there. She walked back over to the table and began setting things back in her bag.

Her hand brushed the handkerchief, and she realized it was wrapped around something. It felt like a bottle. She frowned and picked it up, carefully unwrapping it.

It was a toad.

The toad, the small purple one that Blythe had shown her, what felt like a lifetime ago. Andi wanted to cry, to break down and try to open the door all over again. Instead, she took a long, steadying breath.

"Well, at least Blythe left me with some company," she told the toad. "I'm glad I'm not completely alone."

The toad jerked, its legs kicking against the glass.
She screamed and threw the jar as hard as she could.

Chapter 23: The Assistant

The jar shattered somewhere in the dark.

Andi yanked her lantern out of the sconce, holding it close and backing up a few steps. She was afraid to make it much brighter, not sure she would like what she saw.

A plop.

"This is so stupid," she told her racing heart. "It's barely bigger than your thumb. Step on it."

"Excuse me?"

She screamed again and it took every bit of willpower to not throw her lantern in the direction of the voice.

"Could you stop screaming? Frogs have incredibly good hearing, and I am not adjusting well. How do I…oh!"

Another plop.

"Frog?" Andi took a few careful steps forward. The glass glittered in the lantern light, and sitting in the middle of it was the toad.

"Yes. Hello." The toad scratched at the side of its head with one stubby back leg. "Oh. Yes. That's good. Have you ever had an itch in your soul but no way to do anything about it?"

"I…can't say I have?" Andi crouched down, far enough away that the toad couldn't jump onto her. "What are you? Is…everything in that room actually still alive or…?"

That was a scary thought. Blythe had knocked over the shelf, but it was nothing compared to the destruction wrought by the dark cloud.

"What? No. Don't be stupid." The toad sat up to its full height of maybe two inches. "My name is Bertrand, and I have to thank you for finding my journal. Well, I will thank you, as long as you don't step on me. Reanimating this body was hard. Doing it while stuck in your archive? Nearly impossible. You should be in absolute awe."

"You were in my archive?" Andi had no idea what to do with the information Bertrand fired rapidly at her. None of it made any sense to her. Maybe it was just to much, after everything, but she couldn't be certain that he wasn't talking absolute nonsense.

"Bit slow, aren't you," Bertrand said. "Well, I suppose you got this far, you can't be that dimwitted. Could you pick me up? This conversation is a little disconcerting to have when you're looming like that. I'm a very small frog—"

"Toad," Andi corrected, automatically. "I don't think I should, after you insulted me."

That was the least strange thing that had happened, and she latched onto it.

"All toads are frogs. You're just being nitpicky," he huffed. "Fine, you're probably brilliant, I wouldn't know, I'm sorry. Is that better?"

"Marginally." Andi didn't particularly want to, but she held out one hand and let him jump-- onto it. She braced herself for him to be slimy, but it felt like holding a small, smooth stone.

"There! That's better. Yes, I was in your archive. I transferred my soul to the journal you scanned, so my soul ended up in there."

Andi stared at him. He suddenly seemed heavy, for such a small toad. "That's a forbidden spell."

So forbidden that while she knew of it, the instructions to perform it didn't exist. Not even in her archive.

"Pfft, forbidden doesn't mean impossible," Bertrand waved her off. "If you want to be technical, from my perspective I've done at least three forbidden spells in the last forty-eight hours or so. Tucked my soul into a journal, hitched a ride with you. And then reanimated this little frog toad creature. Not bad for a library assistant."

"Okay, I'm sorry, slow down," Andi said. "You put your soul in the journal—"

"To avoid being a living corpse," Bertrand added.

"You were in my archive." She didn't even like saying it out loud. It made her feel a little weird. She checked for the journal, but it was gone, a tiny void in her magic. Bertrand had to be telling the truth. She wasn't sure what else the truth could have been.

It certainly explained why a corpse had been holding onto the journal.

"Well, not on purpose, you really need to not scan every random book you find, that's dangerous."

"And now you're in a toad? Is that everything?" Andi asked.

Bertrand glanced down at himself. He was a dark purple, with lighter markings, speckled with gold. "A type of harlequin toad, if I'm not mistaken. Am I mistaken? I don't know how versed you are on amphibians."

"Does that really matter right now?" Andi asked.

"Well, several species of harlequin toads are poisonous, so it probably matters—"

Andi dropped him with a squeak and wiped her hand on her skirt.

"Hey! That was extremely rude." Bertrand righted himself. "You can't just drop a person! Who taught you manners?"

"You just said you could be poisonous," Andi shot back.

"Let's start over, I believe we got off on the wrong foot," Bertrand said. "Particularly the one that you were going to use to step on me."

She was more than a little tempted to step on him, right then. Blythe was trapped on the last floor and Andi was stuck talking to a self-important toad who wouldn't shut up.

The absurdity of the situation made her want to laugh. Instead, fat, hot tears rolled onto her cheeks. She stifled a sob with one hand, wiping at her face with her sleeve. It was dirty, but her face wasn't much cleaner.

"Oh no," Bertrand said. "Don't cry. I never know what to do when people cry. I was joking. I know you wouldn't...look. Okay. Starting over for real. My name is Bertrand Kneller. I was formerly an assistant to Silva Graham, head librarian."

"Andrea Madsen." The words came out a little broken and garbled. "You can call me Andi. I'm um. I'm a librarian. And the archive witch for the Rosewood Coven."

"Wonderful, we're introduced," Bertrand said. "Now this is slightly awkward, but I need you to finish what I started."

"And what's that?" Andi had a feeling she wouldn't like what he was about to ask.

"I need you to find Silva and kill him."

"How am I supposed to do that?" Andi's voice was a broken thing. "I'm just an archive witch, I don't kill vampires, I just—"

"See, that's the brilliant thing, that an archive witch ended up here," Bertrand explained, hopping up onto her knee. "That you ended up here. I'm sorry. I'm getting ahead of myself. I do that a lot. Silva did something to the core, I don't know the details, but it cursed this library and everyone in it. I was supposed to return the core to him, but I put it as far away as I could. Unfortunately, the curse took hold before I reached him to finish the job, so I had to bind my soul to my journal. It was the only way I could think of to not do his bidding, and to inform the next witch who came along."

"That's why you were in that library." Andi sniffed. "What does me being an archive witch have to do with anything?"

"Because every witch that ever worked in the library was an archive witch," Bertrand explained. "I…can't access my archive in this form, so some of that information is potentially lost. Any other witch would never have made it this far. I wasn't completely aware, but you've been connected to the library, ever since you used your archive, right?"

"I…I've known where the stairs were," Andi said. She'd stopped crying, but her chest still felt so tight it was hard to breathe. "Are you sure that wasn't you?"

"Oh, please, I'm hopeless with directions," Bertrand said. "My friend Mellie used to say I couldn't find my way to the end of a book and—ah. Sorry. It's…hitting me that it's really been four hundred years."

He was quiet, for once.

"I'm sorry." Andi wished she had something better to say. She doubted there were any words in her archive that would make things any better.

Bertrand shook himself. "That doesn't matter. Well, it does, in a 'if we don't get going, then it will have all been for nothing' sort of way.

"Right." Andi knew she had to keep moving, but standing up seemed incredibly difficult. "The stairs are on the other side of the room. You could ride in my pocket?"

"You have pockets in this thing?" Bertrand asked. He cleared his throat. "I mean, I'd prefer your shoulder, if that's okay. I think I'm only poisonous if you eat me. So, as long as you don't put me in your mouth—"

Andi made a face. "That won't be a problem."

"See? We're good!" Bertrand started clambering up to her shoulder. She picked him up and put him there. "Ah. Luxurious. Your best bet is probably to go straight through. The gardens should have some sun lamps left active. Yes, I see them. It might be the safest place in the whole library."

"The gardens?" She had noticed lights, far off, but she hadn't thought what they might be for.

"Largest indoor garden in the whole continent," Bertrand said, proudly. "Unless they've made a bigger one, since. You'll have to catch me up on the world. Oh! Congratulations, by the way."

"On what?" Andi had no idea what he could be talking about. She'd lost Lexa, and then Blythe, there was nothing to congratulate her on. She was wandering almost completely blind. The best she'd done was survive, and that hadn't been on her own merit.

"On being chosen to be the next head librarian, of course," Bertrand explained. "I am honored to be your assistant. You'll need one. No offense."

Chapter 24: The Greenhouse

Andi almost tripped on nothing.

She stopped walking, turned her head, and stared at Bertrand. As much of him as she could see of him, at any rate, mostly just one minuscule purple hand. She opened her mouth, to ask what he meant, what it all could possibly mean, but something entirely different came out. "How is that not supposed to be offensive?"

"Well, you just don't really seem to have any idea what you're doing, or how the library works," Bertrand explained.

"Because it's been gone for four hundred years and there is very little surviving information," Andi snapped. "This is stupid. I'm not the head librarian. I'm just…I'm an assistant. At the Coven Library, back in Rosewood. And I can't kill some ancient evil vampire."

"I think you can," Bertrand said. "You got this far, didn't you?"

"Not because of anything I've done," Andi said. "It was all people helping me, but I'm still here and they're…they're gone, now. It's just me."

Her voice wobbled and she bit her lip, hard, to keep herself from crying again. It all felt so hopeless, and very little of what Bertrand said made sense. For a moment, she'd hoped he had the answers, but he just left her with more and more questions.

She kept telling herself that Lexa and Blythe were okay, but the truth was she had no idea. She was all alone, and Silva couldn't be far behind. He might be in front of her, for all she knew.

Bertrand was quiet, for a long moment. "You have me."

"Yeah, well." She wanted to say something biting and mean, but all of the fight left her an instant later. That wasn't her. Maybe Bertrand hadn't been helpful, but that wasn't his fault. "I guess I do."

Toward what end, she had no idea. She doubted one lone witch and a very small toad could make it to the core, not with Carmine and Silva on the prowl, not to mention the other two elder vampires could be in the library with her. No one knew anything about Dahlia, but Tana was even crueler than Carmine. She held no court, flitting from place to place seemingly on a whim.

Taking out entire villages on her own.

Andi reached a door of cloudy glass, cut through with wrought iron in a delicate pattern of curling vines, leaves, and roses. The handle was cold.

"Are you sure this is the best way?" Andi asked.

"What do your instincts tell you?" Bertrand asked.

She almost laughed. Instincts? What could they possibly tell her? She backed away from the door. "I don't know. Maybe it's safer to go around."

That felt incredibly wrong.

She ignored it and went to the left, following the slow curve of the wall. The plants changed, but the delicate filigree of iron and glass remained constant.

Bertrand didn't let their walk remain silent for very long. "Andi—"

"The core is at the top of the tree, isn't it?" she asked. "What's the fastest way to get there?"

"Through the library, I'm afraid," Bertrand said. "There are hidden passageways, but I was never made privy to those. I'm sorry. I'm not particularly helpful in that area."

"It's…fine." She sighed. She would have to manage on her own. They walked past shelves full of books on plants, more of herbs that had long since turned to dust, and frames full of dried flowers. "You were in my archive, so I suppose you're at least a little up to date?"

"Somewhat, but I was a little focused on trying to find a body," Bertrand admitted. "I thought that Silva would be the one to find me, that he'd use his magic on the journal, but I supposed he doesn't have magic anymore. Not the way that he did, once. He um. He wasn't always terrible, you know? He did all of this to save Obrye. All of them did."

"All of who?" Andi asked. "Because the only other people I've seen have been…well."

"Him and…right. You wouldn't know," Bertrand said. "Carmine, Tana, Dahlia. Those names mean something to you, don't they?"

"The elder vampires." Andi nodded.

"They weren't always," Bertrand said. "They used to be witches, just like you. Well, not archive witches but they were very strong. Leaders of the respective Covens. They came to Silva for solutions when the Empire of the Dawn landed on our shores."

"And now they're all immortal monsters destroying the very place they swore to protect," Andi said.

"Well…yes." Bertrand was considerably more subdued. "I agree. Unfortunately, the solution has become our downfall. Obviously, I agree. I was going to kill him. If I had been just a little bit stronger…"

"We'd probably still be dealing with this," Andi admitted. "Just…in a slightly less dangerous way."

But Silva had let her go.

She still didn't understand.

"Hey um. Your friend is probably okay," Bertrand said. "I should have led with that. That darkness was the curse in physical form, and she's already cursed, so I bet she's doing just dandy. Maybe even better than dandy. I don't really know exactly, but I think she's fine."

It did help. It shouldn't have, but the tightness in her chest eased just slightly. "Dandy?"

"It means good."

"I know, I just wasn't expecting to hear it." Andi stopped walking. She could feel the dead end ahead, without even being close enough to see it. "We aren't going to get anywhere going this way, are we?"

"I don't know, I told you, I have no head for directions, and now that I'm an inch long at most I think that's going to get worse, not better," Bertrand admitted.

"I mean…what you said before, listening to my instincts," she said. "This isn't the right way. We need to go through the greenhouse."

"I trust you," Bertrand said. "If that's what your heart is telling you, then that's the right way."

Her heart was telling her to find a way to break down a wall, but she doubted that would do anyone any good.

Blythe would find her. She had to trust in that, the same way Bertrand trusted her to not ferry him to a second death.

She hurried back to the door. It took a few tries to yank the door open. It creaked outward, mist billowing from inside of the giant glass structure, swirling around her knees.

She held up her lamp.

Looming out of the mist were trees, twisting up to the ceiling, moss trailing from their branches in long beards. She stepped into the room and closed the door behind her carefully.

Insects buzzed and chirped. Somewhere, a bird warbled. She could hear water, too, rushing somewhere in the mass of dark foliage. Being able to hear something besides her own breathing and Bertrand's prattle made her want to cry.

"Wow, kind of let the place go, didn't they," Bertrand said.

"You really enjoy hearing yourself talk, don't you"

Bertrand spluttered at her. "I didn't have anyone to talk to for four entire centuries."

"You said from your perspective it was only forty-eight hours," she reminded him, finding herself smiling slightly, to her great surprise.

"It's the principle of the matter," Bertrand said. "Besides, if you really didn't want me to talk, you wouldn't answer me. So there."

"I don't think that's true. You'd run a one toad commentary," Andi said. She found a tiny path between walls of bushes and took it. The branches reached out to snag at her skirt. She paused to hook the lantern to her bag again so she could gather the material in one hand. At least it was warm enough she didn't need her cloak.

"Not really dressed for this, are you," Bertrand commented.

"I wasn't exactly expecting to go running around in a giant abandoned library, no," she said. "It was just supposed to be a meeting. With my boss. And...and Blythe. Do you really think she's okay? Couldn't I use my...I don't even know how it all works, but shouldn't I be able to know?"

"Well, sure," Bertrand said. "But I don't recommend it. Not before you forge a proper connection at the core. Then, yeah, go for it."

"So, if I get to the core and connect with it, then I can find her?"

"Well, sure," Bertrand said. "Go crazy. Do whatever you want. Rearrange entire floors on a whim."

"I can do that?" Andi asked.

"If you really want to, but if you're a librarian shouldn't you know this?" Bertrand asked.

She stepped over a root that snaked across the path. "Why would I know that? I told you, there's not a lot of information."

"I mean at your old library, former library, current library until you're official? That place," Bertrand said. "Even if you're an assistant you should know about the core. Every library has one. That's how they're all connected. …They're not all connected anymore, are they?"

"No," Andi said. "…Wait, those crystals are what connects the libraries together?"

"Think of them like seeds," Bertrand said. "Every library is grown around one, expanding its collection from the mother tree. A clonal grove. A forest that's connected by a single network of roots. Wow, see? I wasn't being rude when I said you needed me. I was just being honest! Big difference. Well, okay, not everyone sees the difference, but you get it, right?"

"That's incredible," Andi said. "So you're telling me that every library in Obrye is connected to this one? Or was, once?"

"Well, yes, the library was started as a base of all information on the continent," Bertrand said. "But as the population grew, especially the witches, the need for more places to go grew with it. To accomplish this, cores were generated from the original here, and taken elsewhere, installed into buildings to start libraries there by bringing information over from the original. But that's all

I know about it, so you can ask, but I'll probably just disappoint you again."

"I thought you were an assistant here," Andi said. She still had so many questions, but she bit them back. "I was just hoping you had answers."

"You were hopping I had answers."

She did her very best not to roll her eyes, though she doubted Bertrand could see it. "You're the only one doing any hopping."

"Well, either way, I wish I could help you, but I was kind of new," Bertrand admitted. "Okay, very new. You could even say incredibly new. And that wasn't my area! I worked in the potions floor. Which is right above this one, by the way."

"Then how did you end up being Silva's personal assistant?" Andi asked.

"To be honest, everyone else was dead," Bertrand said. "You know what, you're right. I talk too much. Let's be quiet now. Hey look! It's a stream. You probably need water, right?"

A stream meandered through the undergrowth, crossing the path under a tiny stone arch of a bridge.

She could have cried again, this time from relief. Her throat felt hot and dry. "Yes, I do."

Chapter 25: The Gardener

Andi pulled her canteen out of her bag.

"I wouldn't trust that water," Bertrand warned her. "You have no idea where it's coming from."

"Do you?" Andi asked.

Bertrand thought for a moment. "Well, no, actually. But still."

"I know a purification spell, I think I'll be fine," Andi said. She needed to conserve her magic, but all of the magic in the world wouldn't help her if she died of thirst. She'd been ignoring how dry her throat was, but the inside of her mouth was a horrible desert. She had to stop herself from drinking what remained in her canteen in a few gulps, water dribbling over her chin. It was tepid and tasted of metal, but she didn't care.

Once the canteen was empty she filled it back up from the stream. The water was incredibly clear, burbling over smooth, dark rocks. But she knew it was better to be safe than sorry. Once the canteen was full she flicked quickly through her archive, finding the spell. She drew a circle over the top of the canteen. Glowing sand followed her finger and turned white. It spilled into the canteen and the water fizzed gently.

"There, see?" She took a sip. It still tasted of metal, but it was deliciously cold on her tongue. "Not bad, right?"

"Passable," Bertrand said. "Do you plan on purifying Silva?"

She drummed her fingers against the canteen, the water and hollow space making a pleasant noise. "Would that work?"

"No," Bertrand said. He paused, staring down at the ground. "Or would it? What does a purification spell do to a living being, anyway? Well, an undead one. If we want to be technical. Now, that actually is quite the fascinating question."

"I'm glad you're so brilliant you can come up with interesting theories for yourself. I need a break." Andi pulled off her boots. Her stockings had collected more holes, and the silk wrap around her ankle had definitely seen better days. The bottoms of her feet ached horribly. At least her ankle barely twinged when she rolled it back and forth. She really must have just jarred it when she fell. That, or Blythe had some magic in her wrap.

"My latest theory is you need new stockings," Bertrand said.

"I'll make sure to get right on that." Andi's boots had not been made to run in. She'd never expected to do so much running in her entire life. It wasn't really a pastime she enjoyed.

She undid the wrap and yanked off her stockings, folding them carefully to the side. She sat down on the middle of the bridge and stuck her feet in the water.

It was freezing, sending a shiver all the way up her spine. The greenhouse wasn't cold, almost pleasantly warm compared to the other rooms. The iciness of the water was a shock.

But it felt amazing, like it was washing the pain downstream.

"What if you have to run?" Bertrand asked.

"I can't run anymore." She leaned against her knees. She ached in spots she hadn't known could ache. More than anything, she was desperately tired. She was sure if she hadn't found Bertrand, she would have curled up under the table out in the herbarium and cried herself to sleep.

Sleep was probably what she needed, more than anything. She'd only caught two very short naps, and she had no idea how long she'd been in the library. Days, at the very least. It was hard to tell the passage of time. She hadn't seen a single window in the library proper.

"I don't know you very well, so please don't be offended, but you don't look well," Bertrand said.

She must have looked worse than she thought. "I'm just tired. I need a safe place to get some rest. Know of any?"

"Honestly, there probably isn't one nearby," Bertrand said. "Maybe once we get up to the next floor I can be a little more useful. For now, I know there were sitting areas in the greenhouse. I never saw one myself, but you should be able to find one. It will at least be a place to lie down. The sun lamps should keep Silva away."

"Mm." She reluctantly pulled her feet out of the water. She really didn't want to put her stockings back on. "Probably."

She vaguely remembered lacing up her boots and getting through a tangle of branches into a small open area. There was a bench made of interwoven, living branches that were surprisingly comfortable.

That was the last thing she remembered.

She woke up on said bench with a start.

It was dark, she'd dimmed the lantern down to almost nothing. A light flickered, far away, casting crooked shadows through the tiny hollow she'd stumbled into. Bertrand had curled up above her head.

Above her the bench curved up and over, white blossoms glowing in the faint light. Petals rained down on her, covering her in a strange blanket.

She sat up, slowly, petals falling from her hair. She didn't know how long she'd been asleep, but it must have been hours, considering the amount of flowers she was brushing off of her skirt. She could feel the creases the folds of her sleeve had left in her cheek. Her skull was a weight that wanted to drag her back down onto the bench, back to the depths of sleep. Her brain was cottony and her thoughts sluggish.

She probably needed more sleep.

But something must have woken her up.

She searched the shadows for any hint of movement, for the flash of eyes, but all that greeted her was the dark between the trees.

Maybe it had just been a nightmare. One she didn't want to remember. It wouldn't be out of the realm of possibility.

She couldn't shake the feeling something was wrong.

"Bertrand," she whispered, keeping her voice as low as she could.

"I am resting," he said, too loudly. She wasn't sure how he was talking, now that she thought about it. His little toad mouth didn't move, and his volume was way too impressive for the tiny lungs. "Which is what you should be doing."

"I thought I heard something." She was more sure of that by the moment. She had been too tired to dream. If she had dreamed, it would have been about Blythe. The final moment before…

She couldn't think about it. Not now. She needed to stay alive, that was her only priority.

"It was probably just your snoring," Bertrand said.

"If you weren't probably poisonous, I'd smack you." Her threat didn't hold any weight. She wouldn't actually smack him. Maybe flick him. Gently.

"Well, it is for protection, and see? It works." She could just see that his eyes were open, two minuscule points of reflected light. "Are you sure?"

"I think so." She grabbed her bag, throwing it over her shoulder. The strap dug into her collar bone. "We need to—"

A long, drawn-out scrape interrupted her.

It sounded like metal on stone.

Every hair on the nape of her neck stood up.

Heedless of any potential poisoning, she scooped Bertrand into her pocket. He didn't protest.

She had to crawl out the way she'd come in, through a narrow gap in the branches she could just barely see. She scrambled onto the path.

The scrape again, this time behind her.

She looked back and saw something standing in the path, taller than the bushes, a single eye glowing a bright red. The light flickered again, gleaming off of something vaguely humanoid much bigger than she was. For a moment she was afraid it was Carmine, but the shape was wrong. The back hunched in a way that she couldn't see the elder vampire ever allowing

The bright light of the eye went out.

Scrape.

When the light flickered again, it had moved much closer than she thought possible.

Andi turned and ran.

She careened down the path, not caring about branches catching at her skirt and hair. Her bag caught on one and she yanked it free. She glanced back. The thing was dragging something across the ground, throwing up a shower of orange sparks.

She nearly ran into a tree branch, barely ducking in time. She dashed farther down the path and took the first fork she could find. She followed it for a moment before she crawled into the undergrowth. It was tortuously slow, feeling her way over upraised tree roots and moss covered ground. She got into a hollow at the base of a tree and curled up into as small of a ball as she could.

The screech of metal on stone followed soon after. She pressed a hand over her mouth, desperate to not make a single sound. Her breath was ragged between her fingers.

The lights blazed to life for an instant, just long enough for her to see what was following her through the branches.

It was incredibly tall, even hunched over. Its head was a metal plate affixed over something that must have been a bottom jaw. Its single eye was slightly off center and too large. Its vertebrae jutted from a long neck and down its spine, its chest a curve of more metal. Copper, the same as her lantern, corrosion spreading across the surface.

Except where it had turned black.

It lifted one long arm and slashed through the undergrowth near her with a blade attached to its wrist.

An automaton.

She'd read about them, but she'd never actually seen one. They were old magic, something from the Empire of the Dawn. Their inner workings were lost long before she was born, the few automatons on the continent slowly eroding away to nothing.

It must have been a gardener, once upon a time.

The lights went out again, and all she could see was the glowing red of the eye. An angry star staring down at her from between the branches.

She didn't move, frozen in place, willing herself to become part of the trunk at her back.

After too long it finally turned and moved on, the blade on its wrist scraping against the path.

It was a long time before she could breathe properly again.

Chapter 26: Paths

"How do I get out of here?" Andi whispered.

Bertrand settled on her shoulder. "I'm not sure."

"That is very unhelpful." Her voice was too high, even whispering, too breathy. Any moment now the automaton would find her and cut her down with the massive blade.

"It seemed to stick to the path," Bertrand said. "As long as we avoid the paths, we can avoid it."

"This place is completely overgrown, we need the paths," Andi reminded him. "Well. I need the path. We aren't all one-inch frogs."

"It's not all it's cracked up to be," Bertrand said. "It would take me weeks to reach the other side of this place. At least I have thumbs. They're not particularly amazing, but I digress. Any path in here will have been made by the automaton. Why don't we follow it?"

"And if it turns around?" Andi asked.

"Run?"

It was a terrible suggestion, but she found herself nodding along. There weren't many choices.

It took some time to get out of the undergrowth she'd crawled into, and her skirt ripped with a sound that made her freeze for several minutes, but she made it back onto the path. The scraping had long since fallen silent. The automaton must have moved on.

She hoped.

Her heels clacked whenever she stepped on one of the paving stones, but she didn't dare brighten her lantern or stop to take off her shoes. She gathered her ragged skirt in one hand and walked quickly down the path. The bushes grew thicker and taller on both sides, until she was surrounded by hedges that were well over her head. The light still flashed overhead, bright ambers and yellows, but it didn't reach her anymore.

The spot between her shoulder blades prickled, but when she glanced back nothing was there but the path curling between dark branches full of spiny leaves.

The path split. She knew they were going the right way, so far, but the path turned sharply not too far from where it diverged. The other way curved around thick tree trunks covered in crawling vines.

"What is it?" Bertrand asked.

"These aren't the original paths," she explained. She didn't know how she was aware of that. Maybe Bertrand was right. She couldn't afford to think about it, not when her voice was too loud and any moment she would hear the scrape of the blade against stone. "I don't know which way to go."

"Ah."

"Yeah."

The light strobed overhead, gilding the tops of the trees. A quick succession of day and night. Where she stood was perpetual twilight. Caught between the two like she was caught between the paths.

"And we have no way of knowing which one the—"

"Yes, I know." She bit her lip, hard, to keep her racing thoughts in line, distracting herself with the pain. She couldn't just stand there all day, she needed to choose a path. She pointed to the one they'd been following. "One things, two things, when you have to choose things—"

"You cannot be serious," Bertrand cut her off her recitation of the childish chant.

"I don't know, I thought it would help?" She often chose things that way, usually by realizing she wanted the other choice to be available to her.

"That way goes too far to the right, and we don't know if it comes back," Bertrand said. "So go the other way. If you're wrong, just turn around."

They both knew if she was wrong, it could mean she would die.

Instead of saying that out loud she nodded, steeled herself, and went to the left, following the curve through the trees. Their branches interwove through the underbrush, making it impassible. She could try to separate them with magic, but she only had so much at her disposal, and there was no telling how deep she would get before something found her. The automaton. Or something worse.

The buzz of insects was no longer a comfort, but a precursor to the screech of metal. A bird called somewhere off the path. She jumped so badly she hit her elbow on a tree trunk, pain spearing up into her shoulder and down into her wrist. Air hissed between her teeth and she cradled her arm against her chest until she could move her fingers again without hurting.

At least the path was narrow, but well beaten down enough that she didn't have to worry about tripping besides the occasional errant root.

"That song is still the same." Bertrand's voice broke the silence after far too long.

"The choosing song?" she asked.

"Yes." He sighed. "I suppose not everything can change. Do you know any lullabies?"

"I'll sing some to you later," she promised. "My…my mom used to sing me some old songs. Maybe they're the same, too."

"Maybe," Bertrand said. "Can you tell me what the world is like outside?"

She wasn't sure if he was attempting to keep her mind elsewhere, or if he just didn't feel the danger the same way. Being technically dead and very small, he probably had few immediate concerns about being murdered.

"There's not much left that's safe," she said. "Everything is dark. There are lights in the city, but they were failing when I came here. They could be…everyone could be…"

She'd been trying to not think about it, about the failing lights, the mad chase from Blythe's house, Chrys…

Her breath frayed.

"This isn't working," Bertrand said.

"Are you trying to distract me?" She glanced at him. He'd curled his foot and hand around her bag strap to stay on her shoulder.

"Trying," he admitted. "Failing. I have never been particularly good with people. Or conversation. Or small talk."

"I know the feeling," Andi said.

"I thought the library was the best place for me to work, I've always liked books more than people, but…well."

"A library isn't just about books," Andi said. "It's about what it does for the community. I love books, of course I do, and I want to instill that love in others. And help them learn. Books are wonderful, but it's the people that make a library important."

Bertrand was silent for a moment. "Well. Four hundred years younger than me and yet you're so much wiser. It's no wonder the library chose you."

"I just…repeated what my mentor always told me." Her cheeks grew warm.

"So, when you're head librarian, what are your plans for this place?" Bertrand asked.

"I guess open it up to everyone to use," Andi said. She still wasn't sure it was true, but it did distract her, thinking of plans for a future she most likely would never see. "Start a book exchange with other libraries, update the collection here, start classes…"

"Sounds like quite the undertaking."

She managed a small smile. "Well, luckily I'll have a very capable assistant."

"Luckily, you will."

He fell silent after that, whether because he thought she was sufficiently distracted by what he'd asked, he had his own thoughts, or he remembered that her life was actively in danger, she couldn't say.

She was glad to stay quiet, even if it was only an illusion of safety, but without Bertrand to distract her, her mind spun in circles. From the automaton, to everything outside of the library, to Blythe…

That wasn't what she needed to be concerned with, for the moment. All she needed to worry about was getting out of the greenhouse and up to the next floor.

Staying alive. Avoiding any vampires or corpses.

One thing at a time. She needed to get out first.

Another fork in the path. Both meandered through the trees, she couldn't see which way they turned around the tall trunks and spreading branches.

"Are you going to use the choosing song?" Bertrand asked. The sudden noise startled her.

"I might." She had been about to whisper it quietly to herself. "But I think this way—"

A scrape.

She froze, eyes wide, her fingers tightly around the strap of her bag.

It was close enough that the soft clank of its footfalls reverberated through the path. She couldn't tell where it was coming from. She looked down one path, and then the other, but both seemed likely.

"Andi!" Bert yelled, just in time for her to duck under the swipe of the gardener's blade.

Chapter 27: Chase

The blade lodged into the tree Andi had been in front of a moment before.

She stared in horror for a moment too long. The gardener reached for her with its other hand, its digits too long and sharp. One of the claws caught her sleeve, tearing it like paper.

She ran.

A crash behind her. She didn't dare turn around. Branches snagged at her hair and the brush pulled at the hem of her skirt. She wasn't even sure if she was going the right way. The unflagging compass that had led her so far buried by panic.

Behind her the hiss and screech of metal joints grew louder.

She grabbed a tree branch and swung herself off the path and straight into the brush, barely making it through to the other side. She rolled into rotting leaf litter and down a gentle incline, not stopping until her back hit another tree. Pain flared up her spine, but she scrambled to her feet. The gardener loomed at her back, she couldn't stop. It slashed through the bush and its clawed fingertips hit the loam at her feet, dragging deep gouges through the dirt.

Andi stumbled through the bushes. The light flashed and she just barely ducked under a branch. Her toe caught on a root and she tripped, crashing down into leaf litter and twigs. She didn't have time to recover, up on her hands and knees and crawling away.

The only warning she had was a creak behind her.

She rolled and the blade crashed down where she had been a moment before. She scrambled up to her feet and ran, heedless of any plants she was trampling. She ripped through curtains of moss and slapped branches out of her way, her only thought to get away. Far away.

She slipped behind a tree and stopped a moment to just breathe, to try and get her bearings back. Running away would only work for so long. She needed to get out. Out of the greenhouse. Up the stairs. That was her only chance.

Bertrand was missing from her shoulder.

She patted her shoulder a few times, but no tiny toad appeared.

He must have fallen off, when she tripped, or when she crashed into the bushes, she had no idea.

She edged her way around the tree. The red light blazed in her direction, then swung away.

Andi knew she had to go back. She'd never forgive herself if she left him there.

She tied her skirt up to one side, using the rip, and dropped to her hands and knees. Crawling through the bushes was a little easier than running. She kept one eye out for the red light, but it was turned away from her, at least for the moment. When the light overhead flickered it reflected off of metal, far too close for comfort, and she froze.

How would she find one very small toad amongst the overgrown plants, roots, and dead leaves?

She couldn't even be sure of where she'd tripped. Calling for him would be suicide.

She moved forward, inch by inch, scraping her knees on the ground, the undergrowth catching on her hair and clothes. She didn't dare move faster. Every rustle of cloth or rattle of a bush could alert the gardener. Something crawled over her hand and she bit back the startled noise that tried to escape her. Her fingers slid over roots close to the surface, punching through the dirt in a complicated braille.

She couldn't find Bertrand.

Her pulse pounded in her temples, her breathing too loud in her ears. Every movement was a cacophony of noise. Any moment the red light would shine on her. The blade would come down.

She curled her fingers in, pressing her nails into her palms. The sting grounded her, accompanying the symphony of aches and bruises.

Find Bertrand, get out, get to the next floor.

She knew the steps, but she couldn't move. All she could do was stay there in the bushes, her hands in the dirt, hoping against hope that Bertrand would find her. That her hand would bump into him.

The flickering light did nothing to help, only made the pounding move behind her eyes. She squeezed them shut and tried to get her breathing under control.

Creak.

She looked up.

The single eye was a bloody sun, glaring down at her from a dark sky.

She screamed. It was all she could do. The blade came down and she turned away.

The blade never fell.

She waited a few seconds before she looked again.

The gardener was frozen above her, the blade so close to her head if she moved it would cut her hair. She ducked down farther and scooted away, but it didn't move. Light glared through the trees, gleaming off of the copper that wasn't corroded before it faded again.

A clumsy scramble got her standing again.

"Bertrand?" She tried after the gardener still hadn't moved. Her voice came out breathless and small. "Bertrand…?"

The gardener moved, just enough that the metal joints creaked.

She jumped back, staring at it with wide eyes, ready to run.

It straightened and clicked its long claws together. The blade hung at its side. "Hm. Well. This is different."

She knew that voice. It sounded more metallic, but there was no mistaking it.

"Bertrand?" She didn't move any closer.

When the gardener looked at her again, the eye shone a pale lavender around a yellow center. "Oh. You are not nearly as tall as I thought you were."

"You…you took it over." It was a statement, not a question.

"Well, I figured it was a vessel," Bertrand said. He clicked the claws together again. "Not wild about these hands, let me tell you. I think I preferred my tiny toad fingers."

"Oh, thank goodness." Andi wanted to sink to her knees again, even though her stockings were torn and she'd definitely given herself a few scrapes. The relief overwrote the adrenaline and left her unimaginably tired. "I couldn't find you, and I thought I was going to die—"

"You got pretty close, the toad is right there." Bertrand pointed to it. "I'd grab it but…well. What if I need it again?"

"What indeed." Andi found the small purple toad. Its legs were curled in and its eyes closed. It could have been carved from stone. She wrapped it in Blythe's handkerchief and tucked it in her pocket. "This seems like an upgrade."

She could actually take a look at the automaton. It was about as terrifying as she'd thought. A metal head with a working jaw, the single eye just slightly enough off center to be unnerving. The neck and spine had been fashioned from metal bands, the vertebrae sticking out in long spines as thick as her fingers. It had a simple ribcage, a mechanical heart ticking behind the bands of metal. Its legs were shorter than its arms.

"Debatable," Bertrand said. "But at least I don't have to ride on your shoulder anymore. That was a bumpy ride."

"You could have stayed in my pocket." Andi untied her skirt, letting it fall around her knees again.

He scoffed. "I couldn't see! And it's stuffy in there. And you have so much pocket lint. It's absurd."

She couldn't help but smile. "I apologize for the pocket lint, then. Thank you."

"For what?"

"Saving my life," she said.

"Oh, that was an accident," Bertrand said. "I didn't even know you were there."

"Sure." Andi had a feeling he was lying, but it was harder to read emotions on the automaton than it was with the toad. And she wasn't particularly good at doing it with regular people. She took a step forward and stumbled.

"You're exhausted," Bertrand said. "Let's find a place for you to rest. I can watch over you."

"That would be nice." Andi couldn't think of anything snappier to say. "You got an upgrade."

"Maybe in the keeping you out of danger department, which you clearly need," Bertrand said. "Looks? I'd rather be the toad."

She laughed. "It is a pretty cute toad. Even if it's poisonous."

"Potentially poisonous," Bertrand corrected her. "We actually never came to an accord on that. Besides, I'm sure any poison is long gone, floating in a solution for a few centuries would leech anything too dangerous out. Well. Shall we?"

He held out an arm to her. The one with the claws, which she would have rather avoided, but she supposed it was safer than the blade.

It reminded her of Blythe, down in the laboratory, and the suddenness of it took her breath away.

"Andi?" Bertrand prompted her after a moment. "Do you need the support? I could try to carry you, but I'm not sure that will work out well for you, but I am open to making an attempt providing you don't hold me accountable for any ah. Further injuries."

"No," she blurted it out too quickly. She cleared her throat and tried again. "No. I'm fine. I don't need…I'm fine. Let's find somewhere to rest. For me to rest. Do you rest?"

"I'm a collection of electrical synapses that used to be a person piloting a weird metal suit," Bertrand said. "So…the answer is I have no idea."

"Right." She wrapped her arms around herself, trying to keep all of the hurt that wanted to spill out of her inside.

Chapter 28: Found

ndi's slept restlessly, nightmares plaguing her.

Every time she closed her eyes she saw Blythe, right before the skeleton fell into the dark. Sometimes it was accusing, sometimes terrified, but it was always the same nightmare.

Bertrand left during one of the nightmares. He returned cradling a handful of fruit.

"You need to eat." He tried to hand it to her, but dropped it at her feet. "Okay, I enjoy the mobility, but I need better hands."

"We'll find a way to make you some." Andi picked up an apple, wiping it off on her blouse though she doubted it was cleaner than the ground, and bit into it. It was crispy and sweet, and she quickly reduced it to a core. She hadn't realized she was even hungry. The other half of the granola bar she'd failed to finish earlier joined the fruit. She wasn't quite full, but she almost felt like a person again.

"Better?" Bertrand asked.

"Much." She wiped her mouth with her sleeve and grimaced. "I am filthy."

"I wasn't going to say anything," Bertrand assured her.

"Thanks." She looked down at her hands. There were dark crescents under each of her fingernails. The fruit felt heavy in her stomach. She'd been holding it with her disgusting fingers. It would have been better to just eat it off of the ground. She wiped her hands on her skirt, but it did very little to help. She knew the purification spell could be used for cleaning, but she couldn't waste the magic. She checked on the lantern, she hadn't had the energy to do it before she slept. The light glowed through the glass, still intact despite her flight through the underbrush the night before.

She slung her bag up on her shoulder. They'd taken a rest in a clearing very much like the one she'd first tried to sleep in, with a similar bench and even a small table, though the table was too overgrown for her to actually use. The branches had grown above the back of the bench, lending it a canopy of leaves.

It had been a safe little haven.

"Do you know where we need to go?" Bertrand held up the blade. "I could cut us a path."

"As much as I want to get out of here, please don't do that," Andi said. The flickering light was behind them now, but each flash grated on the surface of her brain. "I think we've caused enough damage."

"Technically the gardener did all of that, and we are completely blameless."

"Sure." Andi decided it was just easier to agree with him. "Let's—"

Bertrand shushed her. "Someone's coming."

"What?" Andi had forgotten, for a moment, that she had things much worse to worry about than a mouthy assistant or a metal gardener. Silva was still there, somewhere. And if she believed Blythe had survived, which she had to, then she knew Carmine must have, too. And anything else that followed her.

Bertrand shushed her and motioned for her to get back, which she really didn't think he should be doing when he had a large blade for a hand, but she stepped behind him anyway.

She didn't hear anything, no matter how hard she tried, and she had no idea if she could sense anything besides where the stairs were. All she could do was wait.

The bush directly in front of them moved and she squeaked despite her best efforts.

Lexa stepped into the clearing.

For a moment it was so strange to see her that all Andi could do was stare.

It felt like a very long time since she'd seen her friend. A whole other lifetime ago, though in reality it was only a few days. Lexa didn't look any different at all, though Andi thought something should have changed. The only thing that had was she had shed her jacket at some point. The black, short-sleeved shirt she wore underneath was tight against her biceps. Her bag was even still over her shoulder and her tri-colored hair was still in its braid.

Andi didn't realize how Bertrand must have looked, standing in front of her, until Lexa was already drawing her sword. "Get away from her."

"Wait!" Andi got between them. Not one of her best ideas. "Wait wait, friends! You're both friends! Please don't fight!"

"Oh." Bertrand stepped back. "Okay. Friends. Got it."

"Andi!" Lexa grabbed her arm and yanked her back, stepping between her and Bertrand. "Get away from that thing!"

"Stop it!" Andi smacked her arm. "He's my friend! Don't hurt him!"

"Are you serious?" The look Lexa gave her made Andi want to take a few steps back. "That thing is not your friend, it—"

"To be fair, it was a very small toad until a few hours ago," she said.

"What?" Lexa made a frustrated noise and sheathed her sword. She grabbed Andi's face in her hands, turning her head back and forth. "Do you have a concussion?"

"No!" Andi tried to push her away, but Lexa didn't even seem to notice.

"Sounds like something someone with a concussion would say," Lexa said.

"I'm fine." Andi's words were slightly muddled by Lexa squishing her cheeks. "What are you doing here? How did you even get in here?"

"Followed some vamps." Lexa finally let go of her face. "I've been looking everywhere for you, and I find you with an overgrown garden tool that could kill you without even trying. That definitely tracks. You are filthy and you smell like blood."

"I feel filthy." Andi rubbed her cheeks, mostly to erase the feeling of Lexa's fingers on her skin. She usually didn't mind, but she hadn't been expecting it. "How are you so clean?"

"I'm a little more careful than you are," Lexa said. "Looks like I had an easier time of it. Just followed them through the walls. They didn't even notice me."

Something about what she said seemed strange. Lexa could be stealthy, when she wanted to, but they were still elder vampires.

"That's good," she said, instead of questioning her. "I'm really glad you're okay. I was worried…"

"You don't have to worry about me," Lexa said. That was normal, at least. "I was more worried about you. Glad you're okay. Let's get out of this weed infested rat hole."

"It's a greenhouse," Andi said.

"Who cares?"

Her tone was cold and sharp. Andi shrank back. She glanced at Bertrand, but he had no expression to give away his thoughts. "You're right. We should go."

"Great." Lexa motioned. "Lead the way. Your…friend can come along."

"How very kind of you," Bertrand said.

Andi frowned again. Lexa usually took the lead, just in case. But Andi knew where they were going.

It occurred to her as she led them to the path that Lexa had no way of knowing that.

They had to walk single file down the path. The branches crossing above them blocked out the flickering light, and Andi's lantern was all she had. At least it was steady.

The undergrowth was sparser, the trees covered in a thick coat of green moss, drenching everything in emerald. A soft bit of purple was easy enough to spot amidst it all.

"Look at this!" She didn't even think, just stepped off of the path towards it. It was a rose, its petals delicately unfurled and covered in dew, shining like diamonds in the light. It was the first flower she had seen. "It's so beautiful."

"We don't have time for this," Lexa huffed.

"Just a minute." Andi held the lantern up. More roses led deeper into the trees. "I think there must be a rose garden over here, if we can just look, it won't take long—"

"Andrea!" Lexa snapped. "Let's go!"

Andi froze.

Lexa had been her friend for as long as she'd been in Rosewood. One of the few people who even tried to understand her. They were closer than sisters.

In the entire time they'd known each other, Lexa had never used her full name.

Whoever stood behind her, it wasn't Lexa.

Chapter 29: Control

"What is the hold up?"

Andi didn't have long before Not Lexa realized she could drop the act. And with it, any guarantee of Andi's safety.

She should have noticed sooner. Lexa hadn't asked about Blythe, or where she was.

Andi thought about running. Fleeing deeper into the roses, hoping for a place to hide.

But even if it wasn't Lexa, there was a possibility it was still physically her. She'd heard of it before — people controlled by a vampire from afar. It wouldn't be difficult for several vampires to overpower a werewolf, especially when there had been no full moon for years. Lexa was strong and fast, but like the witches, she was at her weakest.

Even so, she was still much faster and stronger than Andi.

And if it was her, Andi had no choice.

She had to save her.

Besides, she had no way to alert Bertrand, and she'd crawled through the bushes next to a murderous metal gardener for him, she wasn't going to leave him now.

"Sorry." She injected a cheeriness into voice. It rang hollow in her ears. "You know me. I'm ready to go now."

"Great."

Andi walked down the path, hyper aware of how close not Lexa was. She had no idea how to save her, and she couldn't afford to rifle through her archive. Even if it wasn't obvious she was using magic, it would leave her distracted.

"Who exactly are you, again?" Bertrand asked.

Andi really wished she could tell him to shut up and actually have it work. "Lexa's my bodyguard. And my best friend."

"Yup." Lexa didn't elaborate.

"Since we were kids," Andi had to be sure. "She's known me since I was five."

A blatant lie.

"Yeah." Lexa didn't bat an eye.

Andi was absolutely sure. They'd met when she was twelve and Lexa was thirteen. They'd been in similar situations — both of them had lost everything they'd ever known.

Lexa wouldn't forget something like that. She wouldn't ever let Andi lie about it.

It definitely wasn't her. The last vestiges of hope crumbled to dust.

Andi needed a plan.

"Interesting." Bertrand's tone gave nothing away. "So where have you been?"

"She didn't tell you?" Lexa seemed genuinely surprised. "We were separated, a while back. Of course, I've been doing everything to find her again."

"And do you know where we're going?" Bertrand asked.

Lexa laughed. "What's with the twenty questions? She said we were friends and I'm her bodyguard, isn't that enough? Obviously, we're going to the potions floor. It's right above us."

Bertrand's neck creaked when he tilted his head to the side. "And who told you that?"

"She must have heard it from the vampires, right?" Andi really wished she could kick him without hurting herself.

"Right." Lexa nodded. "And you guys have been heading up, so I just assumed…"

"And what did you assume happened to Blythe? Because you haven't asked about her, not even once. Almost like you already know what happened," Bertrand said.

"What do I care what happens to a vampire?" Lexa sounded impatient. "She joined her little friends. I was trying to spare Andi's feelings by not bringing it up. Thanks a lot."

"Oh." Andi knew it couldn't possibly be true, but it still hurt.

"See? Good job," Lexa scoffed. "What else do you want to ask? For my life story? How I got these scars?"

"If you wouldn't mind," Bertrand said, coldly.

"I don't think I care for this new friend of yours," Lexa said. "What was your name again?"

"Bertrand, and I know you're not Lexa." Bertrand stepped between Andi and Lexa. "I'm sorry, Andi. That's not your friend. She's being controlled."

Andi sighed. So much for having the time to form a proper plan. "I know."

"You knew?" Bertrand didn't glance back at her, but the surprise was obvious.

"Lexa has been my best friend since I was twelve, not five, of course I knew," Andi said. "I was trying to figure out where she was herding us. And keep us both safe."

"…Ohhhhh." Bert lifted the blade. "Well, I suppose the cat is already out of the bag."

Not Lexa's smile grew very wide. "Oh Berty. You were pretty cute back then. Shame you're…this now."

Bertrand's head tilted to one side. "Wait, do I know you?"

"Really, Bertrand?" Not Lexa leaned on one leg, hand on her hip. "It's Tana. The elder vampire?"

"Oh!" Bertrand nodded. "Okay. Yeah. That makes sense."

"Well, now that we all know each other, I suppose there's nothing stopping me from doing this."

With the last word Tana grabbed the blade and yanked Bertrand's arm out of the socket. She was in front of him before Andi could blink, slamming her hand into the rudimentary ribcage and ripping out the mechanical heart.

"Bertrand!" Andi screamed, but the automaton powered down and fell to the ground in a heap of metal and parts, the last magic sparking from the twisted wires that once cradled its heart.

Tana had claws at her throat a second later, Lexa's face twisted into a snarl. "Well. Now that it's just the two of us, how about you get me up to that potions room, hm?"

Andi wanted everything to stop. To take a moment. She'd lost Blythe, she'd lost Bertrand. Lexa was right in front of her, but she was going to lose her, too.

But the world kept passing her by, so fast it was streaks of color on a canvas.

Tana grabbed her collar. She dragged her down the path, not even noticing Andi's heels digging into the mud between the stones.

She glared when Andi scrabbled at her wrist with nails too short and blunt to do any real damage. "Keep that up and I'll yank you around by your pretty red hair."

"I can walk." Andi wasn't going to be dragged anywhere. She knew that nothing good could be waiting for her on the next floor, but she would get there on her own.

"Good." Tana let go of her.

Andi straightened her collar, trying to appear composed and calm, even if she was a hurricane of pain and despair on the inside.

Tana prodded her between the shoulder blades and she started walking down the path. No plan came to her, the only thing she could seem to picture was the collapse of the automaton, completely devoid of life.

Bertrand had put himself into a journal for four hundred years, only for her to come along and mess everything up.

"I wouldn't worry too much. Silva wants you alive." Tana broke through her thoughts. "Something about you fixing the library. I don't really care, one way or another, but I'll let him play his silly little game if it keeps him occupied."

"What could I possibly do?" Andi asked. She was trying to form a plan, but a buzzing filled the space between her ears. Nothing came to her.

"Like I said, I don't care. I say let the whole thing rot."

Part of Andi wanted to agree with her.

The library had brought her nothing but pain and terror. She'd been obsessed with it for so long, but it was a terrible place, twisted beyond recognition.

But there had been some good, too. Fleeting moments of warmth.

Something moved in her pocket.

Trying not to be suspicious, she put her hands in her pockets. The toad body wiggled against her fingers.

Bertrand was still alive.

"Why the potions floor?" she asked, trying to keep her voice even.

"Does it matter?" Tana asked. "That's where I was told to take you. I'm just following orders. Don't hate the messenger, and all that."

"Why use Lexa?" Andi asked.

"You trust her, that's really all there is to it," she said. "Besides, we couldn't have a werewolf running loose. Think of it as a very advanced collar. I'll give her back to you when I'm done with her. No harm, no foul."

"And Blythe? Did she really join the other vampires?" Andi had to know.

"Blythe is dead." Tana's words were an arrow to Andi's heart. She couldn't believe a single thing that was being told to her, it was probably all lies, but it was every fear boiling to the surface. "Stop asking about her."

Bertrand crawled up onto Andi's hand. She lifted her hands to her chest, like she was cold, or hurting. It wasn't hard to push things a little bit.

"Keep going," Bertrand whispered. She hoped quietly enough that Tana couldn't hear. "I know how to fix this. Get to the next floor and we'll solve it together."

Chapter 30: Unstable

Andi slipped Bertrand back into her pocket, silently apologizing for the lint. It was a comfort, just knowing he was there. If Tana noticed, she gave no indication.

Maybe she just didn't care.

It was dark. The distant flashing and flickering of lights barely pierced the interlocking branches. Andi's lantern only lit the path directly in front of her feet. Tana's eyes caught the light just enough that they gleamed when Andi glanced back. It had been comforting when it was Lexa. Now it made her feel like ice was working its way up her spine in a slow shudder.

Something glinted up ahead.

The glass wall on the other side of the greenhouse. She wasn't sure if she was relieved or terrified to see it. Her reflection stared back at her when she moved closer, hollow and wide-eyed. Her hair was a mess, her clothes stained and torn. A ghost of the witch that had entered the library.

Tana lingered behind her, distorted in the glass. A dark shadow with burning eyes.

"Well?" she asked, impatience dripping from her voice. "Open it up."

"Right." Andi put a hand on the door. It creaked open with a gentle push.

She slipped through the opening and slammed the door behind her, so hard the glass vibrated. She wrenched the handle up.

Tana shook the door, her screams muffled by the glass.

Andi dashed across the space between the door and the stairs, her boots sliding on the smooth tiles. She hit the wall with her shoulder, hard enough to jar her. A few books fell around her. She pushed off the shelf and took the stairs two at a time. The rich, dark wood of the staircase was as slick as the floor under her boots. Shelves lined the wall, full of books and vases full of long dead plants.

She didn't have time to appreciate it.

"What did you just do?" Bertrand yelled, slightly muffled.

She didn't have time or breath to answer. The door was still rattling. The glass was thick, and hopefully magically protected.

She reached the top of the stairs, expecting to find another bookcase, but the door was obvious. It looked like a ship's door — metal with a hand wheel at the center instead of a doorknob. It hadn't aged well, but underneath the rust were intricate details. She couldn't take it in. She turned the handle, using both hands, red flaking off onto her palms.

Below her the door crashed open.

She turned harder.

"Put your back into it!" Bertrand yelled.

She had a few choice words for him.

She couldn't spare the breath.

A hard shove got the wheel moving, enough that the metal bars on the door jerked out of place to let it creak open. She slipped through and slammed it shut behind her. She glanced wildly around, found a chair, and wedged it in under the handle.

She stepped back. Her chest burned and her hands ached horribly. Her breath plumed in the cold air that hit the back of her throat and made her cough.

"It's f-freezing," she managed to say through chattering teeth.

"Well, yes, you would want it to be cold." Bertrand didn't sound bothered by it. "Cover that light up. No idea how it will react with some of these."

She pulled her cloak out and wrapped it around her shoulders. She kept it over her bag. The lantern light pooled around her feet.

Boom.

It came from the door, echoing around the room. Andi flinched back. The door boomed again, but it held.

"Do you think that will keep her out?" Bertrand asked.

"No." Andi snagged the tissue and tied it to her cloak clasp. She pulled Bertrand out of her pocket and held her hand up to it. "Here. Get in here. I don't want to drop you again."

He settled into his makeshift sling. "Hey, yeah. I never had words with you about that."

"Later," she whispered. "We don't know who's in here with us. Where do I go? How do I save Lexa?"

Even without the lantern, she could have seen the rows and rows of shelves, all containing bottles of potions. Many of them were faintly glowing. Some shone brightly. Little stars out in the dark.

"Don't be mad, but this might be harder than I thought," Bertrand admitted.

"What do you mean?" her whisper was becoming hysterical. She was very aware that she was still standing far too close to the door.

"I mean, these potions have been sitting around for a very long time," Bertrand explained. "They probably aren't exactly living up to whatever is on the label."

Her heart sank. "So I can't—"

"No, I didn't say that, I just said it would be more complicated than I expected," Bertrand cut her off. "There's another way. We're not giving up. There's a room to the side, on the left. It was for brewing. There should be plenty of ingredients there, including what we need."

"Are you sure?" Andi asked. "If these aren't any good—"

"Andi, I promise you, we'll get her back," Bertrand said. "Trust me. The cabinets have to still be sealed. But we can't worry about that. Right now, we have to get moving. Just one step at a time. C'mon."

She nodded.

There wasn't any way but forward.

She took one step, then another. Her boots were muffled by a thick layer of dust. It swirled and eddied around her feet in a mimicry of mist. Cobwebs on every surface moved like gauzy curtains with the soft breeze of her passing.

The potion bottles were in every shape, their colors brilliant against the dark. Every color of the rainbow shone from each side. Precious jewels in liquid form. Andi knew there must have been some rhyme or reason to how they were arranged, but she couldn't read their labels.

"Just keep moving," Bertrand coached her through it. "Keep the lantern covered. You're doing great."

She wanted to tell him to stop patronizing her, but to her chagrin it was helping. His voice reminded her that she wasn't alone. His presence kept her grounded. Stopped her from spiraling into horrible anxieties.

"A few more shelves and you can turn, it's going to be fine," Bertrand said. They hadn't heard anything behind them, but she knew Tana hadn't given up. She didn't know what lay ahead, either. If Tana wanted her here, she doubted they were alone.

She heard a noise and stopped, straining her ears.

A steady clinking noise, somewhere to her right, but she couldn't place what it could possibly be. Each clink was louder, making her flinch.

"What is that?" Bertrand's voice was so quiet she barely heard him.

"I don't know," she whispered back.

"You gave Tana the slip," a voice Andi recognized echoed through the shelves. Her blood froze. "You're a little more resourceful than I thought."

Andi backed up a few clumsy steps, then dove behind a shelf, pulling her cloak tightly against her. The sun lamp was as low as she could make it, the light wasn't enough to help, but the glass was a comforting warmth against her side.

A clink against the bottle right next to her head.

It was Carmine's nails, clicking against the surface.

"Hello, little archivist."

Andi scrambled away but Carmine was over the shelf in a flash, bottles scattering around them. Some of them shattered with pops and snaps, potions staining the floor in bright hues. Carmine had an icy hand around Andi's neck before she could blink.

She threw back her cloak, but Carmine ripped the lantern off of her bag and threw it away. It clattered across the floor.

Carmine's eyes burned crimson. She was so close that Andi could feel her jaw moving when she spoke. "Silva wants you alive. That's the only reason you're not dead yet. But he never said you had to be in one piece. I'll let you pick which limb you're about to lose. Or maybe I'll burn your face off. You don't need a face to be alive, now, do you?"

Andi was too scared to speak, her mouth felt like it had been sealed shut. Carmine stunk of iron. Like she'd just finished gorging herself on blood.

"Not even going to talk back?" Carmine's voice was silky, even as her grip tightened like steel, her nails digging into Andi's skin. "I have no idea why Blythe would betray me for a little mouse like you."

The lantern flew out of the dark and hit her in the temple with a clang.

Carmine shrieked and dropped Andi, reeling back, her shadow monstrous on the shelf behind her.

"That wasn't me," Bertrand whispered.

"Who's there?" Carmine snarled. "Come out!"

The lantern landed too far away. Andi needed a better distraction.

She snagged one of the potions, glowing a virulent green, and threw it at Carmine as hard as she could.

Chapter 31: Reunion

The bottle hit Carmine in the shoulder.

It bounced off and clattered on the ground, rolling under a shelf.

"Ooh that did not work," Bertrand whispered.

Carmine whirled back on her. "What did you think you could do? You're just a stupid little witch. Your time is over. Your magic is gone. Give up."

Andi scrambled back, hoping to grab the lantern, but Carmine stalked forward too quickly. Her fingers stretched, the bones rearranging with a series of snaps and cracks. Her fingernails extended into wickedly curved claws. The webbing unfurled into large wings. Her face elongated into a snout full of sharp teeth.

She fell forward on her wings. She was inexplicably more massive than before, a hulking monster much larger than the other bat creatures Andi had seen.

She roared. So loudly that the bottles hummed.

Andi screamed.

A dark shape fell from above.

It hit Carmine, who lurched forward and slammed into the floor. For a brief moment Andi thought it was another bat, the way the darkness fluttered around it.

It was Blythe, her coat flaring out behind her.

She kicked off of Carmine and landed in front of Andi, her cane raised. Her coat was ripped up the back. She had a dark bruise near her hairline.

She was so beautiful Andi almost forgot to breathe.

Blythe smashed her cane into Carmine's face, jabbed her in the neck, and then threw her into the shelf with a horrendous crash.

Andi tore her gaze away. She crawled for the lantern. The glass panels were cracked, but it was remarkably intact. She swung it around. It didn't matter what happened to the potions now. They needed light. A lot of it.

The lamp flared in intensity. Carmine howled in pain. She lurched forward. Her skin smoked and bubbled.

She lunged anyway and knocked Blythe against a shelf.

"Oh, we are going to die," Bertrand whispered. "We are definitely going to die."

"Which one of these do I throw at her?" Andi yelled. There were too many potions, and even with the light she couldn't read what they did.

"The yellow one!" Bertrand yelled back. "In the round bottle! But you'll want to get down, it—"

Andi snagged it. The glass was so hot she almost dropped it.

Blythe was next to her in an instant, grabbing it from her hands. She flinched back.

Carmine charged them.

Blythe threw the potion.

Andi yanked her back.

The bottle hit Carmine in the face, hard enough that she jerked back. It landed on the floor.

Carmine looked down on it, picking it up with her strange claws. When she spoke it was with two voices — her own, and one that was so deep it barely registered in Andi's hearing, triggering her fight or flight so intensely that she could barely stand her ground. "You really think this can stop me?"

"Bertrand what was that?" Andi's shrieked.

"Run!" Bertrand yelled. "Go go go go!"

Blythe didn't question that a toad was yelling directions at her from Andi's cloak clasp. She grabbed Andi's wrist and dragged her down the aisle.

Light and sound threw Andi forward. They both tumbled down the aisle, leaves before a gale.

When Andi was aware again, she was crushed up against Blythe. They were wedged between two of the shelves. The room was full of acrid smoke, hanging in a cloud above them. The explosion had caused a chain reaction, most of the bottles were shattered, their contents glowing on the floor. The lantern had rolled away, casting spidery shadows on the wood.

"Are you okay?" Blythe's voice was muffled by the ringing in Andi's ears.

Andi pressed her face against Blythe's shoulder. She still smelled like cloves, somehow. "I thought you were dead."

"What? Did you really think falling a few stories would kill me?" Blythe's fingers were cool on the back of Andi's neck. "I got lucky actually, Carmine was impaled on a rib, and I ran into Chrys and they provided me with a bottle of blood...you're hurt."

"I don't care." Andi's head was throbbing, but it was a distant second to the overwhelming relief burning through her. "Chrys is okay?"

"In one piece and everything," Blythe said. "They had quite a few witches with them. One of them ripped my coat, if you can believe that. They even managed to take care of any company Carmine brought with her. They couldn't get through the darkness, but they're fine. I promise."

Chrys was alive and somewhere below. Andi hadn't realized how worried she'd been until she sagged into Blythe.

"This is very touching, but you're crushing me," Bertrand said.

"Get crushed then, I don't care." Andi did care. She sat up and really wished she hadn't. The pain stabbed into her skull, like her brain had been rattled around and was letting her know that it didn't care for it. She felt something wet on her forehead and her fingers came away red.

"What is that." Blythe stared at Bertrand.

"That's very rude. Obviously, I'm a toad," Bertrand huffed.

"I'll explain later," Andi said. "Right now, we have to save Lexa."

"Lexa is here?" Blythe sighed. "Okay. Right. We just blew up an elder vampire. You probably have a concussion. There's a talking toad. For some reason. Why not save a werewolf while we're on a roll?"

"Yeah, that's the can do attitude we need." Andi tried to use a shelf to pull herself to her feet, but her legs didn't want to listen to her. Blythe stood up with the help of her cane and helped Andi upright. "Berty, what do we need?"

"Must you call me that?" Bertrand muttered.

Andi took a step and sagged against Blythe, who held her up and against her.

"Andi, I don't know—" Blythe murmured.

"Wait. You're really Blythe, right?" Andi didn't have it in her to be subtle. "You're not someone pretending to be Blythe? Or…or you're being controlled?"

"You really did hit your head hard," Blythe said.

"No. I mean, yes, I did. Probably. But not about this." Andi knew she was making very little sense, but the words spilled out of her. "It's Tana, she has control of Lexa. I have to fix it."

"We have to fix it," Bertrand corrected her.

"Right." Blythe nodded. "And how do we do that?"

"There's a room to the left," Bertrand explained. "It's a good thing you're here, actually, I'm pretty sure Andi couldn't have done it on her own."

"Your faith in me is astounding." Andi wanted to close her eyes and just lean against Blythe, but she forced herself upright.

"Okay, I'll get you there," Blythe said. "But you have to explain."

Andi did, as best as she could, with Bertrand interrupting constantly. Blythe scooped up the lantern on the way and Andi dimmed it back down, hiding it under her cloak again. At least her ears had stopped ringing.

Andi was vaguely aware of passing into a smaller space. She was sitting and Blythe was checking her forehead.

"Are you going to lick my face?" She thought that was a fair question, though once it was out, she realized how it probably sounded.

Her head hurt too much to be very bothered by it.

Blythe started. "I…ah…well. It would be the easiest way to clean out the wound…"

She sighed. "Just do it."

Blythe nodded and leaned forward. Her ripped coat fell between them and the rest of the room, giving them some semblance of privacy. She brushed Andi's hair to the side with gentle fingers, cradling her face with one hand.

Andi closed her eyes. Blythe's lips brushed against her forehead, cool but not cold. If she didn't think very hard, Andi could pretend she was kissing her on the forehead instead of licking blood off of her face. That next she would kiss her properly.

If Blythe hadn't been holding her shoulder, she would have fallen out of the chair.

Her emotions being keyed up on high for so long was really not mixing well with her probable concussion.

"Sorry." Blythe pulled back quickly, abruptly. She put a hand to her mouth and looked away. "You still have the first aid kit, right? We should get something on it."

"Right." Andi didn't move. She wasn't sure she could. All she could do was blink owlishly up at Blythe. "I hit my head very hard."

"You did." Blythe gently took her bag from her and pulled out the kit. "But I think you're going to be okay. You just need to give that big brain of yours a break. Leave Lexa to me, okay? I promise I'll save her."

"I know you will, I just need a moment," Andi said. She wasn't quite sure about that. Even the dim light of the lantern felt like needles stabbing into her eyes. She closed them again and let Blythe apply a piece of gauze to her forehead with careful fingers. "I'm not going to make you do it alone."

"Okay, that's incredibly rude, I am still here," Bertrand said. "And no offense—"

"You say that a lot for someone who doesn't want to offend me," Andi murmured.

He huffed. "No offense, but I think I'm going to be a little more useful in this situation."

Chapter 32:
Awake

Andi let Bertrand and Blythe's voices wash over her.

She cracked one eye open. Blythe had moved the lantern away, but the light was just enough to see that they were in what looked like it could have been a very large kitchen, in another life. Wide stone counters, sturdy cabinets, heating elements, and old cauldrons of every shape, size, and material. The one closest to her was blackened silver, corrosion covering it like spots of mold.

The Coven still used cauldrons. She had never been much of a potion maker, but she knew it had something to do with the shape. She almost accessed her archive to double check, but realized that would be a very bad idea on multiple levels.

"Are you sure this is going to work?" Blythe asked.

"As sure as I am of anything," Bertrand insisted.

Blythe did not sound particularly reassured. "And how sure is that?"

"Well, I spent four hundred years in a journal…"

"Honestly, it doesn't matter, I don't trust your judgment either way." Blythe sighed. "You're being awfully helpful, for someone who has no stake in this."

"I'm Andi's assistant, I have plenty of stake," Bertrand said. "Besides, you put the toad in her bag. I suppose I owe you for not picking something worse."

"I didn't…mean to leave her alone." Blythe sounded upset. "I never…I thought it would be funny later. Instead, it's a mess."

"She wasn't alone, she had me." Bertrand puffed up. "And I'm not a mess, thank you very much. I am the best assistant she could ask for."

"She is still very much awake and can hear you," Andi told them. They both jumped, which would have been very funny if her head wasn't pounding.

"You fell asleep for a bit there." Blythe walked over and looked a little too closely into her eyes. "You're not as pale as you were. How's your head?"

"It hurts." Andi wondered if she should be concerned that she hadn't realized she'd fallen asleep. She sat up a bit, and Blythe's coat slid off of where it had been placed over her shoulders. "What are you doing?"

"Well, there's good news and bad news," Bertrand said. She still wondered how she could hear him, especially from where she was sitting. "Salt water should nullify any hold that Tana has on Lexa."

"I'm going to assume that's the good news," Andi said.

"The bad news is, she has to ingest it," Blythe explained. "Oh, and more bad news, I suppose there's no actual fool-proof guarantee that it will work."

"That's…terrible news, actually. Both things." Andi rubbed her temple. It didn't help alleviate her headache at all. Trying to think through the pain was like attempting to wade through knee-deep molasses. She wished that she dared to use a healing spell on herself, but even when she was fully aware, those particular spells had never been something she was comfortable with. "What if it doesn't work?"

"Then we try something else," Blythe said. "I'll do whatever it takes. I promise I'll get her back. No matter what."

That was quite the statement to make. Andi was sure that if she wasn't trying to blink away the fuzziness permeating every thought she would have turned bright red.

"I'm coming with you." Andi tried to stand up.

Blythe's hold on her shoulders prevented her from leaving the chair.

"You are brilliant and capable," Blythe said.

"Sensing a but." Andi narrowed her eyes.

Blythe smiled. It looked a little strained, but it might have been the light. "You need to rest."

"And you'll have an easier time if you're not worrying about me." Andi hated to admit that it would be better for her to stay behind. More than anything, she wanted Lexa back, for her to be safe with them. If staying where she was could help with that process, then she'd sit in a torturous silence for as long as she needed to. "I don't like it, but I understand."

"Good." Blythe pulled the coat back over her shoulders. It wasn't warm, exactly, but it was a comforting weight. "The knives are in the front left pocket inside the lining. If you need them."

"Blythe—"

"I'll be careful," Blythe promised. "And I'll leave Berty with you."

Bertrand grumbled about the nickname but didn't actually object. Andi had a feeling that he secretly liked it. Just a little bit.

"I feel safer already," Andi said.

"I'm pretty sure that's sarcasm, but of course you do, I'm amazing," Bertrand said.

"Of course." Blythe picked him up and put him on Andi's shoulder. She looked like she wanted to say something else, but she gave Andi a swift nod. She picked up a flask of cloudy water and stepped through the arched entryway. She was immediately lost to the dark.

Andi watched the spot where she'd left for a long moment, anyway.

"Are you okay?" Bertrand asked.

"It doesn't feel real," Andi admitted. "It all feels like I'm going to wake up any moment now and…probably still have a headache, but…"

Bertrand slapped his tiny little toad hand onto her cheek. It was disconcertingly wet. She sat very still until he moved it.

"You're awake," he said.

She wiped her cheek with Blythe's coat. What she didn't know wouldn't hurt her. "Don't ever do that again."

He huffed at her. "Honestly. I am trying to help."

"I know, but why are you wet?"

"Oh, I fell in the water," Bertrand said. "It happens to the best of us. Luckily, I'm not a living toad, or I could be in some trouble. There was a lot of salt in there."

She supposed that was true. "You really think this will work?"

"Absolutely." Bertrand tilted his head to the side. "Probably. Tana's abilities as an elder vampire are essentially a twisted version of the magic she could use when she was a living witch. As far as I can tell. She was a master of incense spells."

Andi frowned. She'd never heard of anything like it. "What is that?"

"Oh, it's like…spells, condensed into a solid form, and you burn them, and when people inhale the smoke the spell takes effect," Bertrand explained. "Usually used for keeping people calm during important meetings. I think. It actually wasn't very common in my day. Now it's probably a lost art. I doubt she let anyone who knew her secrets stay alive. She was famous for it, once upon a time. Anyway, the point is, to nullify it you need salt and water. So. Salt water!"

"Okay, that's pretty solid reasoning," Andi agreed.

"Of course it is." Bertrand puffed up again. He deflated quickly. "Providing her magic hasn't changed very much. But I have other ideas, if it doesn't work. I am pretty sure it will work. And Blythe is fast and strong. It will all work out."

"Thanks, Berty." She pet his head with one finger. He closed his eyes and made a tiny rumbling noise deep in his throat. Almost like a purr. She knew that toads didn't purr, and the question of how he was talking flitted through her mind again. She had a feeling the explanation would be long and tedious, and she didn't have the energy for it. "Do you really hate that name?"

Bertrand didn't open his eyes. "I suppose I don't."

She smiled and leaned back in the chair, relaxing a little bit. Bertrand was right. His reasoning was solid, and Blythe was more than capable. Everything would be fine.

Andi drifted in and out of a doze, thoughts fading into nonsensical. She was right on the verge of falling asleep completely when a noise started her awake.

Nothing had changed. The lantern was still lighting up the corner. Bertrand was curled up on her shoulder. She sat up a bit more, disturbing Bertrand and the coat. It slipped into folds in her lap.

"Stop moving," Bertrand muttered.

She shushed him, listening hard. Maybe the noise had been part of her almost dream. She listened for what felt like a long while, but there was no noise at all. With a sigh she leaned back in the chair, closing her eyes again.

Claws at her throat.

She froze.

"Hello again, Andrea." Lexa's voice was in her ear, so close she could feel her breath. "The door wasn't nearly as hard to get open as you thought it would be. And your little friend isn't here to protect you."

Chapter 33: Writing

Andi sat very still. The claws rested on her skin so delicately she could barely feel them. She knew that could change in an instant. "Tana."

Even saying the one word prickled at her throat.

"Did you have a plan?" Tana asked. Her voice was silk sliding over steel. "Was your pet vampire going to expel me?"

"What did you do to her?" Bertrand demanded.

"Nothing." Tana laughed. "Well, nothing yet. I just slipped past her. It wasn't even hard. Your guards are pathetic, little witch. But of course they are. Look at you, sitting here, useless. Relying on a fallen vampire and a little frog."

"He's a toad," Andi snapped. The claws dug in, slightly.

"Leave her alone!"

The claws were gone.

Andi stood up, turning around. She immediately had to lean on the counter across from her, but at least she was on her feet. Blythe's coat crumpled to the floor.

Bertrand bit her, latching onto her finger.

Andi doubted that she could even feel it. True toads didn't have teeth.

"You've both made a critical error." Tana plucked Bertrand off. "Did you forget? I want her alive. But you, oh Berty, I don't need you. And neither does Silva. As amusing as you are, I think it's time we say goodbye."

Andi realized what she was going to do before she stopped talking, before her hand began to tighten into a fist. There was no time. She wasn't steady on her feet. Blythe could be on the other side of the room, with no idea anything was happening.

She only had one thing she could do.

Gold sand smacked Tana in the face. It startled her enough that she dropped Bertrand. With a snarl she swiped magic out of her eyes. "Cute. Really cute. Just for that, I think I'll kill your girlfriend in front of you before I rip out your eyes and drag you up to Silva by your hair. How does that sound?"

"Sounds terrible." A strange calm settled over Andi. Tana's words were designed for hurt and panic. And part of her was scared. That she'd go through with her threats. For Blythe. For Bertrand.

She wasn't scared for herself.

They were in a library. And she was an archive witch.

"No, thank you."

She let her magic go wild.

It yanked books off of the shelves around the room. They flew from counters. The cupboard banged open.

Every book fired directly at Tana. Sand carved pathways through the air. It tingled like electricity on Andi's skin.

Tana shrieked. She batted at the books, backing up a step with every swipe.

Which was when Andi's magic picked up the cauldrons.

They had writing on them.

A book was one thing, but Tana couldn't ignore a corroded iron cauldron flying straight at her head. She ducked, but was immediately pelted by a copper one. Names, dates, and the uses of cauldrons filed into Andi's archive but she barely noticed, intent on driving Tana back.

She was running out of magic. It drained out of her, like the sands in an hourglass it resembled so much. She fell to her knees, the shock of the stone floor not even reaching her.

Everything in the room dropped, including the sand, turning silver before it hit the floor and scattered across the tile.

Tana struggled to sit up. She had a cut across her face that was already healing. "Witches aren't supposed to have magic anymore. No wonder Silva doesn't want you dead."

"I don't care what Silva wants." Andi's head was pounding so badly she was certain that she was going to be sick.

"You should care." Tana climbed to her feet. "He caused all of this, you know. Vampirism, the darkness, the downfall of magic…everything is his fault. He wants to use you to fix it."

Even if Andi's skull didn't feel like it was being slowly crushed by a giant hand, she was certain she wouldn't be able to parse out the meaning. "What does that mean?"

"You'll have to find out, won't you?" Tana grinned at her. There was blood on her teeth. "Good luck."

Lexa collapsed in the pile of books and cauldrons.

"Andi—" Bertrand started to say.

Andi didn't hear him. She was already on her feet, despite the pain, despite the exhaustion. She was across the room without conscious thought, clambering over the pile of magical detritus. Lexa was breathing. The cut on her forehead had already completely sealed up. Her skin felt hot to the touch, but it always did. Especially in that moment, when Andi's fingers were already icy.

She breathed out, slowly.

"Andi!" Blythe was next to her. Andi hadn't heard her come in. She never did. She was on one knee, her face painted with concern. "What…what happened here?"

"Make her drink the water!" Bertrand insisted. "Tana might not be gone!"

"Right." Blythe yanked out the stopper, pulled Lexa's mouth open, and upended the flask over her mouth.

Lexa coughed and spluttered. She surged up, hacking. Dark smoke escaped from between her teeth. Another great, horrible cough brought up something dark splattered on the tile, before it dissipated into the air.

"Ugh." Lexa wiped her mouth. "Oh gross. That was disgusting."

Andi's shoulders slumped and she might have fallen over if Blythe didn't get an arm around her. "I'm sorry. I got to the door and it was open, it took me too long to get back here, I heard…are you okay?"

"Just tired." Andi leaned against her. "Lexa? Do you…"

"Remember everything? Unfortunately." Lexa rubbed her forehead. "Andi, I'm—"

"If you say sorry. I'll hit you," Andi threatened her. It came out wobbly.

She smiled a bit. "Well. Wouldn't want you hitting me again. Fifty or so times was enough."

"We need a place to rest," Blythe said. "Not here. We're too exposed. Bertrand?"

"My old quarters are near here," Bertrand said. "I sealed them, before I left. They should be just fine."

"Perfect." Andi scooped him up. "Thank you for trying to bite her."

"You're welcome." Bertrand leaned his head against her thumb. "I have some notes."

She blinked. "Notes?"

"Yes. Notes." He cleaned his head with one hand. "Sounds terrible? No, thank you? We need to work on your witty come backs."

"Okay." She couldn't help but laugh, even if it sent pain stabbing down her neck. "You're probably right."

Of course I am." He nodded. "Oh, and don't worry, I'm fairly certain that toad's poison comes from the mucus their skin secretes, and I don't do that anymore. So, I'm not slimy or dangerous. That's good, right?"

She smiled. "Very good."

Bertrand found the entrance to his quarters, hidden by a bookshelf in the wall that Andi had emptied. Her magic had scanned each book automatically. She had very quickly acquired all of the knowledge necessary to become a master of ancient potion making. If only she had the skills to back it up, but she could only cook eggs. Potions had always been far out of her scope of abilities.

They followed a short flight of stairs to a simple door. The sealing wasn't a complicated one. Snapping a piece of string in the door frame broke it.

The room beyond was a sitting area. It was nice enough, but clearly not lived in, even before it was sealed. The floors gleamed dully in the lamp light. All of the furniture was made of dark wood.

"The bedroom is through there, I think you should get some rest," Bertrand said. "Maybe a lot of rest. You look terrible."

"He's right, you need sleep," Lexa said. "I have some rations, I'll see about mixing us up something to eat that isn't granola bars. You ate least ate those, right?"

She had eaten a few, so she wasn't lying when she nodded. She regretted the motion. The room spin slowly around her.

"Okay, to bed with you," Blythe said. "I'll get her there, it might be wise to barricade the door?"

"Right." Lexa looked between them. "Did something happen while I was gone?"

"No," they said, in unison, far too quickly.

"Uh huh." Lexa sighed. "You wanna stay out here with me, Berty, or do you want to make sure that Andi actually gets some sleep?"

"I'll stay with you, I don't want you messing up my kitchen," Bertrand said. "Besides, we should get to know each other. I'm very important to Andi, you know."

"Yeah, all right, bud." Lexa accepted Bertrand from Andi. She wouldn't look her in the eye. She hadn't asked to hug her.

Andi knew that it was the guilt, but it still gnawed at her. "Lexa…I'm sorry. That I ran off. And that…that all of this happened."

"What?" Lexa looked at her, finally. She'd wiped the blood off of her face, mostly, though it still clung to her eyebrows and there was a smear on the bridge of her nose. "That's not…you really think I blame you for any of that?"

"A little," Andi said. "Until you said that. And now I'm not actually sure, but…"

Lexa put Bertrand on the table, ignoring his protest. She held up her hands. Once Andi nodded, she pulled her into a very tight hug. Andi hugged her back. She was warm, real, and solid. Just like always.

"I promise we're okay." Lexa pulled away. "Always. No matter what. Even if you throw a cauldron at my head when I'm not under the control of an evil vampire."

Andi flushed at that. "I'm sorry—"

"No, don't be, that was the right call," Lexa said. "Get some rest, Ands. I'll rehydrate some of that terrible soup."

"Eugh." Andi pulled a face.

"Don't eugh me, it's good for you." Lexa patted her shoulder. "Go to bed. I mean it. You look bad."

"So everyone keeps saying," Andi said. "Thanks, Lexa."

Lexa waved her off. "And you, I guess you're all right. Kept her safe when I couldn't."

"Of course," Blythe said. "Thank you for the ringing endorsement."

"That is a ringing endorsement from me." Lexa flashed her a smile.

The bedroom was as simple as the main room - a plain bed with white sheets, a mirror that was thankfully turned at an angle where she couldn't see herself, a chest of drawers. The only bit of personality was a worn quilt on the bed, done in blues, a sunburst of yellow in the middle.

Andi sat down on the bed and everything sank in. She'd never been so tired, and so afraid.

"Can you take off your boots or do you want me to?" Blythe asked.

"I don't think I can move," she admitted. She barely managed to undo the ribbon she'd worn with the blouse, letting the ragged silk hang from her collar. Blythe nodded and without complaint unlaced her boots and set them carefully next to the door.

Andi curled up on her side, the sunburst quilt over her shoulders.

"Rest well." Blythe patted the bed next to her. "I'll be right outside—"

It wasn't really a formed thought that made her hand snap forward and close around Blythe's wrist.

She looked at her in surprise. "Is everything okay?"

"Don't go," Andi's voice was a small, weak thing. "Please don't leave me alone."

"…Of course." Blythe pulled up the chair next to the bed, sitting heavily in it. She leaned her cane against the bed frame. She must have been in a lot of pain, but she was so good at hiding it. Andi wondered if she'd ever learn all of her little tells. She wanted to. She wanted to be there for her. "I'll be right here. So, sleep well."

Andi didn't remember if she answered before darkness folded over her.

Chapter 34: Clean

Andi woke with a start.

She knew she'd been having a nightmare, though she couldn't say what it had been about.

The ceiling above her was unfamiliar. Wooden beams and a diamond shaped light. It wasn't on, but a soft radiance filled the room. She sat up, slowly, remembering where she was.

Blythe was sitting in a window seat. The curtains were drawn back, framing the black sky. It was the first window Andi had seen.

The light came from a row of large, white flowers that coiled around the window. They cast her in a soft glow, like moonlight.

Seeing her let Andi breathe again.

Blythe looked at her when she moved. "Good morning. Or close enough. How are you feeling?"

"Better," Andi said, and it wasn't a lie. Her head still hurt, but it had dulled to an ache. Someone had untied her bun, leaving her hair to flow over her shoulders in a mess of curls. She combed it back with her fingers. "How long was I asleep?"

"A few hours, though it's hard to say," Blythe said. "Lexa crashed out on the couch a while ago, and I think your little toad friend is asleep, too. They're getting along famously."

She dropped her hands with a sigh. "That is the last thing I need."

Blythe laughed, but it wasn't the only reason Andi flushed.

She'd asked Blythe to stay with her while she slept.

And she was still there.

"You didn't have to stay the whole time." Andi looked down at the quilt.

"I didn't mind." Blythe moved to the bed, leaning her cane against the bedpost when she sat down next to Andi. "And I wouldn't want you to wake up alone."

Andi wanted to protest that she was fine. Waking up alone wouldn't have been devastating or terrifying. That she'd grown so used to the horrible tightness in her chest that she hadn't realized it was there until it loosened.

When she did speak, none of those thoughts came out. "I really thought you were dead. Or…or gone."

"Technically…" Blythe gave her a crooked smile. "Sorry, that was not particularly tactful. I won't lie. Carmine's offer was…tempting. It sounds insane. Honestly, it feels insane. But she was everything to me, once. By design, I'm aware of that now, but I didn't need the stars or the moon as long as I had her. When she abandoned me, when I fell, and when Chrys found me in that forest…I thought that my life was over. And I thought I deserved it."

"Blythe…" Andi hesitantly touched her shoulder.

"I know," Blythe said. "Falling…becoming afflicted…it's a moment of weakness. A big moment of weakness. I don't remember it, which is honestly for the best. Seeing that forest again just brought back everything that I lost, made the pain fresh, and I…I will admit I didn't handle it well."

"I already forgave you for that," Andi said.

"I know." Blythe lifted a hand. "Can I touch you?"

Andi nodded.

Blythe's touch was gentle, her thumb brushing Andi's cheekbone when she tucked a strand of hair behind her ear. She was close enough Andi could see the faint tracery of veins under her pale skin. "I like your freckles."

Andi went so red she probably didn't even have visible freckles. "Th-thanks?"

"Sorry, got distracted." Blythe grinned. A flash of fangs. "I was saying something important. Carmine's offer was tempting, but there was no way I would take it. Because of you."

"Me?" Andi blinked at her.

"After Chrys found me, once I'd wrung out all of my anger and grief and betrayal, I don't think I ever really lived," Blythe said. "The ah, obvious reasons aside, I was simply existing. Just staying in that house, waiting for an end. And then I walked into my library and met you."

"And I talked your ear off," Andi said.

Blythe chuckled. A low, soft sound that made warmth pool behind Andi's ribs. "You did. Honestly, I thought you were crazy. And if I'm going to continue being honest, I still think you're crazy."

"Thanks," Andi said, flatly.

"You're also the most amazing person I've ever met," Blythe said.

"Oh." The compliment was so straightforward, so honest, that it left Andi a little lightheaded.

"The fall wouldn't have killed me, but if I wasn't so completely set on finding you, I think that darkness would have consumed me," Blythe said. "So…I wanted to thank you. For saving my life, in more ways than one. For making me want to live again. In a way I haven't for decades."

It was a long time, and while Andi felt elated, she knew the weight of it. She leaned back, slightly. "Blythe…"

"I know," Blythe said. "I'm a vampire, and—"

"I have to break the curse," Andi blurted, knowing it wasn't the time for it. But knowing she couldn't let Blythe keep talking without saying something.

Blythe stared at her. "What?"

"The-the vampire curse," she tried again, sucking in a breath between her teeth. "I have to break it, and I can't guarantee your safety, and…and I can't have you telling me all of this unless you know that, too."

It hurt to say, the words wrenching out of her.

It had to be said.

"I already knew," Blythe said, softly. "I have no delusions that my life is more important than…than everything. This place. The continent. You. Whatever happens, though, I wanted you to know. You should get more sleep."

Andi wanted to say something, to make it better, to tell Blythe that of course her life was more important. They both knew that she couldn't.

It didn't matter that she wanted to. That everything Blythe said was like a counterweight to the rest of Obrye, and the continent was found wanting.

"Actually, I think if I don't have a bath, I will die," Andi said. She was suddenly very, very aware that Blythe was so close to her, and she was covered in blood, dirt, grime, and things she didn't really want to think about.

And Blythe had an incredible sense of smell.

Her self-consciousness could have killed her much quicker than the grime.

Blythe laughed. "Well, I wasn't going to say anything, but since you went ahead and did it for me, yes. Please. Take a bath."

Andi scoffed and pushed her shoulder. Blythe laughed again. She couldn't understand how it was so light, so pure, when the world was crashing down around them.

"Then get out," Andi said. "I need to find clothes."

"I don't have any, and your little bag barely holds your cloak," Blythe said.

"Somehow, I don't think Berty is going to miss a few things." Andi stood up. She was sore, but not nearly as badly as she'd been expecting. "Or everything. I hope it fits me…"

She was short and curvy. She didn't know what Bertrand had been like, centuries ago. She hadn't spared the corpse more than a glance.

"I'm sure you'll find something," Blythe said. "Do you realize he's been naked the entire time?"

"He's a toad," Andi said. "Well…briefly he was a metal automaton. But mostly he's been a very small toad."

"He's still naked, that's a little disconcerting, you can't just leave him naked," Blythe insisted.

"Fine, when I have a chance, I'll make him a very tiny hat to show how important he is."

Blythe grinned again. "That's all I ask. I'll go make sure that soup is heated up. And…it's okay, Andi. It's really okay. I understand."

It wasn't okay. There was nothing to understand.

"Thank you," Andi said, instead. What else could she say?

Blythe smiled one final time and closed the door.

Left alone, Andi wanted to collapse on the floor. Like a marionette whose strings had been cut. She wanted to sit down and wait out the end of the world. Maybe they would be safe, in Bertrand's small apartment.

She knew they wouldn't be. That she had no choice but to keep moving forward.

She turned to the chest of drawers, yanking the first one open. She closed it quickly when she realized that it was Bertrand's underwear. Socks were next, and she helped herself to a pair.

"Well, Berty," she murmured to herself. "At least I got new socks."

She didn't pay much attention to the other clothes she grabbed. A shirt, a pair of trousers that probably wouldn't fit over her hips, a vest. It would have to do.

Chapter 35: Brain Chemicals

ndi frowned at herself in the mirror.

Bertrand's clothes were big enough to fit her, she found out after scrubbing herself with freezing water and accidentally falling right back to sleep with her hair wrapped in a towel. She'd had to roll up the cuffs and sleeves several times.

He must have been tall.

Her blouse and skirt were mangled and stained beyond saving. She'd found more bruises than she remembered getting, dotting her arms and legs.

At least she was clean.

She yanked her hair up into a ponytail and left the room to face everyone.

"Awww, you look cute," Lexa said.

"Are those my clothes?" Bertrand asked at the same time.

"Well, do you need them?" Andi asked, ignoring Lexa's teasing. She knew she looked ridiculous. The clothes were too big, the shirt only not drowning her because of the waistcoat she'd found crumpled in the bottom drawer. The socks were too big, but she was never putting her stockings back on.

Bertrand opened his mouth, then closed it. "Well. No. I suppose I don't. I don't imagine they'd fit now."

"I'll make you a very important hat," she said.

He looked pleased at that thought.

"I like the ponytail," Blythe offered.

"Thank you, that's the first sincere compliment I've heard." Andi glared at Lexa.

Lexa did not seem at all apologetic. "Don't know what you mean. Said you were cute."

"Uh huh."

"I meant it!"

"Right." Andi sat down on one of the chairs. It was high backed and uncomfortable. "I don't know how many floors we have until we reach the top of the tree. Berty?"

"No idea," Bertrand said. "I took the outside route."

"Excuse me, the what?" Lexa stared at him. "The outside route? We don't have to go through every stupid room in this tree? And you're just now mentioning it?"

"To be fair, no one asked me," Bertrand said.

"I like going through the rooms," Andi said. Everyone stared at her, and she realized that probably sounded strange. "If it weren't for, you know, everything that was trying to kill us. It's interesting. There's so much knowledge and history here, some of it completely lost to us, and…and yes. The outside route seems like it might be a good way to go."

"Well, there is the guardian," Bertrand said. "That might be a problem. But you're the next head librarian, so maybe not?"

Lexa and Blythe didn't appear to be surprised by the statement. Bertrand must have been chatting them up while she was asleep.

"I don't know about that," she admitted. "I think I'm just the first archive witch to be here in centuries."

"What is this guardian?" Lexa asked.

"Oh, I don't know," Bertrand admitted. "I never saw it. I just heard about it. It protects the library from outside threats. So, it's probably, y'know, big. I don't think it would consider us threats. If that helps."

"The other problem we have is that we don't know if that explosion killed Carmine," Blythe said. "Tana is here somewhere, and that means Dahlia might be around, too."

"You think all three elder vampires are here?" Lexa looked uneasy at the mention of Tana. "And they all have their lackeys."

"I only saw a few," Blythe said. "Carmine brought the most trusted of her court. Tana has no court. And no one knows much about Dahlia. I've never met her."

Dahlia kept to herself in her own kingdom — in a castle at the very northern tip of Obrye. No one had seen her for a very long time. Anyone who went too far north never returned. She'd heard stories of monsters and beasts. Great eyes like lanterns that stared from the dark.

She shook herself, slightly. Dahlia hadn't been seen for well over a hundred years, and the tree was at the center of Obrye. She doubted they would have to deal with her. It wasn't unheard of for an elder vampire to disappear. Beryl, from the south of the continent, had been destroyed a century ago, her castle burning around her.

"So outside we have a big guardian creature that may or may not attack us," Lexa said. "Or inside, we have at least two, but possibly four elder vampires that will definitely try to kill us and kidnap Andi. I think you can guess which way my vote is going."

"I agree," Blythe said. "Though I imagine it's quite a bit of stairs?"

"Oh, yeah, lots of those," Bertrand said. "Sorry."

"Yes, I'm sure that the stairs that have been part of this library since it grew were entirely your fault," Blythe said.

"I know," Bertrand said, solemnly. It was ruined a moment later when he outright giggled. "Obviously, I wasn't a big fan of stairs, either."

"Andi said when she takes over this place she's going to put in elevators," Blythe said.

Bertrand gasped. "Andi! You're my hero."

"You don't even walk anywhere anymore," Andi reminded him.

"You can be my hero, then," Blythe said. Andi's cheeks flooded with warmth. She wished she would stop doing that.

Blythe had been incredibly open with her, and she'd essentially shot her down. Threatened her existence. Anxiety twisted up inside her chest. She didn't want to have to choose between the world and Blythe. It wasn't fair.

She needed to think about something else. Anything else. "If we survive, sure, elevators. I'll find a way. Where can we get outside?"

"Oh, it's just around the corner," Bertrand said. "There are some reading rooms with outside access. I can show you!"

"Great, that's settled, then." Lexa stood up.

It didn't take very long for them to get their things together and leave. They hadn't been there long, but Bertrand's rooms had felt like a safe haven. Even if that was an illusion, and Silva could have barged in at any time.

Andi was almost sad to close the door. She redid Bertrand's seal, knowing she shouldn't spare the magic. Maybe it was pointless. Bertrand would never be back, not as he had been. The thought didn't stop her.

"Andi." Blythe touched her elbow, briefly, to get her attention. Lexa and Bertrand weren't far enough away that Lexa wouldn't be able to hear every word, but there was some illusion of privacy. "Can we talk?"

She nodded. They might not have a chance, later.

Blythe was visibly relieved. "I'm afraid that I put quite a great deal on you, and I'm sorry."

"You don't have to be sorry," Andi said. "I…I care about you, Blythe. I do."

"I know," Blythe said. "Not very many witches would cut themselves to bleed into my mouth, after all."

Andi hated that it made her blush. "I had limited options."

"You were being chased by a—"

"Don't say it," Andi warned her.

"You didn't let me finish."

Andi tried to make her voice slightly husky like Blythe's was. "Oh, I'm a monster. Oh Andi, how can you bear to spend time with me, when I drink blood. I'm just so terrible."

"That is an incredibly poor imitation of my voice," Blythe cut her off.

"Give me time and I'll get it absolutely perfect, so perfect that you won't even know if you're the one talking or not," Andi said.

"Really? You plan on spending that much time with me?" Blythe's eyebrows rose.

"You invited me to your library," Andi reminded her. "I…I can't pretend that I know what the future holds. Or that everything will be okay. We could die in five minutes. I could fail."

"That would never happen," Blythe said.

"You don't know that," Andi said. "I could succeed, but fail at the same time. I'm scared, and I don't want to…I'd never want to…"

"I know." Blythe's voice was soft and quiet, just above a whisper. "Let's not dwell on what could be, okay? Let's just worry about what's right here and now. And right here and now, I might be all of those things that you had me say—"

"I didn't mean a word of it."

"—Doing the absolute worst job of sounding like me," Blythe continued.

"Oh, that's where you take issue?" Andi rolled her eyes.

"It is, I'm deeply offended," Blythe said. "You really need to work on it, just like you promised. I'd say you should start now, but I don't think my ego can take it."

"You were about to say something nice before you started making fun of me," Andi said. "But now I don't think I want to hear it."

"Or maybe I was just going to tease you some more." Blythe smiled. "You make my heart feel like it could start beating again. That's all I wanted to say. I hope you still wanted to hear it."

"You can't be mean to me and then just say that, it's not fair." Andi's brain stuttered to a halt.

If all they had was right there, right then, what did she want to say? What could she say? Everything that she felt was too big, too bright. She felt like she would have to break open to really express it the right way in such a short amount of time, Blythe had become so essential.

Maybe it was the situation. The adrenaline, the fear, chemicals in the brain becoming confused as to what was terror and what was something else.

"Did I lose you?" Blythe asked.

"I was thinking about brain chemicals," she blurted.

Blythe looked dangerously close to laughing. "Yes, I imagine you were."

"You're important to me," Andi said. "I didn't say that when we talked. And I should have. You're so important to me. And I need you to know that. I've never…I've never been good at feelings, or people, or anything like this. I get lost in my own little world, I know I do. I'm not good at expressing myself and I…I keep talking, I'm sorry."

Maybe she had broken open, and everything was rushing out.

"I think you're amazing, and funny, and beautiful, and I…I've never wanted someone to get lost with me, but I think I'd like it if you did."

That sounded so cheesy Andi briefly considered slamming her head into the door frame and letting unconsciousness claim her before Blythe laughed at her. She looked down at the tips of her shoes. They were scuffed and some of the stitching was coming undone.

Blythe reached forward and very carefully took her hand. "Pretty sure I already have. We should go, before Lexa starts yelling at us."

"You're right." Andi nodded. She wasn't sure what it meant, but Blythe was still holding her hand.

Chapter 36: Outside

The reading rooms fared much worse than Bertrand's apartment.

At one point it must have been lovely. A half moon-room, with window seats all along the outside, interspersed by the natural wood of the tree and bookshelves. There were small tables and chairs, and at one time anyone doing research must have been able to get tea. There was still a cup and saucer sitting alone on one of the tables, waiting for no one.

Some violence had taken place there, muffled by time and dust. An overturned table, a stain on the floor so dark it was still visible, a splintered chair. Books littered the floor, pages like leaves, from an upended bookshelf. One of the windows had broken, letting in the elements for centuries. Moss grew thick around the window frame. A cold wind whistled through the room. It would have been refreshing if it didn't stink of ozone.

"This used to be my favorite spot," Bertand said. "I used to read right over there, by that window. The sun would come in during the late afternoon, all golden."

"There hasn't been light here for a long time." Blythe walked over to the window, peering out. The world beyond the windows was inky black.

Bertrand curled a foot around the strap of Andi's bag. He'd left Lexa's shoulder for hers as soon as she was close enough. Blythe had to catch him before he hit the floor.

Andi pet his head with one finger. He didn't seem to mind when she did it. "We'll fix it."

"Of course you will." Bertrand nodded.

"There's a walkway out here." Lexa opened the door. "It looks like it grew out from the tree. No railing, so be careful, but it should be sturdy enough."

"You walk on the inside," Blythe told Andi.

"I'm not going to fall." Andi couldn't help but smile.

"But in the event one of us did fall, I think I'd be more likely to survive," Blythe said.

"I'm not arguing with her," Bertand said. "I don't know why you are."

"I wasn't arguing," Andi said. "I'll walk on the inside."

It was easier for Blythe, anyway. The way up would put her cane on the outside. Andi was a little nervous. There were a few of the star shaped flowers, but otherwise if it weren't for her lantern, it would have been pitch black.

She still knew it was a long way to fall.

The pathway was just wide enough for them to walk side by side, with Lexa up front.

"All right, here's how it's going to go down," Lexa said. "We get out there and we aren't talking. No long speeches about how much you two like each other, no checking in verbally, use your eyeballs and body language."

Andi's face might as well have been on fire. At some point during her speech she'd forgotten Lexa could hear them.

"Give me an example of this body language," Blythe said. Lexa replied with a very rude gesture and she laughed. "Perfect."

"We don't have a lot of information on this guardian, so our best bet is to avoid it all together," Lexa continued. "So, we're quick and quiet. I'll be up front. Blythe next to Andi. Keep her safe."

"Of course." Blythe nodded.

"Good." Lexa didn't make any comments about Andi's life choices, but she knew they were coming. Probably after everything was over. "It's cold out there, so use your cloak. The wind isn't great. Stay as close to the tree as you can. Blythe, if you need to, move behind. All right, this is the last chance you have to talk before we go out there. Better get the mushy crap out of the way."

"I love you, Lexa," Andi said.

"I love you, too." Lexa's tone didn't change at all. "Great. Mushy stuff over. Let's go."

Andi got her cloak over her shoulders. It still had the little pouch for Bertrand made from Blythe's handkerchief. She held it open for him, making sure he was secure before she followed Lexa outside.

The wind carved around her. It howled down from the upper branches, making the entire tree creak and sway. How they hadn't noticed it inside, she wasn't sure.

It was one thing to be inside the library, knowing she was in a giant tree.

It was another entirely to be outside, climbing up a far too narrow strip of wood. If she could see more, she was certain she would have just stood there for hours, staring in awe. The tree was impossibly large, bigger than she could even fully comprehend.

Blythe touched her elbow, and she started walking.

They were as quick and quiet as possible. It didn't take long for Blythe to have to move behind her, the path getting narrower enough that she didn't have room to walk and used her cane, which she was leaning more heavily on. The path took them right up to another veranda. Lexa had to help her up, and together they got Blythe onto it. The path curved under the veranda and continued on the other side.

Lexa motioned with her head to the entrance. She yanked it open and they got inside. The room was a little less destroyed than the last. Andi was grateful to sink into a dusty window seat.

"Easier with pants?" Lexa asked.

"Well, I'm much less likely to rip them," she said.

"You're welcome." Bertrand poked his head out of his sling.

"Thank you, I needed a break." Blythe sat next to Andi, stretching out her bad leg with a grimace. "Please tell me you have blood in that bag."

"Sure do." Lexa rummaged in her bag and pulled out a bottle full of dark red liquid. She tossed it to Blythe, who caught it effortlessly. She downed half of it in one go. "I have three more bottles, let's ration it out as best as we can. If all else fails, I do have tubing, but I'd really rather not stab Andi if I can help it."

"I would prefer that we didn't do that as well." Blythe took another sip and stoppered the bottle. She handed it to Andi. "You should have this, just in case."

"Right." Andi tucked it into her bag. "Berty, how much farther?"

"Not sure," Bertrand said. "It's at the crown of the tree, where the branches spread from the trunk. So quite a bit higher. And there were quite a few floors. And I was out of it, I don't remember it very well. I just knew I had to get it as far away as possible."

"Right." Lexa nodded. "So quite a ways, then. Let's take five. Andi, eat a granola bar or I swear I'll make you."

"Yes, oh great Lexa, your will is my command," she said as sarcastically as she could. It didn't take much rummaging to find one of her remaining granola bars.

"Damn right it is," Lexa said. "Blythe, you and me need to have a chat."

Blythe sighed. "If this is some horrific posturing with a few threats thrown in because you'll kill me if I hurt her, I think we can skip it."

"It's not." Lexa tapped the bottom of Blythe's boot with her toe. "C'mon."

"If you start fighting, I'm leaving!" Andi called after them. She did not want to hear their conversation. She didn't even want to be aware they were having one. She ate as much of her granola bar as she could and drank some water. It might be her last chance before they reached the core.

She wanted to get things over with, and at the same time she wanted to drag things out as long as possible. If they reached the core, she'd have to figure out how to break the curse. If they didn't, they'd all die anyway. If she broke the curse…

It didn't bear thinking about.

She stood up when Blythe and Lexa came back, without any visible wounds or blood on them.

"Have a nice chat?" she asked.

"Surprisingly we did," Blythe said.

"Mostly," Lexa agreed.

Andi realized exactly what they'd talked about and wished she could hide somewhere. "You wanted to know what happened while you were gone."

"Yup." Lexa nodded. "Figured you wouldn't tell me."

"You figured wrong," Andi said.

Lexa shrugged. "Fine, I figured you'd tell me in the most round about way possible. Now, c'mon, we have a long ways to go. Same rules as before. Same formation. Be careful, be quiet."

Andi could see how Bertrand lost track of where he was. In the dark, everything was nearly the same, just rough wood under her feet, barely lit by her lantern. The only way she could tell that anything was changing at all was the burning in her legs from walking up the stairs and the occasional clump of glowing flowers.

They passed several verandas and entrances. They had just reached one when a deep shudder moved through the tree.

Not the tree. The path.

Andi scrambled up onto the veranda and grabbed Blythe's hand to help her get up when the whole path began to move, slithering across the bark of the tree like a snake.

"...I think I found the guardian," she whispered.

Chapter 37: Spells

"The path is the guardian?!" Lexa shrieked.

Andi ignored her, sprinting towards the door, Blythe behind her. Lexa swore and grabbed the doorknob.

It didn't budge.

"Oh, c'mon!" She yanked on it. The door didn't even rattle in its frame.

"Try pushing!" Blythe yelled.

"I'll push you!" Lexa slammed her shoulder against the wood, but nothing happened. Blythe muttered something under her breath that Andi didn't catch and moved to help her.

Green light shone down on them.

"That's probably not good," Bertrand said.

"I don't want to hurry anyone, but actually yes I do." Andi's words tumbled out into a jumble.

"It's stuck." Blythe stepped back and studied it with frustration. "How is it stuck?"

The light was an emerald sun, filtering through the leaves, descending too quickly. The veranda jerked so hard under Andi's feet she fell to her hands and knees. Twigs showered her hair and back. Blythe grabbed her around the waist and hoisted her back just as a massive branch hit the veranda. It took out half of it with ease, falling into the dark. Blythe pulled Andi closer to the door.

A sound like whale song filled the air. Loud enough it reverberated in her chest. Aching in how beautiful and lonely it sounded. Terrifying in how large.

A face pushed through the branches.

Eyes.

A pair of enormous eyes that glowed like green sunlamps above them. They were set into a fox-shaped face that looked like it had been carved by a master craftsman. It had branches instead of horns, sprouting from thick, shaggy moss.

The guardian opened its mouth, displaying a very impressive row of teeth bigger than Andi's arm. The inside of its mouth was just as bright as its eyes. Andi couldn't look away.

Its entire front was dark and rotten, caving in towards its curved spine, but it didn't matter. It was still too big, too terrifying, to fight.

"Is that a dragon?" Bertrand's question was just loud enough for Andi to hear it.

It let out a hiss of air.

Andi took a tiny step back.

Its attention snapped to her.

"Andi!" Bertrand's cold little hands were at her collar bone. She couldn't glance down at him. She couldn't do anything. "Andi you have to open the door!"

The guardian reared its head back.

She pressed herself against the door, hand scrambling for the doorknob. She found it just as the guardian struck like a snake and turned it as hard as she could.

It moved easily under her hand.

The door swung open. Andi fell through it, landing on her back.

Her landing was softer than expected.

She struggled to sit up. She'd landed in a pit of fine-grained black sand.

Lexa shoved Blythe in after Andi. Blythe caught herself in the door frame, but Lexa shoved her into the sand next to Andi. The guardian slammed into the door frame. The entire room shuddered.

Lexa swung the door closed but the sand drifted in front of it, jamming it open.

"Why is there sand in here?!" She kept shoving the door, but it didn't budge. "Who makes more than one room full of sand? I hate this library!"

"It's imp sand!" Bertrand yelled. "Andi, you can use it!"

Andi had never heard of anything like it.

But she trusted him.

She focused on the sand around her. She could feel something, almost like her own magic. If she just focused, if she pushed, she could meld it to what she wanted.

She wanted every last grain of sand to block them from the dragon.

It rushed between her fingers like a wave pulling out to sea. Sand splashed up against the outside wall, blocking the door and windows. Layer upon layer until it was a solid, glittering barrier.

She stared at it. It had been so easy, almost too easy. Like controlling her own magic, but more refined. More solid.

"How did you do that?" Lexa asked.

"I don't know," she admitted.

It shuddered a few times. Andi put all of her concentration into keeping the wall there, keeping it solid.

"Is that gonna hold?" Lexa whispered.

"Let her concentrate," Blythe whispered back.

A scrape shook the entire room, sand raining down on them from higher above.

Andi did her best to not let it rattle her, tried to keep all of her thoughts on the sand. She threw her terror, her anger, and her sorrow at the wall.

It held firm.

Silence filled the air.

Andi waited for the next bang, the next scrape, anything to show the guardian was still trying to get inside.

Nothing happened.

After a few minutes she let the sand slide back to the floor. It was as easy as breathing, but her hands still shook. The soft, ambient light glittered off the sand like water.

Andi fell to her knees in the sand. Lexa was next to her a second later, helping her back up to her feet.

"Are you okay? Where's that little frog, I'm gonna toss him out there," Lexa threatened.

"No!" Andi covered Bertrand with her hand, willing her fingers to be still. "And he's a toad."

"His suggestion almost got us killed, I'll call him whatever I want," Lexa said. "You said guardian. You didn't say giant tree snake dragon monster!"

"I didn't know!" Bertrand poked his head out between Andi's fingers. "I told you that!"

"And now we're safe again, relatively," Blythe said. "So maybe don't throw our only guide out the door."

"Don't throw my friend out the door!" Andi corrected her, taking a step away from Lexa.

"Aww," Bertrand said. "I mean, yeah! Don't toss me anywhere. You still need me. I'm Andi's assistant."

Lexa sighed, throwing her hands up. "Fine. You guys win."

"Great." Andi knew Lexa would never actually throw Bertrand. At least, she was pretty sure. She decided to change the subject, regardless.

"I suggest whatever we do to the toad, we wait until we're in an area that isn't quite so vulnerable?" Blythe suggested.

Andi realized she was struggling to stand and firmed up the sand underneath her. She received a grateful look in return.

"I guess it's not a bad idea," Lexa said. "You good to go?"

"I'm fine," Andi said. She got a skeptical look. "Really, I just…it scared me, that's all. I really am fine. Where are we, exactly?"

She took in the room properly. A crescent around the side of the tree. Half of it was a pit of imp sand, the other was tiled floor. The wall had a mosaic of swirling color, its detail and luster lost to time and cobwebs heavy with dust. Double doors led to the next room, nearly twice Andi's height. It must have been beautiful, once.

"There are a few practice rooms like this, but I suspect this one is more for show than actual practice," Bertrand said.

"That's dumb." Lexa swept one foot through the sand, leaving behind a groove. "What is this stuff?"

"Imp sand," Bertrand said. "Impression sand. It's infused with magic, so it can be moved at will by witches. Like I said, it's mostly used for practice. You don't have it?"

"No?" Andi had never heard of it. With a thought she made her own library, pulling the shape up. She dissolved the library and made a cliff that she'd seen, once, before the darkness was too far spread. Complete with a waterfall and trees. "Wow. Okay. That's too much fun. We should go or I'll just sit here playing with sand."

At least it was easy to pull from her shoes. She did the same for Blythe and Lexa.

"What sort of practice would require a room like this?" Blythe asked.

"All kinds," Bertrand said. "Control, target practice, effects…we had a big room of this back at the academy. Is the academy in Rosewood…still there?"

"Yes." Andi blinked in surprise. She'd known the academy was old, built before the war, but she hadn't realized it was quite that ancient. "That's where I learned."

"Well, that's not surprising, you're a really strong witch," Bertrand said. "Naturally we attended the same academy."

"Naturally," she decided it was best to just agree with him.

"I just mean that you're smart and resourceful," Bertrand explained. "Those are going to be excellent qualities when you're head librarian."

"Thank you." She figured it was easier to just be grateful for the compliment than try to argue with him. She let her sand cliff slump into the floor. "You're pretty smart and resourceful yourself. The perfect assistant."

"How much assisting can a toad do?" Lexa murmured. Blythe hit her leg with her cane. "Ow. Watch where you're swinging that thing, Fangs."

"Fangs?" Blythe's eyebrows rose.

"Yeah. Can we go?" Lexa raised her eyebrows in return.

"Allow me." Andi made a bridge from the sand, solid enough for them to walk on, all the way to a set of stairs that led up to solid, tiled floor.

The tall doors loomed over Andi, made of heavy looking, dark wood with a golden starburst where they met. The gold was tarnished, but it still gleamed in the lanterns.

"What's in here?" she asked Bertrand.

"I'm not sure," Bertrand admitted.

Andi put a hand on the knob. Despite the dust and grime softening it, she could feel the details under her palm. She exhaled and turned the knob, pushing the door open.

She was greeted by huge glass cylinders, full of light. The room was blinding compared to the others, and she had to shield her eyes for a moment. The cylinders rose from the floor in orderly rows, like truncated pillars, filling the entire floor.

"What is this?" Blythe touched one. It was a delicate, lacy pattern of blue light that shifted to swirl around her fingers. She pulled her hand away it resumed its slow rotation. "It's...warm. It feels like a heartbeat."

"It's a spell." Andi's gaze caught on one that sparkled like diamonds, geometric patterns forming and breaking apart. It was a freezing spell. When she touched the glass frost formed on the other side. "They're all spells. I've heard of this room! Spells are easier to store and study like this, but the art was lost...nothing could have prepared me for this."

The spells came in every shape and color, each one as intricate as the last. The essence of magic spread out before her, each one carefully labeled by what it was and the name of the witch that cast it. A legacy that spanned hundreds of years.

She'd never felt so small and awed. It was facing the vast expanse of the sky, before the dark blotted out the stars.

She forgot about the danger. Her bruises and scrapes faded into a distant thing. She flitted between the spells, reading each one.

"Oh look! This is a healing spell!" She stared at how it twisted and turned. "I didn't think it would be green. Incredible. Oh, and this one! It's a weather spell. They used to predict weather for months at a time with this. Look at that purple! I want to learn it so badly. I hope there's a book. I don't want to interrupt the spell...look at this one!"

She could have stayed there for hours. Days. Maybe even weeks. Just taking them all in. There were hundreds, more than she'd ever expected to see. She wanted to examine each one, trace her fingers over dusty plaques and memorize the name of the witches who came before her, designing new spells, shaping the very future of magic.

She looked up to the mezzanine, lined with books and windows. What would it be like to spend an afternoon there, dust motes dancing in the sun, reading about any spell her heart desired? What must it have been like, four hundred years ago?

It was almost a perfectly clear picture. Honey colored sunlight lancing through the glass, shining through the columns, highlighting the blond notes on the wood, drenching the whole room in gold.

She had to save it. All of it.

Chapter 38: History Lesson

Andi sighed. "We should get going, shouldn't we."

"Are you sure?" Blythe had a gentle hand at her elbow. She was bathed in blue light, highlighting her hair and making her eyes glow azure.

"Yes." Andi nodded, firmly. "It's…it's time. We need to keep moving."

"Good. I want to find Silva and rip his face off," Lexa said. "Maybe Tana first. The other one can get in line."

"Dahlia," Blythe reminded her.

"Do we know if she's here?" Bertrand asked. "What about Beryl?"

"If she's already full of whatever they put in barrels, that one should be easy." Lexa grinned.

Andi knew it was a silly little joke, but she couldn't help it. "Beryl, like the stone. And she's been dead for well over a hundred years, so I doubt she'll be causing any of our future troubles."

"And no one was going to tell me about that?" Bertrand sighed. "Well. Easy indeed. And, just for the record, you can age just about any kind of alcohol in oak barrels."

"Wow, with the two of you around, no one will ever be wrong again." Lexa's words didn't hold any bite. "No wonder you're going to be head librarian and assistant. It makes perfect sense."

"True champions in the fight for information," Blythe teased, but it was gentle.

"You both are terrible people," Andi told them. "When this is my library maybe I won't let you in."

"That's fair and I accept it," Blythe said.

Lexa folded her arms. "Well, I don't. Let me in."

"I don't think they let dogs into libraries." Blythe smiled at her.

"Neither are bats, so I guess we were both being banned no matter how nice we were." Lexa huffed a small laugh. "Funny, she's still letting the toad in."

"I know, it's almost like discrimination." Blythe nodded.

Andi was trying and probably failing to pretend that she wasn't thrilled that they were teasing each other and not at each other's throats. Lexa was her best friend. She wanted them to get along. "I'm not letting him into anywhere. He works here."

"And I'm very polite," Bertrand added.

They moved as they talked. The stairs wrapped around the edge of the room, like they had on every floor Andi had been to. She wondered how many books were on the second level. How many years it would take to read them all.

"You're so small I don't think your behavior matters," Lexa said.

Bertrand sniffed. "I can think of several things I could say, but I won't, because unlike you, I have good manners."

"Try it and see how it goes." Lexa grinned, but it was partly baring her very sharp teeth.

"He's poisonous, just in case one of your threats was going to be to eat him," Andi said. "Even if he's not making his own poison, he was marinated in embalming fluid for a few centuries, I wouldn't recommend it."

"Please don't eat me." Bertrand ducked back into his sling.

Lexa glared at her. "I wasn't going to eat him."

"Are you sure?" Andi asked. "Nothing like 'I'm going to have a frog in my throat, and I don't mean because I'll have a cold'."

Blythe sighed. "Oh good. I was worried it was just me, but it turns out you're terrible at imitating everyone."

"You are supposed to be on my side," Andi told her.

Blythe stepped just a bit closer, taking Andi's hand in her own. She gave her a soft smile, brushing their shoulders together. "My dear, you are incredible at a great many things, but it's a good thing that you're a librarian."

"Is this you telling me to not quit my day job?" Andi pouted. It might have been a joke, but her heart still stuttered at the term of endearment.

"That is exactly what she's saying!" Lexa cackled.

"I am definitely not letting you in. You're both banned for life. No library cards for you," Andi said. She didn't take her hand back.

Blythe didn't let go. "Well, then I suppose I should take advantage of this once in a lifetime opportunity."

"I suppose you will," Andi agreed.

"So, Mr. Assistant. I have a question for you."

That got Bertrand to poke his head out of the sling. "Ask away, I know everything."

Andi refrained from saying that was definitely not true.

Blythe looked like she might laugh. "Why keep spells like this? Don't you have them in books? This seems…dangerous."

"It's perfectly safe, the glass has been attuned to the spell, it won't break," Bertrand answered. "It was common practice when a new spell was formed to store them like this, as well as write about them and teach them. That way it could be studied, refined, or adjusted. The person who made the spell always made a copy of it just like this. I'm assuming that's no longer the case?"

"No one has made a new spell in a very long time," Andi explained. "We've modified existing spells, but nothing new."

The information might be in her archive, but she knew without checking that it had been much longer than she'd been alive.

"Oh, because the library is shut down," Bertrand said. "That's something I learned right away. Spells are made here. That's why they're stored here. After all, the tree is where all ley lines originate, so it's much easier to do magic here."

"That's fascinating," Andi said. "Magic has been fading for centuries, we know that much, and we knew it had something to do with the library and the ley lines. That's why my magic seems to be working better here, isn't it?"

"Yes," Bertrand said. "But that's why it was so dangerous to have this place open when the Empire landed on our shores. With access to the library, they had access to all the magic of the continent."

"That's why Silva hid it away," Andi said. "And they left."

Bertrand nodded. "Silva seemed to think they'd give up. I guess he was right. I assume you've had no contact with them?"

"We've had no contact with any other continent," Andi admitted. She actually knew very little outside of the borders of Obrye. It had been centuries since anyone had shown them any sort of interest. She assumed it was because of the tree.

"That makes sense," Bertrand said. "With the library gone and the vampires…well. And with no head librarian to act as delegate…"

"The head librarian is that important?" Andi asked.

"Yes," Bertrand said. "Silva acted as the go between for the king and the magical community, since the king has always been a normal human. I assume that's the same?"

"We don't have a king," Andi said.

"Ah." Bertrand didn't sound surprised. "Yes. Well then."

"Is this all part of your normal training?" Lexa steered the conversation back on track. "Learning all this stuff, like the head librarian thing?"

"Oh, no, not at all," Bertrand admitted. "Silva explained a lot of things to me that I probably shouldn't have ever learned."

"Were you two close?" Blythe asked.

Bertrand shook himself. "No. Not…not really. Honestly, I barely knew him. It's just there wasn't anyone he trusted at the end, I think. I was new, I didn't have any aspirations to be head librarian. And closer to the end, everyone else was dead. So. That's why he told me. When an archive witch starts to connect to the library, then that means they're most likely the next head librarian. Or something is very wrong. I'm hoping the former. It's probably the latter. Honestly, it's most likely both. Either way, it's a good thing you're here!"

"That's why Silva didn't kill me," Ice worked its way down Andi's throat and spread through her. "He thinks I can…fix whatever is wrong."

"Only an archive witch can fix it, yes," Bertrand said. "Since I'm like this and he's a vampire, you're the only one here."

"She's the only one left," Lexa said. She was uncharacteristically quiet. "There aren't any other archive witches that the coven is aware of."

Andi knew that, but it was always difficult to hear.

"What do you mean?" Bertrand asked.

"Any other potential archive witches were turned or killed," Lexa explained. "Except for Andi. And it was…"

"A near thing," Andi finished for her when she trailed off. "A fluke, maybe."

Blythe's grip on her hand tightened, slightly, and she squeezed back gratefully. It had happened a long time ago. Some days the amount of time didn't matter.

"The only one?" Bertrand's voice squeaked. "That's not right."

"That's the state of things," Lexa said.

"But…but that means you're the only person who could be the head librarian," Bertrand said. "And the only one who can save it. Oh, we need to be way more careful."

"We weren't already being careful?" Lexa sounded annoyed.

Andi only heard her distantly. They'd reached the stairs, Lexa was already climbing them, but she was frozen in place.

"Andi?" Blythe's voice cut through the buzzing in her ears. She stared at her, wide eyed. "Are you okay?"

"I…yes. Yes. I'm fine." She'd already made the decision she had to save it all, didn't she? Knowing she was the only one who could changed anything.

"Do you need to take a break?" Lexa walked back down the stairs and got a little too close to her face.

"No." She pushed past her. "No more breaks."

Blythe didn't move, and didn't let go of her hand, stopping her from moving further up the stairs.

"Blythe—"

"I need a break," Blythe said.

She was lying. Andi knew she was.

It wouldn't hurt to play along. To stop because Blythe said she needed it, when really her world was reeling and she needed to sit down. She nodded and sat on the steps. Bertrand sat on her knees so he could see everyone better. Blythe sat next to her, stretching her leg out in front of her, rubbing her knee.

Lexa sat on her other side. The stairs were wide enough they could easily sit side by side without touching, but they were right next to her, anyway.

Chapter 39: Detour

Andi was grateful no one said anything. Even Bertrand kept silent, sitting on her knees with his legs curled up so he resembled a round purple stone.

The only sound was the hum of the nearest spell, barely perceptible but strangely soothing. The lights danced across the shiny spots on the floor where they'd walked through the dust. Green, blue, gold, then green again.

The weight settled on her shoulders.

The pressure didn't crush her.

She could still breathe.

Anxiety still swirled behind her ribs, but it was manageable.

If she was the only one who could do something, then she had no choice left. It was that simple. Maybe she didn't know exactly what needed to be done, maybe there were quite a few steps she didn't know about, and it was possible her friends had entirely too much faith in her.

The only solution was to try to live up to that faith. To do everything she could.

Blythe took her hand after a few more minutes. She supposed her breathing must have evened out, or her heart wasn't beating as hard as it had been. That was something she was used to having someone in tune with. Lexa always listened. It was nice that Blythe could do the same thing.

"I'm okay," she said. Her voice even sounded steady.

"Good." Blythe made no move to stand up.

She tried again. "We can get going."

"Eat this first." Lexa handed her a piece of orange candy.

Andi held it up. "Did you take this from my desk?"

"No," Lexa said. "You know they pay me, right? Like I get monetary compensation for hanging around witches. I can buy my own candy, thank you very much."

"But you hate these." Andi unwrapped it and popped it into her mouth. It tasted like oranges to her, but Lexa insisted the flavor was nothing like any citrus alive and it made her gag.

The taste was still comforting. A piece of candy didn't make her problems any smaller. It didn't make what she had to do any less terrifying. But it was a tiny bit of sunshine.

That was how her mom always described it, before giving a piece to Andi for scraped knees and childhood woes.

She really missed her mom, in that moment, a fierce ache in her chest. It had been such a long time, but she could still see her stirring one of her large cauldrons, checking the color of the potion against the book next to her.

"Yeah, but I like you." Lexa shrugged. "I stuck a few in my bag, just in case. Glad I did. Blythe, she's crazy about these stupid things, take notes."

"I've committed it to memory," Blythe said.

"I am not crazy about them, I just like them. You two are ridiculous." Andi picked up Bertrand. "Are you going to say something ridiculous, too?"

"I just think you're great," Bertrand said. "And I know everything will be okay."

Andi felt a little deflated. "Well, thank you. You're pretty great, too. I hope you're right."

"Of course I'm right. I've been right about everything so far," Bertrand said. He tilted his head to the side. "Well Everything important."

"You almost got us killed by a wood snake," Lexa reminded him.

"But you're fine, right? We're all fine!" Bertrand waved her off.

"I suppose so." Lexa stood and shouldered her bag. "Let's go. I have some murders to perform."

"I wouldn't want you to be late to that performance," Andi said. She tucked Bertrand into his sling before she offered her hands to Blythe, even though it wasn't necessary, helping her to her feet and handing over her cane.

They headed up the stairs.

Her shoulders were heavy, but it was a weight she didn't have to carry alone.

They made it to the top. Bookshelves rose to a distant ceiling that had some sort of mural, too lost in shadow for her to make out beyond indistinct shapes and colors. The mezzanine had a scrolling wrought iron railing, extending all the way around. A tightly coiled staircase led to the level above them, but Andi knew they didn't need to climb it.

They were already at the way forward.

A door nestled between the shelves. It had silver constellations etched into dark wood. The handle was inlaid with cerulean. It glittered in the light of her lamp.

Lexa reached for it.

Locked.

Lexa struggled with it, then stepped back to give Andi space.

"Worked before," Lexa said.

Andi nodded and put her hand on the door handle.

Nothing.

It might as well have been carved from the wood.

"There's another way," she said, pointing to the left. "It's over here, around the corner. But something about it feels strange."

"In what way?" Blythe asked.

"Like…we're not supposed to go that way," Andi said. "If it's going to be my library anyway, and you're already banned for life, the two of you might as well try to knock the door down."

Bertrand cackled at that.

"Absolutely not!" Bertrand shoved his head out of the sling. "It's…it's pretty. Don't knock it down."

"Do you know another way?" Blythe asked.

"Well, no."

Lexa exchanged a look with Blythe, shrugged, and slammed her shoulder against it with a resounding bang.

She hit the floor. "Ow!"

Bertrand muttered something that sounded quite a bit like "serves you right".

"Are you okay?" Andi kneeled next to her, checking Lexa's shoulder, but the bruising bloomed under her skin and then faded away.

"That bad?" Blythe offered her a hand up.

"Felt like hitting a cliff." Lexa stood up and rotated her shoulder. "We're not getting through that way. Think we're gonna have to try the one that feels off."

They followed the curve of the mezzanine. Andi knew exactly where she was going, even if it felt strange. She wanted to turn away, to try the door again, maybe try the second level.

She knew they wouldn't find anything, but she hesitated.

"What's up?" Lexa asked.

"Check the other level, Blythe and I will see if there's another door," she said.

"You got it." Lexa nodded, taking the staircase two at a time.

"Are you sure?" Blythe asked.

"Something doesn't feel right, I think we should at least try to find another way," Andi said.

That was easier said than done. They had to walk the entire circumference of the tree, and it was massive. She looked down at the spells a few times, leaning a little too far over a railing that hadn't seen any sort of repairs for centuries. It creaked beneath her. She tried her best to focus on the outer wall, instead.

She didn't find another door.

But she did find the one she knew would be there.

She stopped right in front of a shelf. Instead of roses, like the door to the herbarium, tiny, delicate bunches of forget-me-nots had been carved into each corner. She pressed the top right and it swung open.

The room beyond was dark. None of the light spilled into it. She could have been looking at a black wall and she doubted it would have made any difference.

"How did you…?" Blythe looked at her with awe. "Right. Connected to the library. Still."

"I…I think there was a door, between the herbarium and the specimen floor, but Silva hid it when…when it was full of corpses," Andi said. "So why is this door hidden? There's nothing here."

"I couldn't begin to tell you," Blythe admitted. She extended her cane through the door. The end of it vanished, not even the glint of the lantern off of the silver on the end. She pulled it back and it was perfectly whole and intact. "I believe it's safe, but we should be careful."

"Does it smell off?" Andi asked. She couldn't tell.

"Not more than any other room, I believe it's quite small," Blythe said. "It shouldn't take us long to cross."

"Do you know anything about this?" Andi asked Betrand.

"Maybe." Bertrand clambered out of the sling and onto her shoulder. "I think I've heard about it, but I don't think many people use it."

"Nothing up there…hey, you found a secret door, that's awesome." Lexa jogged up. "Wow. Can't see a thing. We sure this is safe?"

"Do we have a choice?" Blythe asked.

Lexa shrugged. "I mean, you can go try to knock down the other door yourself."

"I'd rather not break my cane again," Blythe said. "Andi, if you want, we can keep looking."

It was tempting, to take the time to try to find another door she knew wasn't going to exist. To hope that no one would catch up to them and they'd be safe for another few hours. That Silva would grow bored and unseal the door.

She knew he had to be behind it.

"Unfortunately, I think we're being herded through here," she said. "We won't find another way."

"Hate that," Lexa said.

"We'll follow your lead," Blythe said.

"Right. I know the stairs are directly ahead. Just walk straight, and we'll be fine." Andi squared her shoulders and took a deep breath before she stepped through, despite everything logical telling her to not keep going.

It was strangely warm, but completely black all around her. She couldn't see Blythe, even though she knew she had to be right next to her. When she reached for her hand, she encountered a strange resistance.

"Okay." Her voice felt very close and small, though the room had to be large. "Berty?"

"I'm here." He was still on her shoulder. She scooped him into her hands, holding him close. "Remember what you said. Just go straight. It's going to be okay."

"Okay." She wasn't sure about that. Something about the dark felt menacing. Like she was willingly walking into the mouth of some great beast.

But she put one foot forward. And then another. Her boots didn't make a sound on the floor.

"Just walk straight," she said to herself. "You can do this."

"You can definitely do this."

Bertrand was cold in her hands, but even though he was tiny, his presence brought immense relief. She wasn't alone.

She could almost feel the shape of the room in her mind. A strange, hollow space. The pattern in the middle of the floor on the tiles. The way that the light had left it, fled to better places.

She stumbled.

"Andi?" Bertrand sounded very concerned.

"Just a little dizzy," she said. "It's really warm in here."

She hoped Lexa and Blythe were faring better than she was. Maybe they'd already made it to the stairs, waiting for her.

One more step, but it felt like she'd been running for days without resting. Like one more step would be all she had left in her. She wanted to sink to the floor, surely it would be cooler than the air around her.

"Keep going." Bertrand's voice was a distant thing. She struggled to take another step. Her foot felt glued to the floor.

A glowing figure threw itself in her path.

Chapter 40: Repetition

Andi screamed and staggered back, shielding her face with her hands.

Nothing happened.

"It's okay!" Bertrand yelled. "It's not a person!"

She slowly lowered her hands, ready to flinch back. To run.

The figure was still there. Too bright to make out any details. They looked like they were talking to someone, turned, lifted their hand, and were right back to speaking again.

Bertrand was right, it wasn't a person. They were transparent, the darkness visible through them where the details weren't washed out in white light. Slowly, Andi stepped closer. The warmth from before siphoned from the room, strengthening whatever magic was in front of her. The figure grew clearer, its details more defined, but it never stopped its cycle.

It was Silva.

Not as she'd ever seen him — gray skin and white hair. But as he must have looked in life. A pale man with long, dark hair. He spoke animatedly, using his hands.

"This is the Silva I remembered," Bertrand said, so quietly she almost didn't hear him. "Before I started working here. He came to my school to recruit, and this was what he was like. That's why I wanted to be here. I love books, and magic, and I always have, but I wanted to be this passionate."

This version of Silva looked like the kind of man she would have been happy working for. She understood exactly where Bertrand was coming from.

"I'm sorry," she whispered. Anything else felt too loud.

"It was war," Bertrand said. "In school, I was privileged enough to not be touched by it. We received the news, we heard what was happening, but it was always something happening somewhere else. Far away. And then…it wasn't."

"I'm still sorry." Andi didn't know what else she could possibly say. Obrye had been tearing itself apart since long before she was born, but in the library it barely touched her. "I think I understand."

"Yes." Bertrand seemed lost in thought, staring at the looping figure.

"So this room, it's for…illusions like this?" Andi asked. She looked to where Blythe had been. The light was bright enough Andi should have seen her, but she was alone. "Where is everyone else?"

"Illusions can be incredibly powerful," Bertrand said. "They're probably being affected differently than you are. But I don't think that's the whole story here. I think this is something else."

"Like what?" Andi stepped even closer. She was tempted to touch it, but she was afraid of shattering it.

"I think it might be a memory."

"A memory?" she glanced down at Bertrand.

"A…representation of memory," Bertrand said. "I've seen something similar. But this one is fragmented. Broken. There might be others. Be very careful."

She nodded and went to step around it. The memory of Silva looked right at her. His eyes were very blue.

He turned again.

It was just part of the illusion. Poorly timed.

That had to be it.

She walked forward. When she glanced back the memory was already growing weaker, a flickering candle flame. The next one appeared. It was Silva again, talking to someone she almost didn't recognize. It was Carmine. She was tall, as a witch, but not nearly as bulky. Her blond hair was still pulled back into a plait, but it barely reached past her shoulders. She looked kind.

Silva said something to her, moving his hands, and she responded. The memory stuttered and repeated. It was fainter than the last one, so faint she almost ran into Blythe.

Blythe, who was just standing there, staring at them.

"Blythe?" Andi thought for a moment that she might impossibly be an illusion, too. She touched her shoulder. Blythe started, badly, spinning to face her. Her face was completely neutral, like she'd become the statue she resembled, no expressions available to her.

It lasted only a moment, then her features crumpled to relief when she saw it was Andi. "Oh. Oh, you're here. I couldn't find you, and I tried to move forward, but I couldn't walk, and—"

"It's okay." Andi took her hand, squeezing it. "I'm here now. I'm not leaving you. I promise."

Blythe pulled her closer and rested her forehead against Andi's shoulder.

Andi didn't move for a moment, then lifted her free hand, running it through Blythe's hair. It was short, but soft, parting under her fingers like strands of silk. She leaned her head slightly against Blythe's, just holding her there.

Vampires didn't need to breathe, not if they were just standing there, but Blythe's breath came in soft, raspy pulls for a few minutes before it went silent, her shoulders settling into stillness.

"Thank you." Her voice was hoarser than ever.

"Always," Andi said. The room was terrifying for her, but how horrible must it have been for someone who was used to being able to see in the dark? To being able to sense everything? She couldn't even imagine.

"Why are we seeing this?" Blythe asked. "Is it some kind of trick, or…?"

"It's a memory," Andi said. "I don't want to access my archive here, I can't tell you exactly, but I think there are rooms like this. There were, anyway. A long time ago."

"I can tell you," Bertrand said. "Rooms like this weren't particularly common in my time. I suppose they must not be a thing anymore. It was a place where memories could be accessed. Like a memoir, but in the form of illusions, so I can't attest to their accuracy. The rooms were created to do most of the work. But this one is broken. Because of the library, the state it's in, how long it's been…or maybe Silva broke it himself. It's impossible to say."

"Maybe all of those." Blythe finally lifted her head. Andi missed the closeness almost immediately. "Where's Lexa?"

"Hopefully ahead of us," Andi said. "I can still feel where the stairs are. We're going the right way."

"That's good." Blythe didn't let go of her hand when she stepped back. "I don't particularly want to see this anymore. Let's go."

"Right." Andi glanced back at the memory.

Silva was looking right at her.

It was a jolt, almost painful, but the memory started looping again.

"What is it?" Bertrand asked.

"I thought…" Andi watched the whole loop, but Silva never glanced her way. "Nevermind."

Maybe she imagined it.

The air grew colder the farther they walked. She thought they must be across the room by now, but she had a feeling they weren't crossing an actual physical space.

Another memory.

Silva, again, looking more disheveled, more tired, talking to a tall, large man with mouse-brown hair and a dusty look to him. His clothes were impeccable, and he had a pair of smart, round glasses on, but his hair looked like he'd dragged his fingers through it several times.

"That's…me," Bertrand said.

"You?" Andi glanced down at the waistcoat she was wearing.

It was the same one.

Silva said something to Bertrand, turned, and the memory looped. Bertrand stood slightly awkwardly next to him, shoulders stooped. He was taller than Andi had pictured. At least a head taller than her. He had a softness to him, in the roundness of his face.

Despite the worry pinching his eyebrows together, he looked very kind.

"Oh Berty," she said, softly. She wished she could do something, say anything to warn the memory Bertrand about what was about to happen. To make things not play out the way they had.

"It's…well, it's not okay," Bertrand admitted. "But…it's just a memory. And…I died a very long time ago."

"We'll figure something out," Blythe said, softly. "You won't be a toad forever."

"You're a very kind person," Bertrand told her. "And don't believe anyone who says otherwise."

Andi opened her mouth to agree, when the memory of Silva looked at her.

"You must be the archive witch that's come to take over the library." His voiced echoed, as if from somewhere far away. She glanced over at Blythe and Bertrand, but they were chatting. She could see Blythe's mouth open, but she couldn't hear anything.

"This message is for your ears only." Silva looked tired. His hair was no longer neatly tied back, but loose around his shoulders. His face paler than ever. "I do not know what the future holds, but I am certain that I will not be part of it. Not as I should have been. There are things you need to know. Things only I can tell you. And we do not have much time."

Chapter 41: Explanations

"What do you mean?" Andi knew Silva's memory couldn't possibly hear her.

"I can't respond to any questions you have. I can only try to be as thorough as possible." Silva tugged a hand through his hair. "It's all gone completely wrong. The Empire of the Dawn is at our doorstep, but they don't care about Obrye and her citizens. And why would they? I don't know if anyone will find this, or what state the world will be in, but you need to know that the only thing they cared about is magic."

Andi knew that. It was common knowledge, four centuries later.

"What I don't know is how they found out that the library is at the center of it," Silva continued. "If I'm right, I doubt anyone here will survive. I might not even survive. I don't know what it will do to the coven leaders. I've cut off all contact between the crystals and the core, but that isn't enough. I have to curse the library."

She stared at him.

Blythe and Bertrand had stopped talking, but they were distant to the buzzing in her skull.

"I have no other choice, I've tried everything, and if I don't do this, the Empire of the Dawn will be here. I've tried so many things, terrible things, but this is the only way."

She doubted that. She wanted to scream at him, tell him there was always a choice. That there had to be another way. That if he was so clever and strong as to be made head librarian, he should have worked to find a solution that didn't sacrifice so many. That didn't plunge the entire continent into darkness. That didn't allow the vampires to spread like a disease.

"I am fusing my heart with the core."

Andi froze.

"This will force the library to shut down, and as long as I'm asleep, it will be, too," Silva said. "I have absolute faith that it won't take long for the library to find a new head librarian, someone who can reverse it. I don't know all of the side effects, and I don't have time to find out. This has to be done now. Immediately. The core should be directly above. Bertrand will have seen to it, by the time this message is relayed. I don't know what state you've found the library in, but know that before it was a library, it was the center of magic. You have to keep it alive. No matter the cost. Revive the library, reconnect the crystals, or I fear the world is doomed. If the coven leaders survive, they've been instructed to protect any archive witch they find."

Andi didn't know if that was true, but if it was, clearly those instructions had not been followed.

"If all goes well, it hasn't been very long, and I will be able to take back my heart and we can work together to fix things," Silva said. "But I'm very afraid that all will not go well. Save this place. Save Obrye. Whatever it takes."

The memory started looping again just as Blythe touched her shoulder.

She immediately sat down. Her legs didn't want to hold her anymore.

"Andi!" Blythe dropped next to her, cradling her face in her hands. They were cold, but Andi barely felt them. "Are you okay? What happened?"

"You were just staring at the memory," Bertrand said. "Did you find anything out?"

"Did you know?" Andi asked. She knew she wasn't being specific, that Bertrand had no way of knowing what she was asking.

"Know what?"

"That he…that he used his heart to make the curse?" she whispered. "That he fused it with the core?"

"No." Bertrand sounded as horrified as she felt. She knew he wasn't lying. "What are you talking about?"

"The memory, it spoke to me, it told me, are you sure you didn't know?" She had to ask again. She had to be sure.

"I swear."

She held him in her hands, trying to give some comfort. Trying to help. "I believe you."

"Is that why he had me move the core?" Bertrand whispered.

"He needed it as far away from him as possible," Andi explained, as best as she could. She knew she was skipping things. Blythe stared at Andi, but she couldn't return her gaze. "He thought that as long as he was asleep, the library would sleep, too. But he didn't count on turning himself into a monster. Turning everyone who uses magic into monsters. He killed you! He killed you and he didn't even explain and—"

She had to stop talking. She had to breathe. Blythe had her hands on her shoulders and looked deeply concerned, but she didn't seem to know what to say. Andi didn't know what she needed to hear.

"I'm going to fix it." Andi stood up. "I have to fix it, or…or the whole continent…But not the way he wants. I can't…I can't fix it the way he wants."

She was making very little sense, her words coming out in disjointed sentences, her thoughts too quick.

The center of all magic.

It made a horrible amount of sense. Why spells were created and stored there, why the library had been built.

How it had cursed the entire continent and disappeared for four centuries.

"What are you talking about?" Blythe used her cane to get back to her feet. "Andi—"

"I don't know!" She had no idea what she would do. She needed to break the curse. She couldn't break it. "I don't know. Let's get out of here. This room is horrible. I don't want to be here anymore."

"Okay." Blythe, thankfully, didn't ask anything else. She just took her hand. "Let's go."

"I'm not like him," she said.

"I know." Blythe didn't ask who she was talking about.

"I'd rather let the tree die than hurt you," she said. "I'd rather just not have magic at all. It hasn't done us any good, has it?"

"You know that's not true," Blythe said, quietly. "I don't know what you heard, exactly. I can't tell you what to do. But isn't saving everyone worth it?"

"No." She stopped walking. Blythe could have easily pulled her along, but she stopped, too. "No, it's not."

"Okay," Blythe said. "I don't really understand. Walk me through it."

"I…I have two choices," Andi explained. She took a deep breath. "I can let the curse run its course. Let the tree die. The magic would fade and things would go back to normal."

"And what's the second choice?" Blythe asked.

"I fix the core," Andi said. "I don't know what will happen if I do that. If I leave Silva's heart in there, then the library is still tied to him. All the magic in the continent is tied to him. If I remove it, then…then I think you'll die. You and every vampire and afflicted. You'll all die. The tree will live but at the cost of almost every citizen in Obrye."

Blythe seemed paler. Maybe it was the dark. Maybe it was a lack of blood. Or maybe, she was finally scared. "Are you certain?"

"She's right," Bertrand said. "A curse like this…everyone affected won't survive. But if she doesn't remove the heart, Silva will continue on, and it will be a temporary fix at best. At worst, everyone on the continent will be afflicted. And if she lets the tree die…the result could be the same, anyway."

Blythe's grip on her hand was tight enough to hurt, but she didn't say anything.

"I don't…I don't want to…" Andi's cheeks were wet. She'd started crying. She wiped fruitlessly at her face with her too big sleeve. "I don't know what to do. I'm scared, Blythe. I'm so scared. I'm the only one who can do anything, and I don't know what to do. I don't know what choice is best."

Blythe stepped closer, pulling Andi's forehead onto her shoulder.

"Please, help me." Andi knew she was putting an impossible burden on Blythe's shoulders. That the only person who could make a decision was her, even if it felt too big. Too impossible.

"Of course," Blythe's voice was soft. Her touch was soft, too. "Of course I'll help you."

"What do I do?" Andi's own voice was a broken, pleading thing.

"You have two choices that you can't make," Blythe said. "So the only solution is to make your own decision."

"I can't—"

"I mean, that if both options are too horrible, then come up with another option." Blythe's fingers were in her hair. "Find another way. Make a third choice."

Chapter 42: Planetarium

"A third choice?" Andi's voice cracked. "But—"

"You are the smartest person I know," Blythe said.

Andi laughed, despite her tears, despite the anxiety. It was sad, and a little broken, but it didn't devolve into hysteria. "You know Chrys."

"I do know them, quite well in fact, and you're still the smartest," Blythe said.

"I think you're biased," Andi sniffed.

"Hm. No. I think that my assessment is completely factual."

Andi giggled, despite herself. "Not just because I'm pretty?"

"Oh, well, that's not even a question," Blythe said. "I thought you were cute right away. Insane, but adorable. And now I know you're brilliant, and funny, and amazing."

Andi took a step back, wiping her face with her sleeve. "You're sweet, but I don't feel like any of those things. Just some weird girl who keeps crying on you."

"I would let you cry on me every day," Blythe said. "But I think I'd prefer to make you smile."

"You've known me for what, three days?" Andi asked.

Blythe shrugged. "I think I've made you smile at least three times, so I'm doing okay so far. It doesn't make any of what I say less true. Besides, we already agreed to not worry about what's coming. If all I have is here and now, I want to make you smile. I want to be here for you. I want to do anything I can."

"Thank you." Andi did smile at that, and Blythe smiled back. She was all silver and black, a beautiful brilliance. A moon pinned up in the sky just for her.

"Of course." Blythe nodded. "What do you want?"

"I don't want to be here anymore," Andi said.

"Me either," Bertrand agreed. Andi had almost forgotten he was there, he'd been so quiet. At least he knew when to be quiet. "I mean, here is fine, on your shoulder, but this room is terrible, and I don't like it. Can we go?"

Blythe nodded.

Memories moved around them stuttering and transparent. Ghosts repeating actions over and over again.

Andi ignored them, focusing on Blythe's hand in hers. The lantern light didn't even show the floor beneath her feet. She could see herself, and Blythe, but everything else was lost to the dark. She knew it must be part of the magic in the room, twisted and broken as it was, but it was still unnerving. She could have been walking on air and she never would have known.

Bertrand curled up under her collar, cold through the cotton of her shirt, but she didn't really mind.

She'd never been so happy to find the other side of the room. She leaned her forehead against the stair railing. "This was the worst room."

"Really? Even with the laboratory?" Blythe asked.

"Okay, second worse room, but it's a really close second." Andi didn't move. The smooth metal of the railing felt amazing after a long period of absolutely nothing. Real, solid, and very dusty. That thought made her stand up.

Just as Lexa loomed out of the dark.

Andi squeaked and backed into Blythe, who grabbed her around the shoulders to keep them both upright.

"Wow," Lexa said. "Are you serious right now?"

"You're okay!" Andi grabbed her in a hug. "I couldn't find you, and it was so dark, and I was worried—"

"I've been here for ages," Lexa said. "It's really not a big room. Where have you been? I was about to drag you over here."

"You didn't see the memories?" Andi had a strange pit in her stomach. If she'd been with Lexa, would she have missed the memories, too? She never would have encountered the memory of Silva. Never would have gotten the information she needed.

Would she still feel like everything was moving too fast? Blurs of color streaking around her while she stood, frozen, unable to go forward?

She honestly couldn't say.

"I have no idea what you're talking about." Lexa closed the distance between them in a few strides. "Have you been crying? Did she make you cry?"

"No," Andi said. "I mean, yes, I cried, but not because of her. She helped, actually. But you really didn't see anything?"

"I saw a dark room," Lexa said. "Couldn't see you guys, but you said go forward, so I did. We should have all held hands from the start. Pretty stupid of us to be afraid of holding hands now. You two are always doing it."

"Jealous?" Blythe wiggled her eyebrows.

"Hardly." Lexa rolled her eyse. "I don't want to hold your hand, I bet it's like holding onto a wet napkin."

"It's really not," Andi said.

"I don't really trust you opinion when it comes to her." Lexa shrugged. "You're my best friend, but no. I'm not going to get jealous of some weird vampire just because she wants to hold your hand."

Blythe grinned. "You sound jealous."

"Can we focus, please?" Andi asked. "Why couldn't you see anything? We…we ran into so much…"

"She's not a vampire, or an archive witch," Bertrand explained. "She had no connection to the memories, so they didn't appear for her."

"Okay, someone explain, in an order and with words that I can understand," Lexa said.

Andi let Bertrand tell Lexa all about it. The flight of stairs was short, but it was slow going. Andi could barely see the stairs at all, even on the other side of the room. She glanced back over the railing. A memory of Silva was the last one still active. It was looking right at her. She looked away with a shudder.

"That's insane," Lexa told Bertrand. "What are you gonna do, Ands?"

"I don't know," she admitted. It was overwhelming to think about. "I'll…I'll figure something out."

"Yeah, of course you will." Lexa nodded. "You're the smartest person I know."

"That's exactly what I told her," Blythe agreed. Lexa grinned at her.

Andi managed a weak smile. "You know, buttering me up like this won't work. You're both still banned from my library for life."

Blythe laughed, maybe a little too loudly for the joke, but it made Andi warm all the same.

They reached the top of the stairs and were immediately met with another door. It shone even in the dark — blond wood with a deep blue inlay. Golden stars shone in the wood, moving almost imperceptibly. It made the door they couldn't open look like a pale imitation.

A streak of light shot across the door, disappearing through the other side.

"Shooting star, make a wish," Lexa said.

Andi closed her eyes.

She wished that she would be clever enough to come up with a solution.

That she would be strong enough to protect everyone.

And that when she opened the door it would be an empty floor. Or maybe the top of the tree. That nothing would be waiting for them.

Most of all, she wished that the universe would be gentle to them. To her. Just once. If only one wish came true, she hoped it was that one.

She reached for the door, all of her wishes still held in her chest, and turned the golden handle with a blue constellation she didn't recognize carved into it. It rotated easily under her hand.

The door swung open.

"Color me surprised, it's yet another dark room." Lexa stepped in front of them.

Andi didn't dare turn her light on any brighter, and the lights didn't go on when they walked in. All she could make out was rows of bookshelves on either side of them. When she glanced back the door was hidden by a bookshelf. She tried to remember where it was, just in case.

The room opened up. She turned her lantern up a bit higher. The light glinted on something in front of her. Something huge.

"What is that?" Blythe asked.

"Looks like a giant spider."

"No." Andi took a step back.

"It's not actually a giant spider, Ands, calm down." Lexa sounded like she was probably rolling her eyes.

"Then don't say that!" Andi glared at her shoulder blades.

It did look horribly like an enormous spider crouched, waiting for them.

"It's metal." Blythe knocked her cane against part of it, and the clang reverberated through the open space.

Something whirred beneath them, vibrated the floorboards under her feet. It grew louder and the thing in the middle of the room began to turn, spreading its legs and opening like a flower. Blythe pulled her back before she got hit by one of the arms as it rotated out.

A spark of magic and the middle lit up, so bright that she flinched and shielded her eyes.

It was a sun lamp.

They were inside a planetarium.

One by one the planets started to glow, starting closest to the sun and moving out to the farthest planet, a tiny thing. It turned, slightly, beginning its orbit, but quickly ground to a halt. The earth shone blue and green. The moon was in full view, reflecting the sun's light in a silver beacon.

Another rumble.

It wasn't from under the floor.

It was Lexa.

Chapter 43: Moondust

"Lexa…?" Andi reached for her.

Blythe yanked her back. Lexa snarled and lunged. Blythe barely got her cane up in time, fending her off.

"It's the moon!" Blythe kicked Lexa in the chest, sending her sliding backwards on the smooth floor. Her claws dug furrows in the wood.

Andi whipped her head around to look at the planetarium. The sun shone so brightly it hurt her eyes. Behind it the moon was a pale and glowing shape.

The full moon.

"That's not even fair!" Bertrand yelled.

She ignored him. If she could get to the planetarium, if she could move it just a little bit, it might be enough.

Andi ran. Her boots pounded on the floor in time to her heartbeat. A loud crash behind her, but she couldn't stop. Couldn't even risk a glance behind her.

Something hit her between the shoulder blades. Pain shot up her spine and she hit the ground, hard. She was flipped over before she could even catch her breath.

And looked right up into Lexa's face.

Her eyes, normally amber, paled to a gleaming yellow. Her teeth protruded from her mouth, cutting her lips, too large for her jaw even as it lengthened into a muzzle. She grew taller, her back hunched, her arms so long she could touch the floor, her fingernails curved claws. The growl in her throat rumbled in Andi's ribcage.

Andi only had seconds before Lexa finished her transformation.

She hadn't had one in years.

Andi yanked her silver dagger from the sheath on her bag. She sliced through the air in front of her. Lexa reared back, enough that she could sit up and scramble back, somehow finding the strength to get to her feet.

Lexa roared, a horrible wave of sound, and leaped at her.

Blythe slammed her cane into Lexa's shoulder, knocking her back into one of the arms of the planetarium. It made a hollow ringing sound.

"Go!" Blythe screamed.

Blythe drove Lexa back into the shelves. One toppled over, slamming to the floor, loose pages exploding into the air.

Andi scrambled to look for controls, a way to at least turn the contraption around, but there was nothing in the room with them. She didn't even know how it worked. She didn't have time to send her magic into it. She pressed her shoulder against one of the corroded copper bars with everything she had.

It didn't budge.

"Uh, Andi, I think you need to move!" Bert yelled.

She sheathed her dagger and clambered onto the bar, corrosion flaking off on her hands, staining her palms blue and green.

The supports were just close enough to the ground she could climb them like a ladder. She clambered up through the mess of bars. The earth was large enough to hold her and she gingerly stepped down on it, afraid it was hollow. It dipped down beneath her foot, and she held onto the bars so tightly it hurt her hands.

"Can you move it?" Bertrand asked.

"The moon is only completely full for an instant," Andi said. "But a transformation lasts all night. I don't think I can move it enough to matter."

"So, what, knock it down?" Bertrand suggested.

"Moon set, or close enough," Andi agreed. She tried not to think about how far away the floor was. How if she didn't die from the fall, an angry and out of control werewolf would be on her in seconds to finish the job. Silver knife or not, she didn't have a chance of surviving.

When they were younger, Lexa's wolf form hadn't been dangerous. At least, not to her. Andi spent plenty of time with her as a wolf.

But that was before the dark, before the moon had been hidden behind a thick layer of clouds for years.

Lexa couldn't have the same control. It was a miracle she hadn't killed anyone already.

All she could do now was try to save her friend.

She reached the bar that connected the earth to the moon and kicked it. The impact rattled up to her knee.

The moon stayed serene and full.

"Oh, come on," she whispered.

A rippling growl directly below her froze her to the support.

Lexa was slowly circling the floor directly beneath the moon.

She was a hulking mixture of human and lupine. Thick gray and brown covered her completely. Her spine curved and hunched to accommodate her longer arms. She lifted her muzzle and stared up at Andi, her eyes glowing like candles in her dark sclera.

Andi couldn't see Blythe anywhere.

"Andi…" Bertrand's voice was tiny.

"I see her," Andi whispered back. Lexa's large ears twitched. Her lips pulled back and she bared her significantly larger teeth. A growl rumbled in her throat.

And Andi was stuck on an ancient copper bar, far above the ground. Her bag threatened to pull her off the side, but she didn't dare drop it. The lantern was still attached and she had a feeling she was going to need it.

She refused to die here.

No one was going to die.

Lexa continued to circle, her skin twitching as her bones stretched and changed. Her shirt and pants ripped, boots destroyed. She'd lost her sword. Andi didn't think it mattered, not with the length of her claws.

"Maybe we're up too high?" Bertrand suggested.

Andi shook her head. "We're not."

The only reason they were still alive was because Lexa wasn't done changing.

The second the transformation was finished she'd be up there with them. Andi still had the dagger, but even if one tiny silver blade could fend off a full changed and out of control werewolf, which she highly doubted, she didn't want to hurt Lexa. Silver could poison her, could kill her.

There had to be another way.

Another choice.

"Berty, I'm going to do something really stupid." She pulled him off her shoulder and put him in her sling. She hoped it held.

"Andi—"

"It's a sunlamp, and th-the moon must be coated in moondust," Andi said. "If I can break a chunk off, then—"

"No!"

Whatever the rest of Bertrand's protest was, she didn't hear it. She pushed herself off the earth and leaped over to the much smaller moon.

She made it, just barely, scrabbling to stay on top. The whole structure shuddered. The bar let out a horrible, creaking groan.

It held.

She lay flat on her stomach, craters giving her fingers just enough purchase to hold on. The moon was barely big enough to hold her.

She felt like a piece of cheese on a stick.

Her hands were shaking so badly she cut herself on the dagger blade when she freed it from its sheath and nearly dropped it. Her blood made the hilt slick. She got a good enough grip on it and smashed the pommel against the moon.

A deep, hollow boom.

Lexa reared back, clapping her misshapen hands over her ears.

Andi hoped for a crack, or at least a dent, but nothing had changed. She tried again. Another boom. That time the hilt pulled on the cut on her palm and jarred out of her hand.

It clattered far, far below. Bertrand was saying something, but she couldn't make out the words. It was too much, the growl beneath her, the sting on her hand, her aching ribs from her jump.

She was bleeding badly. Her hand could have been on fire and it couldn't have hurt more. Red soaked into the moon dust, pooling in a false crater underneath her hand.

Shifting her weight to take the pressure off the bar groaned again.

Lexa threw back her head and howled.

The noise was horrific, much worse than her hitting the moon a few times. The high, almost sing-song call of a wolf, underlaid by a deep, pulsing explosion of sound that twisted itself in Andi's guts, flattening her further against the surface.

Lexa jumped from the ground directly to the moon's support in one smooth motion.

Andi screamed, trying to move, but she had nowhere to go. The moon bobbed underneath her. There was a planet below her, a globe of blues and greens that glimmered with its own light, but it was too far away. She'd never reach it.

She'd lost the knife. She hadn't damaged the moon at all.

Lexa slowly crawled towards her, hand over hand. Almost lazily, knowing she had all the time in the world.

"Lexa." Andi had to try. She had to do something, anything but sit there and wait to die. "Lexa please. You know me."

If Lexa even recognized her own name, it didn't show.

It had been too long. Andi's archive flitted through her mind, like a life flashing before her eyes, but there wasn't a single spell in there that would save her.

A crack.

The entire structure let out a terrible grating. Andi scrambled to hold onto the rough rock.

The moon dipped, bounced up, and both the earth and the moon snapped off their supports.

A scream was ripped from Andi's throat. She was weightless. Her stomach was somewhere above her.

The earth hit the floor with a tremendous crash. The impact knocked Andi off of the moon. She rolled across the floor. A reddish planet slammed into the floor inches away from her head and bounced off.

She covered her head with her arms and waited for the crashing and banging to stop.

It didn't for a long time.

Chapter 44: Dust

Silence.

Andi dared to move her arms. Her wrist banged against one of the support columns. She bit her lip to stop herself from swearing, tucking her hand up to her chest.

The bars formed a tent over her, leaning against each other.

It was the only thing that had stopped her from being crushed.

"We're alive," Bertrand whispered, his words muffled.

She didn't dare reply. She wiggled her way out of the debris. Her skirt never would have survived. She was certain none of her current clothes would be in any shape for rescue. Focusing on that kept her from thinking about what waited beyond the metal supports.

Her bag caught a few times, and finally she left it where it was. She unhooked the lantern and carefully pulled it out with her.

The giant sun lamp had gone out.

The lantern was the last light she had.

She struggled past cracked planets and spots where the floorboards had broken into jagged teeth. She couldn't hear Lexa. She didn't know where Blythe was.

Thick dust filled the air like fog. Even with the lantern she could barely see. She coughed and dragged the collar of her undershirt up over her mouth and nose. The sour tang still coated her tongue, but at least she could breathe.

"Are you okay?" Bertrand whispered.

"I don't think anything's broken." She didn't bother whispering. If Lexa was conscious, she'd know exactly where Andi was. She hurt all over, but nothing stood out from the overall ache except for her hand, but she couldn't worry about that. "Got lucky. What about you?"

"I mean, I'm not lost, so I'm doing better than expected. Let's find the others."

"Lexa?" She tried to call. Maybe her friend was somewhere in the rubble, already conscious. Her ears were still ringing. "Blythe?"

Bertrand shushed her. She froze, wrapping her arm around her lantern to keep the light dim.

Someone picked their way carefully through the debris.

It might be Blythe. It could even be Lexa.

Andi knew it wasn't either of them. They would have called her name. They would have found her by now.

She crouched behind the fallen rings of one of the planets. The dust burned her throat and stung her eyes. She bit her lip hard. She needed to brighten the lantern. She needed to swing it up and around. If it wasn't Lexa or Blythe, it must have been a vampire. She could fight off a vampire, at least for a little while.

Her fingers trembled.

She couldn't force herself to move any more than that.

No matter how much she screamed at herself to get up, to fight, to do anything, she stayed exactly where she was. Crouched down behind a piece of the planetarium and praying that whoever it was gave up.

A hand shot out and grabbed her ponytail.

She shrieked and clawed at it. It made no difference. She was dragged out into the open.

She swung her lantern and the hand let go of her hair to grab her wrist.

A massive, gray-skinned hand.

"Hello again, little witch." Carmine yanked her back. She was missing an arm. Her face was horribly burned on that side, and she limped when she dragged Andi through the debris. "You know, Silva wanted you alive. You could have just come quietly. But you had to go and make a big old mess, didn't you?"

"Did you do this?" Andi's voice was too high, too shaky.

"Silva went on and on about how the moon was so realistic it could affect a werewolf. I just wanted to see if it was true." Carmine bared her long, white teeth in a horrible parody of a smile. Her eyes glittered like rubies. "And there it was. I was hoping the bitch would finish you off, but at least it's just you and me now."

"If Silva wants me alive, why are you doing this?" Andi had to think quickly. She was all alone with an elder vampire. Even with one arm, Carmine was incredibly dangerous. Maybe more so than she had been before, and Andi couldn't think of a single thing she could do to stop her.

"Do you have any idea what I did for him?" Carmine snarled. "I've been killing archive witches for centuries. I've been keeping his stupid little library asleep. And now he's awake and what, he thinks he's in charge again? I can't believe one of you survived."

Her grip tightened and Andi poured magic into the lantern. The light flared, sending jagged shadows across the floor. Carmine lurched back, letting go of Andi to cover her eyes.

Andi scrambled back. She needed a weapon. Anything that would keep Carmine at bay. Her hand landed on a piece of support and she held it up. The point wavered unsteadily, even when she tucked it under her arm.

Carmine barked out a laugh. "You really think you can kill me?"

"Just stay away from me." Andi's voice was as shaky as her hands. "Just leave me alone."

"Oh, but I can't do that," Carmine purred. "After all, you're the one that got away. I have to make it right. How did you survive, anyway?"

"I hid under the floorboards when you slaughtered my entire village."

Andi's terror slowly burned away to anger. A burning rage that she hadn't realized she still carried with her, every day. Carmine had killed everything she'd ever known. Everyone she had ever cared about. And for what? To hold onto power for a little bit longer?

"Ah. Well. That's too bad," Carmine said. "Too bad you weren't as brave then. If you'd come out, maybe I wouldn't have killed them all. Or maybe I still would have. I guess we'll never know."

"You're a monster," Andi spat at her.

Carmine laughed again. "Oh, sweetheart, but you're the one that's getting all cuddly with a vampire. The same thing that killed your whole family. She might have been there. Honestly, it all blurs together after a while."

"Don't talk about her," Andi snapped.

"She wants you to think she's some knight in shining armor, that you can rely on her, but she's just like the rest of us," Carmine said. "She's always been like that. Nothing has changed."

"You don't know her at all."

"Oh, we were together for a very long time, I know her pretty well," Carmine said. "After all, I'm the one that turned her. But you know, despite everything, I'm in a generous mood. My arm will grow back, so no harm no foul."

Andi was confused, but she kept the bar up, even though it was heavy. Even though her hand was still bleeding, leaving red streaks on the metal.

"You don't get it, do you," Carmine was directly in front of her before she could blink, ripping the bar out of her hand and throwing it to the side. She grabbed Andi's face, her claws biting into the skin at her jaw. "I'm willing to compromise, just to piss Silva off. It's a pretty good deal, for you. No more worry, no more fear, and you have an eternity with your little girlfriend. Or at least until you get bored of her."

"No," Andi whispered.

"I'll even turn you into a proper vampire," Carmine said. "Aren't you lucky, running into an elder vampire now. Don't worry, it'll only hurt for a moment."

"No," Andi said it louder. More broken. The terror doused her anger.

"I'm not asking for permission. I think this will be fun." Carmine opened her mouth. Andi tried to swing the lantern, but Carmine didn't even notice the sizzle of her own skin.

"Leave her alone!" Bertrand yelled, his voice too tiny in the cavernous silence.

"Quiet, unless you want to be crushed."

Andi covered him with her hand, it was all she could do. One of them had to make it out.

Her fangs were needles. She turned Andi's head to the side, exposing the vein on the side of her neck. Andi whimpered and closed her eyes.

She'd lost everything. She hadn't saved anyone.

A meaty thunk filled the air.

There was no pain.

Andi dared to look.

Sharp white points protruded from Carmine's chest. She let go of Andi to touch one.

"You," she choked out. "How…?"

"We never really saw eye to eye, Carmine." Silva's voice was even and calm. His shirt was open, his ribs stabbed through Carmine's back. "Pity. We were friends once. Goodbye."

"You—"

Carmine never got a chance to finish. She shriveled into nothing, so quickly that Andi didn't have time to look away. Gone in seconds.

Silva's ribs folded back into his chest, the skin sealing up into an ugly looking wound. He unhurriedly did up his shirt, then waistcoat. "Apologies, for that unpleasantness. Hello, Andrea. I believe you met my memory, but I will ask you again. Will you help me?"

Chapter 45: Breathless

Andi stared at the spot Carmine had stood, just a moment before.

"Andrea, did you hear me?" Silva asked.

"Where are Lexa and Blythe?" Andi didn't want to agree to anything he said, let alone help him. He was just as monstrous as Carmine. Maybe worse. He'd been a monster before he ever even turned.

"Blythe is safe," Silva didn't elaborate. "Lexa…well. I wouldn't worry. I'll have Tana find her. She must be under here somewhere."

Andi's hands hurt from her gripping the lantern handle.

"The same Tana that controlled her?" Bertrand asked. He'd poked his head from between Andi's fingers.

"Ah. Bertrand." Silva's expression shifted from vaguely curious to completely blank. "How good to see you."

Bertrand snorted. "Can't say the same."

"As for Tana, yes, it will be—"

A wisp of smoke curled in the air and formed the shape of a woman, blowing away in an instant and leaving behind a beautiful elder vampire. She was taller than Andi but just as curvy. Her plunging neckline left little to the imagination, a silver chain glittering between her breasts. Her white hair fell straight down her back like a shower of silk. Unlike Carmine and Silva, she had pale green eyes. Phosphorescent in the dark.

"One and the same." She gave him a little wave, smiling wide enough to show off her fangs. "Hi, Berty. Don't worry. I won't control the little wolfie unless I'm asked."

"Find her, don't control her," Silva said. "Andrea, come with me. We need to take care of your hand."

"I could help with that." Tana's smile grew impossibly wider.

Andi shook her head. "No, thank you."

"Pity. Pleasure to make your acquaintance formally," Tana said. "I hear we'll be working together in the future."

"Now, that's not set in stone," Silva reminded her, still too calm. "Come along."

Andi had no choice. She had to follow Silva. They picked through the debris. Lexa had to be okay. Werewolves were strong, resilient, and incredibly fast healers even in human form. Once she was pulled from the rubble, she would be fine. She had to be.

All Andi could do was hope Silva wasn't lying.

But he had lied about so many things.

She tried to find Blythe, amid the wreckage of the planetarium and the broken room, but she didn't see anything. No gleam of her hair, or a glint of her cane.

Silva walked back into the stacks, moving slowly so Andi could keep up. She was getting dizzy, each step seemed to take too long, but she had to keep moving. Her friends had protected her so many times. She wouldn't let them down when their lives were in her hands.

Silva opened the shelf and stepped inside, onto the delicate curl of a spindly staircase. Darkness encroached on the edges of Andi's vision, but she followed him up, step after step, trying not to think about where she was going.

A dark wood door awaited them on the next floor, laced with a filigree of golden leaves. Silva opened it and stepped back, gesturing gallantly into the room. "After you."

She didn't want him behind her.

Not that it made any difference.

She bit the inside of her cheek hard enough to sting and stepped inside.

Candles flared to life the moment her foot cleared the threshold, painting the office on the other side in a cozy glow. It was much bigger than she expected, but the only detail she had eyes for was Blythe.

She was standing at the other end of the room, surrounded by glowing red glyphs.

"Blythe!" Andi ignored Silva and the inherent danger, hurrying to her.

"Andi." Blythe stepped forward, but the glyphs glowed harshly. She bared her teeth and smacked her hand against an invisible barrier. Her cane and coat were missing, and she had an arm around her torso. "Are you okay?"

"I'm...I'm okay." She was alive. They were all alive, for now. "How...?"

"Lexa got me pretty good." Blythe smiled, but it was more of a grimace. "Woke up here. I'm so glad you're okay, I heard a crash, and I was terrified..."

The initial relief was gone, and the words Carmine said floated through her mind.

Looking at her, Andi couldn't imagine it.

"Andi?" Blythe's eyebrows drew together. "Are you sure you're all right?"

It had been a long time ago, and she had been a full vampire. Did that excuse it? Did that make things okay?

Andi had known, deep down, that of course Blythe had done things that she couldn't possibly agree with. But she wasn't that person anymore. She hadn't been for decades. Maybe she had never been that person to begin with.

Andi had to let it go, or she would be consumed by what ifs and maybes.

She had to believe that everyone had the capacity to change. Even a vampire.

Silva stepped up behind her. "We have things to discuss."

"Let her out, or I won't listen to a word you say."

"Fine, if you insist." Silva snapped his fingers. The glyphs sputtered out and Blythe lurched forward, grabbing Andi's shoulders, looking her up and down. "I think that it goes without saying that if either of you try anything, I'll tell Tana to kill your friend."

"Is she okay?" Andi had to ask, even if she didn't believe the answer.

"She'll survive, if you don't do anything foolish."

"Right." Andi nodded.

She'd left Lexa back there.

With the vampire that had controlled her.

What else could she have done? All of her choices were being made for her, things moving too quickly.

"It's okay," Bertrand whispered. "It's going to be okay."

"Sit down." Silva indicated a plush emerald chair. She sat gingerly, but it wasn't dusty. Silva's office must have been sealed the same way Bertrand's rooms were. "Put down that lantern."

She set it in her lap.

"Hold out your hand."

Silva took her hand, turning it over. "Not as bad as I feared. A clean cut. Unfortunately, I no longer have access to my spells. Luckily for you, I'm always prepared."

He moved to the large desk and procured a medical kit from one of the green cabinets behind it. He opened the kit and pulled out several dark glass bottles and a square of gauze and a few strips of clean cloth. He poured the contents of one of the bottles onto a cloth. It smelled like disinfectant, though she couldn't read the spidery handwriting on the label.

He gently cleaned the cut on her hand, along with a few scrapes on her face. She closed her eyes, waiting for the sting, but the effect was more cooling than painful.

He placed the gauze on it and wrapped it up, carefully. Clinically.

"There. I'm no healer, but I became quite adept in the art in my later years," Silva said. He sounded proud. He didn't ask if she was still hurt. Blythe stood behind her the entire time. "We will have our discussion when I return. I need to tend to your friend."

"Why are you doing this?" Andi's voice broke at the end of the question.

Silva just smiled and left the room. The door clicked shut behind him.

Blythe helped her to her feet and hugged her, carefully. Andi rested her forehead against her shoulder, like she had done so many times in the last few days. She breathed in candle smoke and cloves.

It didn't matter. The Blythe who had cool fingers cradling the back of her head wasn't the one that Carmine had twisted into something that fit her needs. Maybe she wasn't a knight in shining armor, but she was kind.

Andi's shoulders relaxed. They weren't out of the woods, but the tear she hadn't realized was waging war in her chest closed.

"I don't know what he's trying to pull, putting us all in danger like that, and—"

"It was Carmine." Andi didn't lift her head. "She…she was still alive."

Blythe stiffened. "Oh."

"She tried to turn me," Andi recounted. It shouldn't have been so easy, but the words slipped out of her like water pouring from a cup. "Silva killed her before she could."

"…Oh." Blythe sounded like she didn't know how to feel. "Well. I…I won't miss her."

"You don't have to," Andi whispered.

"I know. I feel like I should," Blythe admitted. "But I won't. She was a monster. I should have realized a long time ago."

"It's hard to see, sometimes," Andi said. She'd been afraid she'd been in the same position, but in that moment, she knew she hadn't been.

"I suppose so." Blythe nodded. "What does Silva want?"

"He hasn't said," Andi said. "But it must have to do with the core. With the…the magic. I don't have a third choice yet. I don't know what to do. I can't leave it. I have to do something."

"You'll figure it out," Bertrand said. Andi leaned back enough to let him hop onto her hand. She put him on the arm of the chair. "You're the smartest person I've met."

"Oh, really?" She had to smile a bit.

"Well, technically I haven't met myself, so yes." Bertrand puffed himself up. She laughed at that. It was a little high, a little thready, but it helped.

When she looked back at Blythe, the smile on her face was achingly gentle.

"What?" Andi asked.

"I have to admit, I'm terrified," Blythe said. "But I trust you. And if now is the last moment we have alone, if this is it—"

"It won't be," Andi said, quickly, though she had no idea if that was true. She didn't know what the next few minutes held, let alone hours or days.

"But if it is, then I just need one thing." Blythe's fingers brushed her cheekbone, gently, tucking the errant strand of hair that never stayed back behind her ear, cupping her cheek. "May I?"

Andi leaned forward and kissed her.

Her lips were cool and soft. She cradled Andi's face like it was the most important thing in the world.

It wasn't a deep kiss, or a long one, but it left Andi lightheaded, anyway.

Blythe pulled away and rested her forehead against Andi's. Her eyes closed. Eyelashes snow dusting her pale cheeks. Impossibly still, a beautiful marble statue.

Andi didn't say a word. She didn't want the moment to end. If she could make it stretch on, impossibly long, then she would have.

But maybe it was all the sweeter because it ended, Blythe leaning back when the door opened.

"Your friend will be fine." Silva swept into the room. He snapped his fingers and chairs pulled up on their own, one for Blythe next to her, and another so he could sit across from her. The glyphs on the furniture glowed red, burning into the wood like they would go out any moment.

"If she gets hurt…" Andi started to warn him, though she had no idea how she would finish it.

"She'll be awake soon, I've told Tana to fill her in on the details," Silva said, like it wasn't a terrible idea. Like Tana hadn't possessed her. "Now. We have something important to discuss, and it can't wait a moment longer. The library is dying."

Chapter 46: Core

Andi knew he was telling the truth. She could feel it, deep down. "Because of your curse."

"Precisely." Silva folded his hands. "While my actions did save the library and the continent initially, clearly it had…unintended and unforeseen consequences."

"Yeah, unforeseen," Berty muttered. "Because sticking your rotting heart into something wouldn't have any bad consequences at all."

"Oh, Bertrand, you've grown quite the spine, considering how very small and insignificant you are."

Silva didn't move, but Andi scooped Bertrand up, anyway, holding him close. "What can I do?"

"So, you'll help?" Silva leaned forward.

"I never said that." She had every intention of doing something, of trying to fix things, but she wasn't going to promise to do what he wanted. She couldn't. "I asked what you think I can do about it."

"You can reconnect the core to the tree," Silva said. "That will ensure the tree's survival. The continued survival of the entire continent. You're the only one that can, thanks to Carmine's…escapades. I want you to know that I had nothing to do with that. I asked her to keep the archive witches safe. If I had it my way, we would have an entire team for this endeavor. Unfortunately, it's just you. I cannot help, and neither can Bertrand."

"What about the curse?" Andi asked. "This much darkness can't be healthy for anything."

Anything but a vampire, but even they would eventually wither and die when there was nothing left for them but a dark, barren wasteland.

"I cannot say, I imagine the inclusion of your magic and the core being reconnected would lessen it, at least somewhat," Silva said. "Breaking the curse is out of the question. I believe you've already figured out why."

"Everyone afflicted by the curse would die," she said.

Thousands of people, gone in an instant.

"Precisely." Silva nodded. "Is it really so bad? Immortality? I know Carmine offered it to you. I know that you considered it."

Blythe jerked, like she wanted to move, but she pressed herself back into her chair instead.

Andi knew some part of her had considered it. Immortality was a temptation. There was no question about that. It didn't matter who a person was, and she knew she was no different. The amount of work she could do, that she could study and read, was staggering. An entire eternity ahead of her, full of anything she wanted.

With Blythe at her side. Forever.

Never changing, never aging.

An endless nightmare.

Things were sweeter because they ended.

"No, thank you," she said. "I'll help save the library, but I don't need that."

"Of course, it is something that's best left as a discussion for later, anyway." Silva stood. Blythe's cane was in his hand, even though it hadn't been a moment before. He must have tucked it behind his desk. "You should be aware that if you decided to allow me to turn you, some part of your magic would stay with you. Something that you found…particularly useful. Mine was being able to absorb anything I desired. You know of Carmine and Tana's. It's nothing you can consciously choose, but you wouldn't be without. If that might sway your decision."

Andi knew it didn't matter what she said. He would assume that was the decision she would make.

He tossed the cane at Blythe, who caught it with ease.

"Do you need rest?" Silva asked her. "We have little time, but there should be time for that."

Andi shook her head. Time wouldn't help her. "I'm fine."

"Splendid." Silva stood up, offering her his hand. She didn't want to touch him, but she let him assist her. Better to suffer unpleasantness than irritate him.

His hand felt like dead leaves.

She wanted to wipe the sensation away the moment her hand was free. She didn't dare. Blythe stood without help, but she leaned heavily on her cane.

"Can you go with Blythe?" she asked Berty.

He nodded and hopped onto Blythe's hand.

Andi picked her lantern up from where it had fallen into the corner of the seat.

"You won't need that," Silva said.

"Please, I…just let me have this," she whispered. She knew it wouldn't help her, but it was comforting to hold. The only bit of insurance she had, for whatever it was worth.

"If you must." Silva opened the door, holding it open for her. "After you, my dear."

She kept her face as neutral as she could. She couldn't let her revulsion show. Silva wouldn't hurt her, but that wasn't what she was afraid of. She glanced at Blythe.

"Your friend is welcome to come," Silva said. "It might provide you with some incentive to make the right choice."

"Thank you." Andi didn't know what else to say. The words were stones in her mouth she wanted to spit out. Silva let Blythe walk between them. Andi knew it didn't matter. If he decided he wanted her dead there was nothing that could save her.

She wanted to go to the core anyway. If he wanted to lead the way, then she would let him.

The wall gave way to an enormous window. An inky darkness lay beyond, occasionally cracked in half by a flash of red lightning. Andi could just see their reflections. Even Silva had one. She'd once heard that elder vampires cast no reflection. Maybe that was only in mirrors.

Emerald light glowed through the glass. The guardian moved ponderously across the window. She stepped away.

"It won't harm you," Silva said, quietly.

Blythe sounded less convinced. "It tried before."

"It's injured, and confused, but it will listen to me," Silva said.

Andi hoped he was right.

They walked up a few flights of stairs, winding back and forth through bookshelves. An enormous clock made of an assortment of metals glittered in the light. The hands were frozen in place, at a time near either noon or midnight, the moon dial forever trapped at a waning crescent.

Nestled beneath it was an archway, curling over a bare piece of wall.

"Go ahead and touch it," Silva told her.

Andi barely rested her fingers on the wall before it folded out like a flower. The howl of wind and the creaking of branches replaced the stifling silence.

"Interesting." Silva's tone didn't betray what he was thinking. She wondered if he was aware of what Berty had told her. What it might mean for his future.

Andi stepped into the crown of the great tree.

A thick layer of rotting leaves slid under her feet. The silver lace of spiderwebs glinted in the lantern light. A cold wind tugged at her hair and whistled through the branches above.

The core lay ahead.

In another time, the core would have looked exactly like an enormous version of the crystal in Blythe's library — a white orb surrounded by golden rings.

She could still see the ghost of what it used to be.

It was tainted a dark red, spreading in spidery veins across the surface. The rings were dark and corroded, barely rotating at all. She could feel the curse from where she was standing, thick and dark as the miasma that covered the sky. It stole her breath, a pressure in her chest.

The guardian crawled up onto the crown with them, circling around the core.

It was all the same. The core. Silva. The guardian.

The moment the heart had been placed in the core a slow, quiet death had begun. For all of them. Silva wasn't a vampire, not the way the others were.

He was a walking corpse.

"There it is," Silva said. He didn't know. He didn't realize what he had done with his curse. "Well? Go on. The tree will guide you. It always does."

She knew that it wouldn't happen.

Giving the tree magic wouldn't save it. It would just prolong the inevitable. For a year, maybe ten, but very little time in the grand scheme of things. And eventually, it wouldn't be enough.

Breaking the curse wouldn't work, either. The core was too far gone. The tree would follow it soon after. No matter what she did, the tree was dead.

"What are you waiting for?" Silva asked. The guardian lifted its head, baring its teeth at her.

"I need a minute, it's a lot." It wasn't a lie. She stepped closer to the core, even though it repulsed every part of her. It smelled like rot and disease.

"Andi, if you need time…" Blythe didn't finish what she was saying. Andi wasn't sure if she knew how.

"We don't have time," Andi said. She knew it was true, even as she said it. "You were right. What you said before."

"I was?" Blythe asked, quietly.

She nodded.

She needed a third choice.

Chapter 47: Mycorrhizal

Andi closed her eyes, trying to think. She didn't want to access her archive, Silva would know in an instant if she did.

It had to be her, and her alone.

The sky rumbled, but she didn't think it was thunder.

"Andi—" Blythe started to say.

"Fix it or I'll kill her." Silva stretched out one arm. With the pop and twist of bone it morphed into something like the wings Carmine had in her other form, fingers lengthening into horrible claws.

"I'm fixing it," she reassured him. "Just…don't hurt her."

It took everything Andi had to get closer to the core. She had to do something. Anything. Up close it was much bigger than she'd anticipated, several times her height. Each metal ring was as big around as her arm. It spun slowly, a few feet off the ground.

The great metal rings twisted, creaking and whining with each rotation. A broken, rusty machine. When she was close, they ground to a halt, leaving an open space for her hand.

Right where the heart was, still pumping, a beat against her mind. Out of step with the world.

She set her hand just above it.

The surface of the crystal was icy cold. It felt like Silva's hands — something rotting and long dead. The gold of her magic glimmered against the deep, awful red. Sparks of light danced across it, brilliant as stars.

There was nothing for her magic to hold on.

The core wasn't dying.

It was already dead.

Silva's heart was the only thing left, pumping along and keeping the library alive. One stutter in its beat and the whole thing would fall apart.

"It's not that difficult." Silva appeared next to her, one arm still transformed. He grabbed her wrist with his normal hand and forced her to touch the heart. It squirmed under her fingers, slimy and cold. Bile burned her throat. She tried to yank her hand back. Silva's grip was an iron shackle.

"Let me go!" she struggled against him. She tried to swing the lantern at him, but he caught her other wrist, claws curling around her arm. He bent down just enough that they were eye to eye. His face was twisted pewter. His teeth pale needles.

"Just pour magic into the heart," he snarled. "Revive the core. The library will take care of the rest. This is all you need to do."

"And then you'll kill me?" Her voice cracked.

"That entirely depends on you, doesn't it?" He smiled, like he'd just said something completely reasonable.

Something under his shirt moved. Andi recoiled as much as she could in horror.

He was going to force her to pour all of her magic into the core and then he would kill her, taking anything that was left. With Carmine gone, he had no one stopping him from finding every archive witch on the continent as they were born and repeating the process over and over again.

Obrye would be a land of eternal night and death.

Blythe's cane came down on Silva wrist with a snap. He jerked back. Andi swung the lantern. It hit him in the face. He shrieked and jerked back, hiding the damage with a hand.

The guardian roared in pain and anger. It struck like a snake, and only Blythe slamming the end of her cane into Silva's chest and pushing off saved them. The guardian twisted around, its enormous trunk encircled them.

Andi held the lantern up with shaking hands. The glass had shattered on one side, the shining pieces scattered in the leaf litter at her feet. The copper bowed in, nearly touching the light.

"Whatever you're going to do, you need to do it," Blythe said.

Andi barely heard her, staring at the lantern. It had seen her through so much, it hadn't even broken when Carmine threw it.

"Enough of this nonsense," Silva said. "As…satisfying as it would be to kill you, I believe Carmine had the correct idea. It would be so much more satisfying to force you to help me keep this place alive, don't you think?"

"I don't want that," Andi whispered.

"I don't give a damn what you want," he snapped. "Fix the core. Fill it with magic. That's all you're good for."

"Shut up," Blythe told him.

"If you don't want to spend an eternity without her, then you'll do what I ask," he said. "Both of you. Or I could kill the frog. Would that be incentive enough?"

"I'm a toad actually," Berty murmured. His voice shook. He clung to the shoulder of Blythe's coat.

"Don't hurt them. I…I need magic from the library to get it to work. You're lucky I have something right here." Andi shook the loose glass from where it was sitting in the frame. She scooped the tiny bit of sunlight into her fingers. Warm, soft magic played against her skin, like the petals of a flower on a soft breeze.

"Very well," Silva stepped back. His arm folded back into itself with a crack.

"Andi…" Blythe looked terrified.

Andi couldn't blame her. "It's going to be all right."

"No, it's not, you can't do this," Blythe said.

"If I don't, the tree dies, the curse isn't broken, and everyone else will follow," Andi said. "Please, Blythe. I asked you to help me. I'm asking you to trust me now. Both of you."

"I trust you," Bertrand said.

Blythe looked nothing like the vampire she'd first met. Her hair disheveled, eyes wide and scared, her clothes torn. The elegant, aloof, sarcastic woman no longer seemed to exist. What was left was a scared, genuine person that Andi cared about so much the realization made her heart ache.

Her past didn't matter. The future didn't, either. The only thing of importance was that moment.

Blythe leaned her forehead against Andi's, briefly. "I trust you."

Andi kissed her, just a peck on her cheek. It was all she could do. It was all the time she could spare.

"If you're quite done?" Annoyed and impatient, Silva spit the words at Andi.

She didn't have any time at all.

"Yes," she said. "I just…In case…in case I didn't make it."

"Good." Silva didn't reassure her.

She held the light in her hands, just in front of the heart. It was magic from the library, something that had been there long before she was born. And her own magic, obvious in the gold that dusted her palms. They'd been twined together into something new, something that radiated between her fingers. Warmth and life pooling together with something ancient and steady.

Her third choice.

She lifted her hands.

The light spun in the air, suspended in front of her. At one point, hundreds of lines of magic must have run to the core. But one remained, flowing straight to the heart, pumping its dark magic into the tree.

She inhaled.

On the exhale, a soft sight, she pressed the light into the heart.

It beat faster, the chambers thrashing with the force of it. The sound so loud it filled her bones.

A crack.

A dark, jagged line worked its way over the core's surface, snapping and chattering like ice in the spring.

"What are you doing?" Silva straightened. "Tell me what you're doing, you little—"

He reached for her.

His arm ceased to exist.

He screamed.

The guardian struck at her, unfurling into leaves and sparks of old, dead magic as it moved, until all that passed by her was a gentle breeze.

The heart shuddered to a stop, turned black, and fell to the ground.

The great rings dropped, crashing all around her. She paid them no mind, focused on the light in her hands, the tiny spark of life that she was weaving, her magic dancing around it, specks of gold. Stars shining in the dark.

The single point of magic flared brightly. A sprout pushed its way through the dead leaves at her feet, green and bright. It grew quickly, until it was tall enough for her to place the light in its branches. A handful of leaves broke away, yellowing as they spiraled around the light.

It flashed again, so brightly Andi had to look away, shielding her face with her arm.

When she could see again, the light had crystallized, the leaves had become golden rings no thicker than a thread, spiraling around the crystal slowly.

With a groan the old core slowly fell to the leaves, crumbling apart, forming a crescent at the back of the new sapling, cradling it like a mother.

"What have you done?" Silva was on his knees, clutching his stump to his chest. His skin had shifted from pewter to the fine white of ash, flaking in places, a deep crack running from his hairline all the way to his chin.

"It's a mycorrhizal network," she explained. He looked at her with lost eyes. The red faded from his irises, leaving a dull gray in its wake. "It's when trees help each other thrive. It's kind of like people. But I guess you wouldn't understand that."

Far away, above the mountains, the sky turned pink. Sunlight — true sunlight — gilded the very top of the tree, bare branches shining gold.

Silva looked into the first sunrise the library had seen in centuries.

He closed his eyes, a small smile on his face. "No. I think you're right. I don't understand."

He crumbled into ash and dust.

Andi stared at the spot for a moment, but there was nothing to mourn. That man had been dead for a very long time.

She turned to Blythe instead. She was still standing there, leaning on her cane, staring at Andi like she'd never seen anything quite like her. Her hair was still white, her skin pale, but her eyes seemed darker. Maybe it was distance. Or the light.

"Are you okay?" Andi took a step and the reality of everything that she had put herself through caught up to her. Her legs simply refused to support her anymore and she started to fall.

Blythe caught her before she could, holding her closely. Tightly. "I think I should be asking you that."

Her voice vibrated in her chest.

It was accompanied by the faintest beating of a heart.

Chapter 48: Seedlings

"Are you sure this is going to work?"

Andi glared over her shoulder at Lexa. "I'm the head librarian now. You have to respect me."

"I don't have to respect anything." Lexa pushed off from where she was leaning against the table. "You woke up two hours ago, you were asleep—"

"For three days, I know," Andi had heard the same words several times.

"And you left me in a pile of rubble," Lexa reminded her.

"That was three days ago, get over it." Andi focused back on the task at hand. "I know what I'm doing."

"You sure?"

"If you don't let me focus maybe I'll blow up the whole library and then we'll see how focused I can be."

"That won't happen," Bertrand said from her shoulder. He'd been curled up next to her when she woke up, the first familiar face she saw. She'd been placed in a temporary set up in the library.

She'd never been happier for Chrys to be the second person she saw. They'd sat down and gently explained everything to her.

Carmine and Silva were dead.

No one had seen Tana.

No one knew where Dahlia was, or if she'd been at the tree at all. Andi suspected she'd never been there.

She hadn't broken the curse, not entirely. She'd cleared the skies above Obrye and the darkness had lifted from the library, allowing Chrys and their team to move up to the top of the tree.

The regular vampires had fled before the sunlight.

But the biggest change occurred in the afflicted.

When dawn broke over Obrye, they'd been standing in the street, confused. Chrys had received word from one of the Coven healers that they were back to more or less normal - the curse lifted like a sickness.

She'd been more concerned for Blythe.

Chrys didn't know what she had become. Neither human, or a vampire, but some hybrid of the two. Alive, able to withstand sunlight, but just as fast and strong as she had been. Whether she was dependent on blood or not remained to be seen.

Andi had left for Blythe's manor soon after. Now she stood in her library.

"And why do you have to do this right now?" Lexa asked.

"I told you, libraries and trees both thrive on networks," Andi explained. "These crystals? They're like seedlings to the mother tree. But it's not sunlight and water that they're sharing, it's magic, and people, and information. Cutting off the other libraries might have kept the Empire of the Dawn from reaching the main library, but it also isolated the tree. Even if…it would have died, eventually without those things. So! I have to fix it!"

"Okay, that makes sense, I guess," Lexa said. "But why this library in particular? Why not the one in the city?"

"Well, um. You see. There's already a connection to the city." Andi floundered for an explanation that wouldn't be incredibly embarrassing. "At that school."

"Really? No other reason?" Lexa grinned at her.

"It's because Bly—"

Andi grabbed Bertrand before he could finish his sentence, cupping him in her hands. "Well. It's close by."

"Really? Nothing to do with me, then?" Blythe stepped into the library. She was still relying heavily on her cane, but otherwise she was radiant. The sun coming in from the open windows was bright on her hair, painting it in gold light and blue shadow. The sight made Andi's heart race, and everyone in the room could hear it, even Bertrand.

"Nothing at all." Andi smiled at her. "It's just convenient."

"A convenient little escape route to your girlfriend?" Lexa asked.

"I don't know what you're talking about, you're both still banned for life," Andi tried to sound haughty, but her cheeks were on fire.

"I don't mind you slipping in here whenever you feel like it." Blythe grinned at her. Andi's face all but combusted.

She cleared her throat, but her voice still came out a little wonky. "Just. Stand back. And don't distract me. Here, Berty, hang out with Lexa."

"As much as I like you, little guy, we have to get you a more mobile body." Lexa put Bertrand on her shoulder so he could hold onto the strap on her shoulder.

"How about a snake?" he suggested. "They're more mobile, right?"

"No hands, though."

"Hmmm, good point, not that these hands are particularly useful. I think hanging on would be easier—"

"One thing at a time," Andi warned them. "I've never done this before. I could actually blow up the library."

"Wait, what?" Blythe sounded mildly alarmed.

Andi ignored her, placing her hands on either side of the crystal. She closed her eyes, sensing where the connection it must have once had used to be. It didn't take her long to find it. The action reminded her of searching through her archive.

Then again, the library was essentially her giant archive now. She'd created a new core, and while it wasn't strong enough yet to keep the entire library going, it was a start.

Connecting the seedlings would make it stronger.

It was harder to make them connect. She wasn't exactly sure how to do it, and the magic kept shying away from her, until she realized they needed to connect through her.

Light shone through her eyelids. When she opened them again the crystal had split. Emerald leaves grew through the split, until it was a tiny tree. Her magic slid between the rings and sparkled on the tree.

The crystal sank into the bookshelf behind it and a doorway appeared.

"…Wow," Lexa said.

"I did it!" She threw her hands up in the air. "I actually did it, I…woah."

A wave of dizziness hit her. She sank into a chair, holding her head.

"This is why I told you to wait," Lexa said.

"It couldn't wait," she said. "It already waited three days. It needed to be done. And I need to find more. As soon as possible."

"Well, how about you rest first," Lexa said. "I'll…let you do that. Yeah. Just be in the other room. The room clear at the other side of the manor, where I can't hear you. C'mon, Berty, tell me about those weird jellyfish."

"So, they're actually not jellyfish at all, not even related, despite the resemblance," Bertrand's voice faded as Lexa left the room.

Leaving her alone with Blythe for the first time since Silva died.

"So." Blythe sat across from her, leaning her cane against the table. "It's over."

"Well, not entirely," Andi said. "I do have to find these seedlings. I don't even really know how many there are, but the more there are the stronger the library is, and the stronger our connection with the rest of the continent is. No one has seen parts of Obrye for…for ages. Who knows what could be waiting for us? And there's still two elder vampires, and—"

Blythe put a hand over hers. Her fingers weren't as cold as they once were. "Sounds like you'll be busy."

"I guess," Andi said. "For a while. I have a lot to learn, too. I still don't really know what I'm doing."

"You haven't even been awake for very long," Blythe reminded her. "I was really worried. The healers said you were fine, Chrys checked on you themself, but…I'm glad you came here, first. Even if it was just convenient."

"We both know it wasn't convenient at all," Andi admitted.

"Not at all?" Blythe smiled a bit. "We're not trapped in a library anymore. There's nothing pushing us together anymore. And you know I've done…I've done terrible things. Things that I have to make up for. So…I understand if it was merely the first place you thought of."

All things Andi had already thought about. Things she'd wrapped up neatly and put away.

"I know." Andi stood up. She moved closer, her hand still in Blythe's. "There's a lot of work to do, to get Obrye back up on its feet. I don't know where this will take me. And I don't really know how long it will be. So. Maybe you could start to make up for things by coming along."

"What?" Blythe looked up at her.

"I care about you, a lot," Andi said. "I think I might even…well, I like you. I want to see where this goes. So. If you'd like to join me, to see where things go, and to see what we can do to make things better…then I'd consider unbanning you from the library."

Blythe laughed and pulled Andi down into her lap with a flurry of her skirts, pressing her face against Andi's shoulder, her arms around her waist. "Oh, well, if that's what it takes."

"It does." Andi threaded her fingers through Blythe's hair. Still as soft as silk.

"Then yes," Blythe said. "I want to be with you, no matter what. No matter how you'll have me. I believe I've fallen in an entirely different manner than the first time."

"Oh?" Andi froze, suddenly hyper aware of everything around her. Of the ticking of a clock nearby, the sun coming through the window, a soft breeze catching on the empty branches of the trees in a bare garden outside.

"Would it be too much to say it?" Blythe teased.

"I swear, I'll never let you in the library if you are going to be mean to me right now—"

"I would never," Blythe cut her off. "I love you."

Andi could have been floating, and she wouldn't have even noticed. The earth could stop spinning, sending them crashing through the window at a thousand miles an hour, and it wouldn't have made any difference at all.

"You did make my heart start beating, after all," Blythe's voice was quiet, vulnerable. She still hadn't looked up from Andi's shoulder. "It's only fair that you get to keep it."

"Then I'll gladly take it," Andi murmured.

Blythe lifted her head to kiss her. It was longer and deeper than their first kiss. Blythe's lips warmed up under hers.

It left Andi breathless, leaning her forehead against Blythe's.

She still smelled like cloves and smoke. She had on a coat that could have been the twin to the one she tore in the library.

Andi pressed a hand to her chest, right above her heart, and felt her heart pounding.

"Just making sure it's still working?" Blythe asked with a very soft smile. Her eyes were a darker gray than they had been.

They were beautiful.

"Something like that." Andi kissed her again.

Acknowledgements

This book is very near and dear to my heart, and I have a lot of people to thank for making it a reality!

First and foremost, I would like to thank Carmilla, for encouraging me to write this and enjoying the story so much. It wouldn't have happened without you!

Huge shoutout to Brooklyn and Jennifer for hyping me up and keeping me motivated to write.

To Em, for inspiring me to write it in the first place.

To everyone who subscribed while it was on substack and for everyone who commented, you guys are awesome!

And of course, to Cloaked Press, for believing in this book and in my others!

Last, but not least, to you, dear reader. I hope you enjoyed the story, and please remember to review! It really helps!

Thank you all again!

About the Author

A. Lawrence lives in Idaho, where long stretches of roads through nothing but hills of yellow grass and abandoned cabins have always inspired them.

When they're not writing, they are drawing or being forced to relax by their geriatric and demanding cat.

Tumblr: akidoodles
Instagram: akidoodles